FROM RUST

THE HOLLOWS

FROM RUST
THE HOLLOWS

DANIEL JAMES CLARK

PRESS

Published by Vulpine Press in the United Kingdom in 2025

ISBN: 978-1-83919-679-9

www.vulpine-press.com

To anyone who, despite all the evidence, continues to hope.

Open Channel Radio Burst Log: Unencrypted Band
Subject: Intercepted Communication
Parties: 002
Receiving unit: Command and Control Unit 1215685577565

[Begin Log]
0812:14
"Um, hello? Is anyone still broadcasting on this frequency?"
0812:17
"This is an automated response from the United Entities Military Security Commission. A level [silence] attack has been reported in the following [long transmission as multiple locations are read over one another at the same time]. Radio communication exceeding 470Ghz are not recommended."
0813:01
"An automated fucking tower broadcast. Great. Anyone out there with a radio have any information? We've been sitting here waiting for days."
0813:10
"This is an automated response from the United Entities Military Security Commission. Sender is advised to cease radio communications above the 450Ghz range recommended for close tactical use. This station has been able to pinpoint your location with an accuracy expectation of [long pause] three miles. Enemy capabilities may meet or exceed this accuracy expectation."
0813:42

"Alright, fuck all of you. I know you're listening. We can't let these people keep us quiet. We need orders, or this shit is going to be over before my unit can mobilize."

0814:03

"This is an automated response from the United Entities Security Commission."

0814:08 [Simultaneous Reception]

"Okay, fuck off. Fine."

0814:08 [Simultaneous Reception]

"Further broadcast is highly discouraged. This station has been able to pinpoint your location with an accuracy expectation of [long pause] sixteen meters. Enemy capabilities may meet or exceed this accuracy expectation."

[End Log]

CHAPTER 1

The wind moved across the desert like hot breath, pushing and pulling a small campfire rhythmically. Mark had given up trying to avoid the smoke and simply waited for it to pass. He turned a coin on a chain over in his fingers, feeling the smooth, round shape as he stared into the flames. Occasionally, the moist branches of the burning sagebrush sputtered, sending bright orange sparks into the night sky, where they died out against the backdrop of the universe.

It had been days since he left the smoldering wreckage of his command mech in the valley where they'd been ambushed. Mark was following the trampled path the enemy mechs had left behind, headed north. They—and he—were headed to what Mark assumed would be an enemy stronghold in a mountain range he couldn't even see yet. What he'd do once he got there, he wasn't sure. He only knew that someone would have to pay for what happened. He'd find some way to take down as many of the Harbingers as he could.

Turner, and the rest of the cadets might have retreated to any number of places. They hadn't followed the enemy, or they'd have overtaken him already. A mech, even a slow or damaged one, still moved faster than one man. No, they'd probably given up the chase and either headed back for Tonopah or even all the way back to Taycher Mechanized Armor Base, whatever was left of it. There was even the remote possibility that someone from the tattered remnants of the United Entities government had finally gotten in touch with them and given orders.

Zak and the rebel woman...well, he didn't want to think about that. Not now.

He held the necklace out in front of him to catch the light of the fire. It was an ordinary coin, a penny with a year marked on it that now only meant something to him. There was a hole drilled into the top, and a ball chain fed through it. It had been his graduation gift to Brooke, before the attack at Taycher. He didn't have the courage to put it on. If he did that, it would be admitting she was gone. So long as he held it, it remained an item he could presume to return someday.

Mark closed his hands around the coin and held it to his chest, returning his gaze to the fire before him. Soon he would crawl into the small tent he had set up and fight his way into sleep.

~

Alison looked up from her notebook and saw Zak regarding her from across their campfire. It made her uneasy having a government soldier with her, but the alternative was dying alone in the desert. As much as it infuriated her, she needed Zak in order to find Eva, and at least he seemed committed to the task. They'd managed to find her belongings among the scattered debris from the truck. Her tattered backpack and satchel held everything she now owned, including the notebook containing her hand-drawn maps of the various supply caches along her routes and the revolver her father had given her.

"Where to next?" Zak asked as he added a dry branch to their fire.

"There should be a cache of supplies and an ATV about ten miles out." She looked down at her notebook again. "It's not a supply stop I've used before, so I hope my intel is right."

Discussing her plans with someone else was a foreign experience for her. For years, she'd been a courier for the Harbingers of the Fall, ferrying information across the vast deserts of the western United Entities. Her only companionship had come from her contacts at either end of her routes and the occasional respite between assignments. Typically, she spent those with her family at their home in the woods near Tonopah.

A shock of almost physical pain went through her. That home was gone now. In one night, she'd lost her anchor point, her reason for fighting against the United Entities. Now, the only thing that mattered was getting back there. The fragile thread of hope that Eva may have survived the attack kept her moving. If her injured leg didn't hinder their progress too much, she should be able to make it back to whatever was left of her home in just a few days. But, no matter how quickly she moved, it wouldn't be fast enough. The thought of Eva, scared and alone, haunted her every waking moment. She needed to know, needed to get back.

Another fire, another place. John tended this fire with care, making sure it burned cleanly, with little smoke. In the cab of the truck behind him, a little girl slept soundly. He'd found Eva tucked safely inside the makeshift clubhouse in the woods near her home, scared and alone. She'd been well stocked with food and may have been safe enough, even if he hadn't come along. It had taken her a day or so to warm up to him, but as soon as he mentioned knowing Alison, things smoothed out dramatically.

John hadn't had the courage to tell her he didn't know where Alison was, or if she was even still alive. He had made a promise, though, as much to himself as to Eva. If Alison was alive, he would reunite them. If he could do only one thing with his time left, he would do this one good thing. Nothing could absolve him of what he'd created when he wrote the words that the Harbingers now used as their core doctrine. Nothing would cleanse him of the things he'd done in the name of the United Entities. He wasn't even sure which he needed absolution for.

Behind him, he heard the door of his truck creak open. He turned away from the fire to see the girl, five years old but tall for her age, step to the ground while rubbing her eyes.

"I have to pee," she said, and stood patiently.

"Just a minute," John said, working against his bad leg to get up from the ground. "Let me find the flashlight."

He reached into the bag beside him and pushed aside various supplies and accumulated travel junk to find a large black flashlight. He walked over and handed it to her.

"Watch Meeple," Eva said. "Keep her safe, okay?"

"Sure, hon," John said. He peered into the backseat of the truck. It was there; a bright blue stuffed whale she'd claimed in one of the abandoned gas stations they had stopped at a while back. He picked it up and put it into the crook of his arm as Eva walked off a few yards to find a private place to relieve herself.

While he waited, he patted his breast pocket before remembering he had no cigarettes. Instead, he looked out at the night sky and wondered how people who didn't smoke filled these inconvenient spans of time. It took him a minute or so to realize that looking up at the stars and thinking about something was probably exactly what they did. He let out a short laugh.

"Did you laugh?" Eva asked suddenly from beside him.

"Wow, that was good," he said, messing up her already jumbled brown hair. "You got me this time. You're either getting better or I'm starting to lose my hearing."

"Why did you laugh?" she asked, clearly tired but trying to stay up.

John tried to think of a way to explain his thoughts but decided it was better to just scoot her back into bed.

"Here's Meep," John said, handing her the blue whale. "Climb in and go back to bed. We're going to hit town tomorrow, and I need you to be awake when we do."

"Is Allie going to be there?" She asked, the sleep in her voice fading away for a moment.

"I don't think so," John said. "I mean, not yet. I'll let you know when we're getting close. I promise."

"You don't even know where she is," Eva said with an air of assertion as she pulled at the blue fur on Meeple.

John didn't know what to say. Clearly, he had underestimated the girl's insight.

"You're right," he said. "I'm not completely sure where she is. But I promise you I'm looking for her. We'll find your..." He almost said "mother" but caught himself. Eva still believed Alison was her sister, and it wasn't John's place to tell that secret. "We'll find Alison."

Eva shrugged and continued looking down at the whale.

"You shouldn't lie, John." She looked up into his eyes as she said this, and, confusingly, she smiled. "Just tell the truth. It's the best policy."

John laughed and shook his head. He picked her up and, with some strain on his bad leg, placed her inside the truck.

"Sure, I'll keep that in mind next time," he said. "But I do promise you I'm looking, and we are going to find her."

"Okay," she said, already falling back to sleep.

He shut the door carefully, trying not to rock the truck as he did. She was probably already asleep, but the action came naturally. He'd always made sure to close his own daughter's door slowly and carefully. When she was very little and sleep only came at the tail end of a tedious ritual, the last thing he needed was for a door to wake her back up. As he returned to the fire, he wondered how many other habits he had that could be traced back to a version of himself that no longer existed.

He sat down, reached into his coat pocket, and pulled out a folded photograph. He opened it and was just able to see the smiling faces of his daughter and wife in the firelight. On the other side of the crease in the photo, he stood with a matching smile. He hardly recognized himself in the image. Would they understand the man he had become? He was old and tired now, broken down by time and pain. He'd managed to ignite something with his writing. The Doctrine, as the Harbingers of the Fall had started calling his collected essays, laid out the framework for the chaos that was now gripping the world. The Harbingers had managed to pull off a widespread synchronized series of attacks.

He shook his head and tried to push past a dark core of guilt growing inside. A new purpose had to take precedence. He couldn't change the damage he'd done as a member of the United Entities military forces. Nor could he control the seeming wildfire of chaos the Harbingers of the Fall were unleashing around the globe. It was out of his hands now. What he could do was help Eva find Alison. He looked down at the faces of his wife and daughter once again and hoped this small act would be enough.

Turner and the others had waited at the rocky base of the nearest mountain range to see if Mark or anyone else would return to them from the valley. The short battle—an ambush, really—had ended, and Turner thought it wise to rest anyway. The next morning, he'd sent two of their remaining mechs out to check the wreckage. The team had managed to return with ammunition, food, and medical supplies, but they hadn't found anyone alive. They did find tracks leading away from the mech, however. A single line in the sand indicated that someone had managed to pull one of the off-road motorcycles from the shattered vehicle bay.

Turner didn't think pursuing the Harbingers of the Fall any further was worth the risk, and so he set a course back to Taycher. With the show of force the enemy had unleashed on them, the best they could hope for would be to regroup somewhere and try to find reinforcements.

They made good time, traveling almost continuously, and only stopping for brief rest periods. Taycher Mechanized Armor Base, the home of the United Entities Mechanized Armor Academy, was close by now. They'd left it behind mere days ago, but it felt like they were returning from a full tour of duty in some faraway land. They would be in visual range within the next hour, if their calculations and sensor sweeps were accurate.

He used the radio inside his mech, a bulky Ursidae class mech named the Nanook, to call out orders to the other units in his small core. "Icarus, press ahead for a bit. We're gonna need some solid eyes up front. Turn around and report back when you've made visual contact."

"Yes, sir," a voice came back. "Don't go running off on us."

Turner felt like he should say something witty but couldn't think of anything fast enough. Instead, he kept his tone even and flat. "We'll be here when you get back, Icarus. Keep comms low. We don't know who's out there."

Turner sat back in his chair and took a deep breath. He was still surprised that the others looked to him for leadership in the aftermath of the ambush. They'd lost two leaders in just a few short days, and nothing official indicated he was next in line. Still, he was the one that gave the order to retreat, and that seemed to be enough for now. After vying for leadership back at the Academy, he finally had it and it didn't feel quite right. It was like wearing a flight suit tailored to fit a different person. He was doing his best, though, and hoped things would get easier with time.

They had been traveling in a shifting formation since they left, and Turner was scanning more frequently than they were used to. They'd lost their command mech, and with it, the luxury of their most advanced sensors. He also sorely missed the comfort the huge gun on top of the command mech had brought. Turner thought bitterly that if Mark hadn't charged toward the enemy down in the valley, they might have been able to at least salvage some of the sensor array on the command mech. Mark's mad scramble *had* given them enough cover to escape, though, Turner had to admit. Without that sacrifice, they all might be dead.

He sat up straight and asked Payne to run another scan at the sensor and comms station. Kalen was also with him in the Nanook, manning the weapons station. It was cramped in the cockpit, but it was more room than the lighter mechs had to work with. He was at least thankful for that.

"Yes, sir," Payne said, and ran a scan of the surrounding area.

While their command mech had sported a full array of sensors, the Nanook had only one advanced frequency scanner. It allowed them to scan the area periodically for radio sources, even faint ones, that might indicate an enemy unit trying to communicate in the vast desert landscape around them. Turner kept communication between his own units minimal and at very low intensity, to minimize any imprint on enemy sensors. He routed most messages through the radio but had managed to send out some direct communications to other pilots using their optical implants when conditions were right.

"Nothing weird on the scans, sir." Payne sounded emotionless and flat, a product of the stress from the last few days piling up, no doubt.

The nearly constant state of awareness needed to keep what remained of their core safe and organized hadn't been easy. Everyone was tired beyond anything they'd trained for at the Academy. Turner hoped when they finally got the base in sight, it would be in friendly hands. He watched out his cockpit window as the Icarus continued to amble nimbly off into the distance. Soon it was beyond a dune and out of sight.

It wasn't long before he saw the Icarus headed back toward them. Their calculations were right, the base was close.

"Base looks abandoned, sir." The voice from the Icarus came through, weak but clear. "But that doesn't mean anything."

Turner thought through his options. Sending a single mech out to make contact might mean never seeing it or its crew again. No, they would just have to approach all together and hope for the best.

"Spread out in a standard attack formation," Turner said. "Keep out of each other's line of fire. Let's get the base covered by as many angles as we can by the time we get there. If it's got an enemy presence, we'll have a better chance of taking them out or forcing a surrender."

The mechs around the Nanook shifted into a wide line, then began advancing on the base. The Icarus fell into the formation as they approached. Turner could feel his pulse quicken as he anticipated the need for quick action. Progress was slow as the units on the outer edge of their formation advanced more swiftly to get into the curved shield that would best protect their advance. As they crested the high ridge around the base, Turner saw for the first time the true scope of the damage that had been done.

The high walls, once tall and pristine white, were now charred and crumbling in large sections. Only one of the guard towers, which had seemed at once both oppressive and comforting when he'd lived inside, remained intact. A light smoke still rose from the interior of the compound into the clear blue sky. At the center of the base, the building that contained administrative offices and living quarters for base leadership still stood tall above the desert. However, the sleek black glass that had once adorned the sides was shattered and sloughed off in many places. There was no sign of movement, not even the speck of a guard in the remaining tower. Looking to his left and right, Turner watched as his meager core of units continued to advance.

"All stop," Turner said over the radio. "I'm going to see if anyone is home."

If the enemy had taken the base, they already knew where Turner and his team were. If the base was still held by friendlies, he might be able to persuade them he was telling the truth. He opened a wide channel. There was no sense masking his signal now.

"Taycher Mechanized Armor Base, this is—" He stopped for a moment. Admitting he was just a cadet wouldn't do him any favors. Neither would admitting that the units they were piloting were merely training mechs. "This is Captain Hiroki Turner with the United Entities Mechanized Armor Corps. Stand down and surrender, or I will be forced to engage."

Kalen spoke up from the weapons control station. "Oh, a captain now, are we?"

"Shut the fuck up, Sam," Turner said, kicking down at him. Then, back into his radio, "I repeat, this is Captain Hiroki Turner. Anyone home?"

"Sure we are, *Captain*," a familiar female voice came through the radio. "You're clear to approach. The base is still under United Entities control. Use entry bays one and seven. See you inside."

"Uh, Base," Turner said. "The bays you mentioned are completely destroyed."

"What? No!" The voice came back through the radio—dry sarcasm impossible to mistake—then cut off.

Kalen chuckled to himself down at his console. Turner resisted the urge to kick him again. Instead, he moved his mech toward the crumbling western wall of the base. The other units soon followed and came into a column formation around him. As their mechs reached the outer perimeter, the destruction wrought inside the base became clearer. His pulse seemed to stutter and a chill shot through his body. All but one of the cadet barracks were charred husks, and the one that did remain was heavily damaged. He could scarcely believe he was looking at the same place they'd left just days ago.

The five mechs worked their way carefully through a crumbled base wall, and Turner directed them to the open parade yard. Up until the attack, they'd all gathered there every morning for company inspections before being released for classes. Turner remembered the feeling of being in formation with so many other cadets. It had always been freeing in a way, like becoming a small part of a larger organism. Only a small group of people stood together on the yard now as the mechs approached.

Turner brought his unit to a halt and keyed his optics off the controls. He turned his seat around and disengaged the rear hatch. A rush of air, laden with smells both familiar and foreign, invaded the cockpit of the mech. He stepped out and used the marked foot and hand holds to descend the twenty feet to the ground. Before him was a group of cadets, officers, and other base personnel that looked more tired than any group of people he had ever seen, including his own team. Some were standing, waiting to greet the new arrivals, while others were seated on crates or in the trampled grass.

Kalen was the next to climb from the Nanook, closely followed by Payne. The occupants of the other four mechs also disembarked into the eerie silence of the destroyed base. As they approached the new group, Turner began looking for the person he had recognized on the radio. He spotted her quickly, and she seemed to recognize him as well.

Oksana Vesnina was a dark-skinned woman with round features that made her look innocent, almost out of place in her military uniform. She was, or she had been, a second-year cadet at the Academy. He'd only met her because of an elective course on Structured Group Social Dynamics, which had turned out to be a fancy way of saying "office politics." Still, the course had been useful in some ways, until it had been cut short by the

Harbinger's attack. He'd been paired up with her on more than one occasion for some of the inevitable group assignments and he liked her wit and dedication. He was glad to see she'd survived the attack.

"Vesnina?" Turner called out to her as he approached the new group of people. "Is that you, Oksana?"

"How are you, Captain?" she asked with a smirk and an exaggerated wink as he walked up. "I wasn't aware you'd been promoted."

Kalen laughed and Turner felt the urge to turn and run an elbow into his throat.

"Hey, I didn't know who could be in here." Turner spread his arms and dropped them. "It sounded like a good idea to keep as much information back as I could."

"Well, you may as well be a captain," Vesnina said. "You're looking at a Lieutenant."

"You've got to be fucking kidding me," Turner said. "I mean, you've got to be fucking kidding me, sir. I guess."

"Watch it," she said. "But you should talk with Banks. He's the actual Captain. Over there." Vesnina pointed out a tall man in a worn officer's uniform near the back of the group. That man was eyeing the new arrivals, seeming to scrutinize every detail. Turner took a moment to compose himself and approached Captain Banks.

"Sir, Cadet Hiroki Turner, returning to base." Turner saluted and stood at attention.

"At ease, cadet," Banks said. "I'm sorry about this, but I am going to have to place all of you into custody while we try to verify your identities. I can see that Vesnina vouches for you, but you understand."

Banks nodded to his group, and in a series of swift movements Turner hadn't thought the tired soldiers capable of, they fanned out with their weapons drawn. Some members of Turner's team went to reach for their own weapons, but a quick gesture from him to stand down was obeyed. Any firearms or other potential hazards were removed from each of them, but no one was put into restraints. Turner appreciated this small courtesy at least.

"Things are worse than you may understand," Banks said, looking past Turner to survey the scene. Turner saw his eyes land on each of the mechs in turn, seeming to assess their value. "We can't take anything at face value anymore. But, preliminarily, I want to thank all of you for bringing these machines back to us. We're going to need them."

CHAPTER 2

Katherine walked up the narrow stairs of the massive eight-legged command mech they had stolen from the Academy and found Jim on the command deck. He was standing in front of a metal plaque bolted to the bulkhead near the back of the room, his fingers resting lightly on the polished brass letters.

His eyes were closed, and he seemed to be deep in thought, so Katherine read what she could of the plaque and waited a few moments. At the top, it read "UEMAC Neith 459-089-DNJ." In the center of the plaque, in larger letters, was the name of the mech: "ANANSI." Underneath that were the names and ranks of the previous commanders, each one engraved on a thin piece of gold metal, with ample room for more to be added later.

"What's going on in there, Jim?" she asked, finally stepping closer. "You trying to read that with your fingers?"

"We should keep the name." He opened his eyes and looked at her. "Anansi was a trickster god, able to overcome overwhelming odds to outsmart his oppressors. Makes you wonder how they name these things."

"I was on the naming commission for the Jotun-class mechs they rolled out two years ago," she said. "And I can say with authority that we let our aides handle it. I'm sure someone just ran a search for famous spiders and put the names into a hat."

"All the same, this one fits." He let his hand fall away. "Anansi also lost his head because he defied the gods on more than one occasion, so I guess we'll see."

"Sure, we'll keep it," Katherine said. "How do you even know all that?"

"Just one of the stories my mom used to tell me." Jim shrugged and looked back at the plaque. "She always had a ton of them. She was studying anthropology when the Decline started, so she always had the best stories for me at bedtime."

Katherine was quiet for a moment, not sure if she should ask him another question or move on.

"Sorry," Jim said. "I get spacey when I'm up too late." He shook his head and turned away from the bulkhead. "I'll be back to relieve you in a few hours, yeah?"

"Sure. Any communication from out there?" She gestured out the front glass of the command deck. "We've got to be getting close to something."

"Nothing yet. If you do hear anything, send someone to get me, please."

"Sure. Get some rest. And I'd like to hear more about these stories sometime. It'd be better than staring at a damn screen for hours."

Jim nodded and headed for the stairs at the back of the command deck. Katherine shook her head and examined the plaque more closely. She reached out and touched the cool metal. Through it, she could feel deep vibrations as the mech moved with great strides across the desert.

19

Katherine wondered why John had made them sand off all the names that had been carved under the bunks in the berthing compartments if he was just going to leave this plaque up. Surely, if the names of the soldiers who'd served on this mech before were to be scrubbed, the names of the commanders should be as well.

She recognized a few of the names on the small brass plates at the bottom. Many of them had already retired, but one or two were still high-ranking officers she'd been in high-clearance rooms with. She wondered if they knew she'd defected yet, if any of them had defected with her, how many of them were dead.

She scratched at her forearm in a quick, repetitive motion, then stopped herself. By relaxing her hands and closing her eyes, she fought off the momentary shock of emotion. It wasn't quite panic but was more closely related to sadness, or shame. In reality, it was probably a unique cocktail of thoughts and reactions she alone would ever really know. Most emotions were, she mused, simply personal shots of various neurotransmitters and neural pathways lighting up in unique ways. Each one no more than a malfunction of sorts, if she decided to treat them that way.

She ran through a mental checklist to make sure she had herself back in complete control. She allowed the thoughts to wash over her and let them each have their moment, then pushed them away.

She'd betrayed a lot of people, and many of those people were dead now. If the strategies John had written were being followed to the letter, a whole lot of people she'd never even met were also dead. But the only way to take down institutions as large and complex as the United Entities was to do it all at once. Their tactical position would never again be as good as it was in the moments after their first major actions. The benefit of striking first meant they had been able to take down preselected targets with absolute precision. These were assertions she'd read in one of John's earliest essays.

Katherine had no concrete indication that the Harbingers were following all of John's strategies, but the evidence she'd seen so far indicated they were following the broad strokes at least. Another advantage the Harbingers had was that their end-game scenario was different than nearly any other revolutionary movement in history. Their aim was to bring about the intentional collapse of civilization. It was that simple. If she believed in this cause—and she did—death was an inevitability. Feeling regret over the deaths of people whose faces she'd happened to see in a room once or twice was not logical.

The Fall had begun, and she was but a minor player in the final spastic jerks of society as it finally crumbled beneath its own weight. The Harbingers of the Fall was an organization designed to destroy itself as swiftly as it was supposed to destroy everything else. And, since the Harbingers had decided to begin their attacks on the United Entities, it meant the other world powers would be dealing with all of this too. Bringing down the UE would have been a worthless endeavor if another world power could just walk in and take the throne.

She had chosen her side, and she would carry out her part to the best of her ability. With the full force of the Harbingers, she would ensure the rotting tower of society was sufficiently razed.

They would establish new, level ground from which to begin anew.

Katherine opened her eyes. The names on the plaque stared up at her coldly, and she stared back with her own intentional indifference. She reached to her belt and removed a pocket multitool. She flipped out the flathead screwdriver bit and slid it behind the first name at the bottom of the plaque. The engraved brass plate was secured with two metal brads. With one jerk of the screwdriver, it came loose and clattered to the deck. She slid the tool behind the second name and pulled it free, allowing it to fall as well.

The two people on the deck manning the sensor array and weapons station turned to stare at Katherine, but she paid them no attention. Four more names fell to the ground, and then there was only one more. She pried at it and found it more stubborn than the others. She looked down at the name and was immediately stunned. A man named Garrin Kingston had evidently been the first person to command the Anansi. More importantly for her, he had also been her first instructor when she'd joined the Homeland Security Force. The Mechanized Armor Corps hadn't been founded yet and was in both of their futures back then. Garrin had been tough. That was his job, but he had also been cruel. Cruel in ways that did not befit a commanding officer.

Katherine allowed anger to well up from within her. She attempted to maintain control as feelings of guilt and shame threatened to follow. These were not useful feelings, so she pushed back against them, and removed the screwdriver. Then, instead of prying the name off, she scraped at it. She continued, brass shavings peeling off and drifting to her feet, until the name was gone.

~

John drove with Eva down a dirt road and entered the outskirts of Tonopah, a mid-sized city mainly important for the information transfer hub that used to be located in its Enclaved center. That hub was gone now. He'd been on deck when Katherine gave the orders to take it down. When he'd still been with Katherine and the others, they'd cut a swath of destruction through the center of the city as they'd fled Taycher.

Eva had one hand out of her window, riding the wind as the shapes of trees and occasional rooftops slid by. The buildings looked abandoned, but many must have housed residents too afraid to come out. A large sign, standing resiliently in the sky, advertised gas, snacks, and beer. John brought the truck to a stop below the sign. He needed a moment to collect his thoughts before getting too far into the city.

"Are we stopping for today?" Eva asked.

"No." He shook his head and reached over to tousle her hair a bit. "Just give me a minute, okay?"

She glared at him, then smiled and let him think. She was young but seemed more aware of her surroundings than others her age. Perhaps he'd just been away from children for too long and this was how they all acted. Either way, if she was going to survive in the world that awaited her, she'd need to grow up fast. She reminded him of Alison, and not just because she looked like her. The same wiry athletic build was already evident,

23

somehow suited to the desert in ways he would never be. It was her eyes, though, the color of honey, set in a sun-bronzed and freckled face, that were nearly identical to Alison's.

His leads on Alison's location were slim, bordering on contrived. Her last known location had been inside the Tonopah financial district, where she'd left the safety of an armored truck and run off unexpectedly toward the enemy. She'd just been witness to the destruction of her family home, so his first thought had been that she would try to make her way back to the house. He had waited there with Eva for two days, though, and had seen no trace of her.

His second lead—or assumption—was that she had gone off to enact revenge on the soldiers that had killed her family. Perhaps she, like John, had thought there was no one left alive at the home and simply went off to do as much damage as she could. If that was the case, someone in the area must have seen or heard something. John put the truck in gear and started driving again.

"Seatbelt, John," Eva said from beside him. "Safety first."

He sighed but pulled the belt across, clicking it into place and rolling his eyes theatrically. The last time he'd tried to argue, she'd given him a look of disappointment probably borrowed from her mother. John drove the truck along the debris-strewn streets, the massive gray edifices of ruined financial buildings rising around them to meet the sky. He made his way toward the hole in the skyline where a rebel mech had been ambushed by government forces. The brief battle had created a martyr for the Harbingers of the Fall. John had seen to that with a sufficiently dramatic speech before he left.

24

As he turned onto a broad road leading through the financial district, he saw the twisted frame of the downed mech in an intersection three blocks ahead. Light from the rising sun glittered across the metal hull. As he approached, two people sprang up from the wrecked machine with tools in their hands. At first, it looked like they were going to run away, but one of them shouted something to the other, and they stood their ground.

"Get down," John said instinctively to Eva as he got closer.

He pulled up a good distance away from the mech and turned so he could call out to the figures. He'd interrupted them working on breaking the mech down for parts. John removed his gun from the center console and held it out of sight, just in case. It was an older model he'd kept from his first years in the field. He'd even reluctantly had it converted to use the newer magnetic ammunition when traditional gunpowder cartridges had become harder to source.

"Any chance I could ask you a question?" John called. "I'm looking for someone. I'd really appreciate some help."

One of the figures, a woman in overalls and a dirty wide-brimmed hat, waved a tool at John dismissively. The other, a short man with a distinct forward curve in his back, said something to the woman and turned toward John.

"If we've got an answer, you'll have to give us something," the man said. "Strange times we've got going. Can't be giving anything away for free."

"Sure," John said, and took a moment to think of something to trade. "I've got food, some spare blankets and the like. Any of that interest you?"

"Nah," the man said. He approached close enough for them to talk more easily, but stopped before John got anxious. "Got plenty of that stuff. What I don't got is a truck to haul this junk outta here."

"I hate to tell you this, but I'm kind of attached to this one," John said, chancing a glance around him. He was more exposed than he'd like, and the open windows in the buildings around him made him nervous. Through some of them, he could see faces peeking out from behind tattered plastic sheeting or tarps.

"I'm not gonna try and take it from ya. I'm not exactly in fighting shape," the man said with a laugh. "Just need help getting some stuff from here to somewhere else. I've got gasoline, too, back at the yard, if that sweetens the deal."

John thought for a moment, weighing his options. The man seemed confident enough that John could tell he'd made similar deals with people before.

"Sure. If it's not too far, I can do that," John said. "If you've got answers worth having. And any fuel you can spare would be good for the days ahead."

"Of course," the man said. "My name's Conrad. That over there is Bee. Don't need you to go far. I've got a scrap yard on the edge of town. We're not the first to scavenge from this wreck, but we're definitely the smartest. Last crew left the core in it and everything. Should have it out by tomorrow morning."

"Did you see what happened here?" John asked.

"Nah. Heard it, though," Conrad said. "Just about everyone in the country must have. What's left of the country, I guess. No, me and Bee were working one of the downed jets a few miles that way."

Conrad pointed in one direction, then rethought it and pointed in another direction. "Got some good stuff out there too. You need a central control module for one of those new Finch jets? A parachute?"

"No, just looking for some answers," John said. "So, you weren't here when it happened, but do you know what happened?"

"Oh, sure." Conrad pointed to the people in the windows. "Most of these people are pretty nice once you get to know 'em. Told me the whole thing. A bunch of big bots came stomping through here a few days back. Tore through the Enclaved portion of the city. Most of that's gonna be gone by now, I suppose. Then they took out some government buildings. Anyway. Later, a smaller group of mechs came up from the same way, out by the base?

"Yeah, so there was one straggler in the city, I guess, and these newcomers really laid into it." Conrad jerked a thumb back at the collapsed heap of the mech. "But, like I said, lots of meat left on the bones. That all you wanna know? I'm sure you coulda guessed most of that just by looking around with your eyes open."

"No, I'm interested in what happened after," John said. "You said you weren't the first one here to poke at these bones."

"Yeah, sure. There were at least a couple of crews here before us," Conrad said. "The first one, group of military types, took mostly ammo and some medical supplies from the cockpit. Apparently, they had a hell of a time getting it, though. Heard there were some rebels around. Some Harbingers, if you believe the

27

gossip. Really made them work for it. Only ones that died were rebel types, though. Shame, if you don't mind my saying so."

John didn't say whether he minded or not, and instead continued his line of questioning. "The ones that were killed. Did their bodies make it anywhere in particular?"

"Sure. I mean, they're not here anymore." Conrad scratched his chin and looked back toward Bee. "Where did they say they moved those rebel bodies, Bee?"

"In the old courthouse," Bee said, not looking up from her work. "Took them and as many as they could find from the collapsed apartment building down there."

John took a moment to check on Eva and looked down at her tiny form on the floor of the passenger's side. She was holding her stuffed whale tightly to her chest and looked up at him with concern.

"I'll just need to check that," John said to Conrad. "Then I'll be back in the morning to take whatever it is you need."

"Sure, take your time," Conrad said. "I'm not going anywhere. I'll do my best to have it out here before you get back."

John loosened his grip on his gun and returned it to the center console. He reached one hand down and placed it gently on Eva's head before shifting the car into drive and heading up the street in the direction Conrad had said the courthouse would be.

"I'm sorry about that," John said quietly. "Eva, she's probably fine. I just need to be sure."

"I said," Eva managed through her tears, "no lying."

CHAPTER 3

Turner sat on top of a wide desk inside a relatively undamaged classroom. He'd been escorted there on Banks' orders and left there alone. The others in his group had been put in different rooms up and down the hall. A bedroll and a gallon jug of water left for him was indication enough that he might not be leaving any time soon. This room had once been a science classroom, sparsely decorated with posters depicting the atomic elements and other important basic information. The various mechs of the United Entities fleet, or the ones they'd once had, ran on a wide range of energy sources. Some light mechs carried electric charge in banks of replaceable batteries. The larger mechs, like the eight-legged Neith- class command mechs, ran on nuclear cores. The principles of these and a dozen or more unique energy core designs would have been just one of the many courses taught in this classroom. If he ignored the spray of bullet holes punched along one wall, he could almost imagine it was just another day at the academy, and he was early for class. Turner had disliked this room even before the attack and liked it even less now.

He spent his first few hours opening every cabinet in the room, looking for something to cut the boredom. He wasn't

29

looking for a weapon or a way out, of course. Banks' concerns were justified. If they let every group of people who said they were allies join their ranks, they'd all be murdered in their sleep. Someone would be along eventually to let him know they'd found his service record and that he was free to go. Or they wouldn't.

He didn't find anything interesting in the cabinets. They'd been smart enough to take anything dangerous out of the room before locking him inside. He did find an assortment of old dusty plastic beakers, one of which he'd cleaned out as best he could to use as a drinking glass.

He'd just begun to think about how he was going to use the bathroom when there was a knock at the door.

"Come in," Turner said. "I guess?"

The door opened and Vesnina walked into the room. She didn't smile at him, but simply gestured for him to take a seat at one of the student desks.

"Seriously?" Turner asked. "You know I'm not a goddamn rebel. This is ridiculous; we brought mechs back, for fuck's sake."

"Just sit down, Turner," she said. "We've talked to the rest of your group and need to establish a timeline to verify your story."

"Okay, sure," Turner said. He hopped off the desk at the front of the room and sat in the one she'd indicated. "Where should I start? What about Social Dynamics? Did you finish that paper for Professor Coville?"

"As a matter of fact, I did," Vesnina said, rolling her eyes and smiling. She looked down at a pad she'd brought with her. "But no, we'll start with the night of the attack. Where were you when it began?"

"Fuck, sleeping, I guess?" Turner leaned back in his chair. "Yeah, I was asleep. The first explosion didn't wake me. Someone hit me, though, hard, and I was up. Everyone was getting ready for something in a hurry, and I didn't know what the hell was going on.

"I got hooked up with some other cadets. We barricaded the door, drew up a quick plan with some chalk on the floor. Fuck, all this feels like it happened to someone else. We had two teams, and we were going to try and gather as many forces as we could and get ourselves out to the live piloting training yard. Get the training mechs powered up."

"The ones you brought back?" Vesnina asked.

"Yeah. Well, some of them." Turner closed his eyes and continued. "We lost Zimmer before we even left the base. There were these squads of Harbingers working from barracks to barracks. By the time we got out of ours, it looked like they'd been through most of them already. A few of the buildings were already on fire."

"Why didn't you go after the squads?" Vesnina asked somewhat sharply.

"We thought our time would be better used by getting to the training mechs. I didn't think about it much." Turner looked back at her. "But you did. You went after them, didn't you? You and the others."

"Um, yeah, we tried," she said, and began nervously picking her cuticles. "Some of the officers managed to get a good

31

counterattack going in the chaos. We tried, but so many people were already dead."

"I'm so sorry," Turner said. "I can't even imagine."

"We did what we could." She took a deep breath and refocused on her pad. "Back to you. Once you got to the training mech hangar, what did you do?"

"We laid Zimmer up in one of the classrooms. Fuck, is his body still there? We didn't have time to bury him,"

"We buried a lot of people," Vesnina responded. She waited for him to continue.

"Yeah, okay." He shifted uncomfortably. "Well, we got the mechs armed and powered as quickly as we could, and we went after them."

She looked at him directly and asked her next question. "You just armed a small core of training mechs and set off after some of the most advanced mechanized units in the country?"

"I mean, yeah. We thought we'd get on their trail and eventually be joined by other forces." He held up his hands, realizing now why she was asking. "Hey, I get how this might look. We're not defectors. We went after them because someone needed to. Hell, we're probably the only units that got anywhere near them. They took out a wing of fighters that came in from the east. I still don't know how they did that. Someone said they must have stolen some tech from the base?"

"This is good," Vesnina said. "That information isn't widely known. It's worth noting that you gave it to us without pressure."

"What's that worth, like ten points toward my release?" Turner laughed, the sound echoing in the empty classroom. He cleared his throat. "Well, yeah. It looked like they hit a barrier in the sky. We ended up rescuing one of the pilots, Barkley. He was with us when you took us into custody. I mean, we followed them for a while. We took one of their units out in the city. We kept going. We eventually sent out a scout team."

"Did you get any useful information?" she asked. "How many there are, or anything like that?"

"I led us right into a trap." Turner laid his hands on the desk and said the rest as quickly as he could. "My mech got hit, and we were able to find cover. We radioed for help and waited. Everyone knew it was a trap, but they came for us anyway. Goddamned hero shit. I couldn't pilot my mech. The first hit nearly knocked me unconscious, and they moved me down to one of the trucks."

For a long time, Turner stared at his hands, turning the next part of the story over in his mind.

"It should have been me in that mech," he said softly. "It was my team. I led them there. When the rest of our mechs arrived, everything happened so fast. Our units took hits, but they managed to turn the tide and take out the enemy and get to us. We thought…I thought we'd won. I started thinking about which medals they were going to give all of us, and then the rest of the enemy forces came over the ridge. There were so many of them. They must have cleared out the entire hangar back here.

"Our mechs took heavy losses. My mech, Brooke, was in there. Fuck, it went down, and Mark just lost it. He started advancing on the enemy mechs with our command mech. I did the only thing I could think of. I pulled up a map of the valley and found the nearest defensible position and ordered everyone to retreat.

"We waited for Mark or anyone else to come after us. When no one did, I sent out a small team to scavenge for supplies in the wreckage. When they came back, they told me they hadn't seen anyone, but that some of the supplies had already been lifted from the wrecks.

"I figured we'd seen enough losses and decided to turn back for Taycher. We made our way back here, and you promptly locked us all up." Turner slapped his hands on the desk and leaned back in his chair.

Vesnina took a moment, seeming to process everything he'd said. She took some final notes on her pad and then looked up. "Okay, that all matches up with what we've got from the others. I'll be back in a bit. Shouldn't be much longer."

She stood and walked out of the classroom. As she left, Turner could see an armed soldier standing at the door outside. He waited in the room for ten minutes, then the door opened suddenly.

"Come in," he said under his breath.

Captain Banks walked into the room and Turner stood up. When he moved to stand at attention, Banks waved him off.

"I really am sorry for all of this," Banks said, and Turner got the impression that he meant it. "You have to understand what we've had to deal with here since the attack."

"I would understand if someone just told me. We saw some shit, too, and we didn't hold you at gunpoint in order to have a conversation."

Banks raised an eyebrow and looked at him sternly. He sighed and relaxed his shoulders. "I don't owe you an explanation, but here it is." He motioned for Turner to sit and took the seat Vesnina had earlier. "Those of us who survived managed to regroup after the rebels moved out. That night, we woke up to more gunfire. They'd left people behind to further thin us out. People we'd trusted. For all I know, there are still some of them in my ranks, but there's nothing I can do about that now."

Banks closed his eyes, seeming to be pushing himself past the memory of that first night. He took a deep breath and continued.

"We spent the next few days digging pits so we could bury our dead and theirs. By the time we thought to check the training mech hangar, we found that those units were gone. It would have been nice to have them here for defense, but we assumed the Harbingers had taken those as well.

"When we saw you out there on the ridge, we assumed you were rebels returning to finish us off. Vesnina believes your story, and the rest of your crew have corroborated it. So, you're going to fall in with the rest of us. Because you were the commanding officer, the third in just a few short days as I understand it, you're getting a battlefield promotion."

Turner widened his eyes in surprise. The shift from a thorough dressing-down to a promotion had been sharp. He actually felt like taking a seat now.

Banks continued shortly, "So, Lieutenant, please gather your people and meet me out on the parade grounds in twenty minutes. Your flyboy, Captain Barkley, will be tasked with other duties, so don't expect him."

"Yes, sir," Turner said.

He waited for the man to clear the hallway, then stepped out of the room himself. To his relief, the guard that had been by his door was gone now. Up and down the corridor, his own people were out of the other rooms, engaged in conversation. When they noticed him standing in the hallway, they all quieted down, evidently looking to him for direction.

"On me," he called to them. "We've got a bit to discuss."

CHAPTER 4

John stepped out of the truck and looked over the courthouse before him. The building was a grand marble structure, scorched in many places and heavily damaged in others. Still, the massive stone pillars in front remained intact. The front doors were open, and he could see that natural light permeated the space inside. He turned back to the truck and debated his options. Surely what was inside the courthouse would be disturbing to anyone, especially someone as young as Eva. Leaving her outside wasn't an option, though.

After thinking through the alternatives, he opened the passenger side door and gently lifted Eva from the truck. He turned her so that her face was buried in his neck and walked with her in his arms up the white marble steps of the building. At the top, he could see people inside. Their quick and efficient movements belied some sort of power structure and order. That was a good sign that he might be able to get some help.

He passed through the entryway and waited for his eyes to adjust to the semidarkness. Countless shards of broken glass, glittering with color, littered the red velvet carpet beneath his feet. John looked up and saw that the building had once featured an ornate stained-glass ceiling, reduced now to merely the wrought iron frame. The frame stood stark against the bright blue sky, like a spider web, or perhaps a cage.

One of the people moving around spotted John and Eva and stopped in his tracks. The man was covered in dirt and sweat, a griminess that didn't seem to match the quality of his shoes.

"She's not…" The man looked tired and anguished. "Not another one."

"What?" John asked and readjusted his hold on Eva. As he did, she moved her head and put her arm around his neck.

"Oh, thank God," the man said. "I've buried too many children already."

"No," John said. "I mean, yes. She's fine. Someone up the road directed me here for information."

"We don't have any medicine, sir," the man said. "This stopped being a hospital days ago. We're just trying to keep up with the dead."

"That's why I'm here, actually." John could feel the tears Eva was crying into his shoulder as they soaked through his jacket. "I'm looking for someone. A rebel woman."

"You mean from the night of the attack?" the man asked. "Sure, but we buried them already. Except there wasn't a woman. Not as far as I know. Just three men."

"Are you sure?" John asked. "All men? You're sure?"

"I can't tell you with a hundred percent certainty, but yes, they all appeared to be male when I added them to the log." When John didn't reply, the man wiped off his palm and extended his hand. "Carlos Yamana, my name. I'm a doctor."

"John Phillips," John replied, shaking the man's hand.

"I can show you our logbook, if you like," Carlos said. "We have been able to verify the identities of most of the bodies that have come in. Usually, it's a simple matter of checking their papers or any registered implants they might have."

"Yes, sure," John said. "Thank you."

Carlos walked away, and John followed after him. When they reached a stairway, John leaned over and set Eva down. He'd been moving more in the last few days than he had in years, and his bad leg was aching. "You're going to have to walk for a bit. I can't carry you up these stairs."

Eva nodded, held her stuffed whale closer to her body, and allowed herself to be led up the stairs. When they reached the second floor, Carlos went into an office and returned with a three-ring binder filled with papers.

"This is everyone we've gotten through this building," Carlos said. "It's not alphabetical, but it is thorough. The Harbingers have their own tab here." He opened the binder for John and flipped it to a single sheet of paper. "Not a lot of them yet, but I'm sure that will change. There were the three that came in after that mech went down a few blocks away. All of them died from gunshot wounds."

John scanned the names, recognizing two of them from his time with them on the stolen command mech before he'd left. These were his people, and Alison wasn't on the list. For a moment, he allowed himself to hope. If she hadn't been found dead with these men, she could still be alive.

"Did anyone see how these men died?" John asked.

"If you ask some of the people around here, you'll get a lot of answers," Carlos said. "I've heard stories saying they killed a dozen government soldiers before they fell. I haven't seen a government soldier through here yet, though, so I doubt that's true. More likely, the other story I've heard is closer to the truth."

"What's the other story?" John asked.

"That they died in a firefight, out by the wreck of that machine." Carlos waved his hand generally in the direction John had driven from. "They tried to sneak up on some government soldiers and paid for it. I've heard a rumor the government crew took one of the rebels as a prisoner to escape. It all sounds very dramatic, but that's the story that makes the most sense to me. All the hero crap is just that—crap. But, if it helps these people to have something to believe in, I'm not going to argue with them. They've been coming in daily to pay their respects."

"Can I see where you buried them?" John asked.

"Be my guest," Carlos said. "Downstairs and out the back door. You won't miss it. Listen, I need to get back to work. Find me if you need something else. I hope you find whoever you're looking for. I just hope you don't find them here."

John nodded and handed the binder back. "Thank you."

"Hm, sure," Carlos said, seemingly already distracted by whatever task he was set to do next. He went back to the office to replace the binder.

John and Eva walked back down the stairs. At the bottom, they turned and headed outside through the open set of double doors where Carlos had directed them. Behind the building, John could see the scale of what Carlos and the other people at the courthouse had been doing. A large plot of undeveloped land had been turned into a cemetery.

Neat rows of closely packed graves were marked with wooden planks at the head of each one. On each of these, a date was written. Many also had a name and a date of birth as well. Toward the back of the lot, he saw the graves Carlos must have been talking about. They were adorned with candles and all manner of decoration. The Harbingers must be popular with those left in the city.

"She's not here?" Eva asked quietly.

"I don't think so," John whispered. "I'm just not sure where to check next."

"Didn't the doctor say they took someone?" Eva asked. "To escape?"

"Maybe. But if that was Alison, I don't know if there's anything we can do to catch up to her. They're at least a few days away by now. I think our best bet is going to be asking around here a bit longer. Then we should get back on the road. We have a schedule to keep."

Eva looked at the ground and kicked some dirt around. Together, they worked their way toward the rebel grave markers. John was relieved someone had decided to make taking care of the dead their job. The alternative John had envisioned was looking through a room of corpses for Alison's face.

The graves were marked with the same names John had seen in the binder upstairs. Somehow, seeing them here was harder. He looked down at the three names and placed his hand on the rough wooden planks one at a time. Crawford, Simms, and Samson. The sound of his skin on the wood was soft, like falling sand. John understood on some level that their deaths were not his fault alone. Taking responsibility for them would be to assign himself more power than he ever really had. He was just a man with a talent for words who occasionally got drunk in his room and typed without thought of consequence. At least, that's what part of him believed to be true.

John looked up from the three decorated graves and took in the whole graveyard for the first time. There were scores of bodies beneath the soil here. All across the United Entities, the world, there must be fields like this. Graves like the ones he'd dug out at Alison's family home. The true cost of a fresh start was buried beneath his feet. What began as mere words had undergone a metamorphosis through brutal force and finally terminated here in death. John thought coldly that this was what the foundations of society crumbling looked like up close.

~

"We should have heard from someone already," Jim said, knocking on the communications display with his knuckles. "It's been too long, and we're too damn close."

Katherine stood at the front of the command deck, looking out over the landscape. It was beautiful in a way that felt almost staged to her. They were moving through what must be one of the last preserved woodland areas in the northern hemisphere. Most agriculture had been put behind so many walls and checkpoints that the farms could hardly be called natural anymore. Some were not much more than brightly lit warehouses that spanned over miles of arid land forced to yield.

The vista before her, though, was green beyond her understanding. Trees as tall as the command mech itself sprawled for miles in all directions. As they moved through the redwood forest, she took care to divert her forces through the lanes that would cause the least amount of damage. Ancient power line roads and off-road trails were easy enough to follow. When they did need to push through a section of wooded earth, she managed to get them into a tight formation.

She shook her head and returned her thoughts to the mission at hand. Jim was right; something was wrong. They were close to Ember Springs, the mountain town they'd been ordered to reach at any cost. Why they'd been directed there, neither Jim nor Katherine knew, exactly.

Perhaps someone else in their party was holding onto the next set of instructions, but until a trigger event occurred, they may have been ordered to keep it secret. There had been aspects of the plan thus far that Katherine had needed to keep to herself, but she was at the end of her checklist now. Her orders ended in Ember Springs. Given Jim's displeasure, he didn't seem to have the next piece of the puzzle either.

"We haven't reached the town yet," Katherine said. "Maybe we'll get orders when we arrive."

Before Jim could respond, there was a commotion at the rear of the room. Someone was trying to convince the door guards to let them pass.

"You know, this is actually great," a woman said. "I was hoping we'd end up dying today. Fuck off and let me through, Carl."

"What's going on?" Katherine asked, walking toward the argument. "Let her in. She's not going to do any harm."

Carl, one of the people posted at the door, stepped aside and resumed staring stoically out into the corridor.

"Jesus fuck," the woman said as she stepped into the room. "Authorization phrase, Lemon Armchair."

"Excuse me?" Katherine said. "Did you just say, 'Lemon Armchair'?"

"I didn't pick the goddamn phrase. Don't look at me," the woman said. She was short and solidly built, wearing an outfit that looked like she'd had too much time to put it together. She looked like a rebel that could have come from any era or region. "I'm Sima. They told me to say Lemon Armchair, at least I think that was it, and give him this." Sima pointed at Jim with a sheet of paper and waved it back and forth in the air impatiently.

"Must have forgotten to tell me about the citrus furniture, I guess," Jim said. "But I will take that."

The woman handed over the scrap of paper and waited while Jim read it. Katherine felt a surge of emotion that she worked to keep hidden. The phrase "Lemon Armchair" was her kill phrase. She'd received the phrase before the attack on Taycher. Her orders ended here. Soon, it would be someone else's turn to take control, and she wasn't sure how she felt about that.

"These are new frequency encryption keys," Jim said. He walked to the communications display. "No wonder we aren't getting anything."

As he entered the new codes, Sima stood in front of Katherine, shifting uncomfortably.

"Was there anything else?" Katherine asked. "If that's it, you're dismissed."

"Yeah, that's it," Sima said. "I just want to know what's going on. We're all just sort of waiting for any information down below."

"You can wait a bit longer," Katherine said. "Thank you for the codes. We will call on you if we have any further questions."

She called for the guard, who stepped away from the door, and motioned for Sima to leave. Sima did so slowly, looking out at the landscape in awe. Katherine left her to gape for a few moments, trusting that their guard would escort her off the command deck.

Jim had nearly finished inputting the new codes when Katherine reached him at the comms station. "Maybe they'll have a welcome-home party," he said. "There, that should do it. What should we say?"

"You heard the woman," Katherine said, smirking and gesturing at the radio. "Lemon Armchair."

"Lemon. Armchair," Jim said clearly and slowly into the radio. "Fuck, I hope she remembered the phrase right. If that was wrong, we might have some trouble."

A few moments of silence went by as they awaited a response from whoever was out there among the trees.

"Copy that, Lemon Armchair." The voice that came through the radio was clear and crisp. Very close. "Proceed along your current bearing, and you'll come up on an escort soon."

They continued for five minutes until the light mech Katherine had leading the formation came to a stop. "Command, we've got a mech, a few miles up," the pilot in their lead mech came in through the radio.

Jim reflexively switched the comms over to their local group and handed the receiver to Katherine.

"Do not engage," she said. "Looks like we've made it, everyone. That's our escort. Approach and follow wherever they lead."

"Lemon Armchair, really?" Jim laughed and shook his head. "First thing I'm doing when we stop is figure out who's assigning codenames."

A new voice came in over the radio. "This is Escort One. Lemon Armchair, please take position with your command mechs at the top of the hill marked with red smoke. Instruct the rest of your units to follow me to the secondary garage within the mountain. Welcome to the Hollows, comrades."

Katherine didn't need to instruct the other mechs to continue following the escort mech. The order had been broadcast over the main channel. Deferring to her was only a courtesy.

"You heard them. Follow your escort," Katherine told her pilots. "I'll see you on the inside."

She took her seat at the controls, piloted her mech up a shale slope, and stopped once it reached a smoke location marker. A massive steel door was set into the mountain in front of them, camouflaged to look like the rock surrounding it.

"I've reached the marker," she said through her radio. "What should we be doing now? I've got just above two dozen crew on board. The other units have similar crew complements."

"Power down, engage the automatic sensor sweeps, and disembark." The order came from the radio. "Someone will be out to direct you inside shortly."

Katherine relayed the information and powered down the Anansi. The silence that washed over the command deck once the engine cycled down was eerie. They'd been running the engine continuously for so long she'd completely forgotten the sound of it was there.

"I guess that's it," Jim said. "Let's all head for the cargo ramp and await our hero's welcome."

"Sure," Katherine said. "You all go on ahead. Gather everyone below deck and head outside. I'll finish up here and meet you."

Jim eyed her with concern but turned and led everyone else off the command deck. Once the sounds of boots on stairs faded to almost nothing, Katherine paced the metal floor of the command deck. She stayed there for a while, trying to pinpoint why she felt hesitant to leave the Anansi. She stood at the front of the command deck, looking out over the expansive mountain range.

"Katherine." Jim's voice startled her out of her trance. "We're all waiting for you."

"Sure, yeah." She turned and studied Jim's face. Faced with the prospect of actually leaving, she found words for what was bothering her. "You know, I've been in command for a long time, Jim. Even before I ran that school I was in combat for years, making major decisions that destroyed a lot of lives. I've done so much from a position of power to make things worse. Being here on this machine was the first time I've felt good about my orders in a long time."

"You don't *have* to give orders right now," Jim said. "You can just feel relieved for a bit. We're here. We made it, and now it's someone else's show for a while."

Katherine shook her head and smiled briefly, but she didn't feel any better. "Sure. Someone else's show."

As they headed down the cargo ramp, Katherine saw that the huge blast doors had parted just enough to allow a team of armed soldiers to exit the mountain. They stood menacingly still with their rifles ready but not raised. One figure, a man dressed in a black suit who looked out of place in the natural landscape, approached her.

"Do not be alarmed," the man said. His voice was cool and even. If his tone was trying to soothe her, it wasn't working. "We can't be too careful. Uncertain times and all that, you understand. Please place your firearms on the ground and allow yourselves to be taken into our custody. None of you will be harmed. As soon as we can verify your allegiance to the Harbingers, you will all be released and allowed to continue your work, whatever that ends up being."

Those in Katherine's group didn't immediately comply, so she removed her own pistol from its holster and placed it on the metal of the cargo ramp. It made a sharp click as she laid it flat, and that encouraged everyone around her to do the same. The armed group of soldiers moved carefully toward them, then removed any other items they were carrying. The soldier tasked with frisking Katherine removed a multitool from Katherine's belt almost apologetically.

The squad of soldiers then led her and her crew toward the doors leading into the mountain. Just before they entered, they came to an abrupt stop as a team of people dressed long gray lab coats rushed out toward the command mechs. She turned to watch them, but she already knew what they'd be after. They headed toward one of the other command mechs. The Ston device they'd stolen from Taycher along with the mechs, had been their primary extraction target. Katherine understood its significance only because it had somehow protected them from any kind of aerial assault during their entire trip.

Before the attack, her security clearance had only allowed her minimal access to information regarding the science labs at Taycher. The most she'd ever been able to glean from the reports she accessed was that something of vital importance was being developed there. She had once been given a heavily redacted file that referred to the project by name: Project Ston. She'd looked up the name in the records to see what else she might find, but had only found references to an ancient city somewhere far across the globe. She'd been as surprised as anyone else when the device had protected them so utterly from incoming aerial attacks. Not knowing the range of the device, she'd made sure to keep their forces bunched up as much as possible during their long trek north.

Someone else they'd scooped up at Taycher must have held more information about the device than she did. Compartmentalization of information: standard operating procedure for the Harbingers of the Fall.

She passed through the doors, and they began to close immediately behind her. It took a few moments for her eyes to adjust to the darkness as she walked to the front of her group. Shapes began to assert themselves, first as dull shadows, but then as more recognizable silhouettes. They were inside a vast cavern carved from the rock. There were dozens of mechs along the walls and in neat rows before them. Her mechs, the ones she'd pulled over hundreds of miles of desert, would certainly bolster these forces, but the Hollows were already well equipped.

Above, on a catwalk, were the familiar shapes of pilot training simulators. The scene was so reminiscent of the central garage at Taycher that she was momentarily disoriented. How had they been able to steal this many mechs? Where had they gotten those training pods?

Of course, she reasoned, they had obtained the schematics and software for these machines and simulators years ago. They couldn't have the resources to physically build the parts for these mechs inside the mountain though. With her next thought she found a solution. The Harbingers had simply been siphoning parts from the assembly lines to build their own fleet. She'd been party to at least a few of those thefts, she remembered. She'd falsified orders for replacement parts for the mechs the cadets used for training. The orders had been so specific, though. At the time, she'd assumed the Harbingers were building a single mech. Clearly, they'd been busy pulling in parts for a while.

The soldiers stopped her and her crew. Katherine looked for the man in the suit, but he must have slipped off once they'd gone through the doors. The soldiers lined everyone up and led them one at a time down one of the dozens of hallways that branched off from the hangar. She managed to work her way back toward Jim, reassuring her people as she walked.

"How did they...did we..." Jim asked in a whisper as he stared up at the mechs. "How the hell are we this well armed? How can this place exist without the United Entities knowing?"

"That's a good question," Katherine said. "If we can do this, I have to wonder what else has been going on in here."

"You," a stern and direct voice called through the thinning crowd. "Scholl, you've been assigned to another location."

"Guess I'm headed to the principal's office." She attempted a smile but could only manage a nervous grin. First patting Jim on the shoulder, she turned to greet the two men who were coming to escort her. Being inside this well-organized and well-armed stronghold should have brought a deep sense of relief. Instead, Katherine felt uneasy. She'd expected more fanfare and a less rigid structure. There wasn't anything explicitly wrong with how things were proceeding, it all just seemed a little too organized for a revolution.

The two men didn't attempt to guide her physically. At least she was spared that discomfort. She did note that both of the men had their rifles held firmly in hand. As she walked away, her crew continued to be led off, one by one, down a different hallway.

She was taken to a passage marked with a green line on the wall, part of some wayfinding system, no doubt. The command mechs used a similar system below deck to guide wayward soldiers. As they walked, the bare stone walls gave way to more polished and painted surfaces. Eventually, they came to a room with the door open, and she walked inside. She turned around to ask the two men what she was doing here, but found the door shut firmly in her face before she could get out a single word.

Katherine turned back around and realized she was in a large living space. A wardrobe, bed, and desk were placed efficiently around the room. In one corner, there was a small bathroom complete with a shower.

"Okay," she said to the empty room. "I suppose I'll make myself at home."

She walked to the bed and sat down, resting her hands on the crisp white sheets. They were cool and smooth, much different than the rough bunks she'd been sleeping on in the Anansi. She moved her hand and saw that she'd left a visible smudge of grime on the sheets. Katherine looked at the shower and contemplated how many times she would need to bathe before the residue of the last few days fully washed away.

CHAPTER 5

The cool desert air whipped around Alison's all-terrain vehicle as she and Zak pushed through the evening air. Their vehicle, meant for only one rider in ideal circumstances, was covered in dust from miles of open-desert travel. She knew traveling in the dark was dangerous, but her mind had been a white-hot blur since she realized someone may have survived the attack at her home. Zak was seated behind her, holding onto the cargo boxes strapped to the back of the vehicle as they bounced along the rough desert trail. Occasionally, he would turn around and pull one of the straps tight again.

They should be nearing their destination soon. During their last short break, Zak had asked her to wait until morning to cover the final stretch, but she hadn't been able to bring herself to stop. Every minute she'd spent captured was another moment Eva could have been alone, waiting for her, waiting for anyone.

"Alison," Zak yelled above the wind and the drone of the engine. "If you don't slow down, we're going to lose some of the supplies!"

Alison said nothing and poured on more speed. She knew he was right, though. If she kept this speed any longer, they'd lose more than their supplies. She held the throttle for a few more seconds, allowing the dirt road below her to become a river as the tires drifted along. After savoring the feeling for a moment more, she let go of the throttle and the ATV coasted to a stop. The fine dust cloud they'd been pulling up behind them for miles washed over them, limiting their visibility.

After the dust cleared, Alison stepped gingerly off the ATV, taking her key and satchel with her as she did. Her leg still ached from her injury, and the cast on her leg made movement hard. She limped off the road and away from Zak as he busied himself with the task of pulling the various containers off the vehicle. With any luck, he would have their meager campsite set up by the time she returned.

For her part, she clicked on a flashlight and worked to gather a small bundle of firewood and tinder to keep them warm through the night. As she walked, she occasionally picked up a stick or small log and added it to a growing bundle in her arms. Once she had enough, she turned toward the south and looked at the hills in the distance. Just beyond them, her family home and the community where she'd spent most of her life waited for her return. It was technically an illegal settlement, and had only been allowed to continue to exist because they were useful. Her father had been one of the more useful members of the community. He'd given the patrols that passed through weekly more in contraband produce than they could ever hope to acquire themselves. In this way, her father and a few of the other industrious individuals in the area had managed to keep the community invisible.

That was all over now, though. Her home had burned to the ground before her very eyes as three enemy soldiers managed an escape. Three soldiers, and one of them was with her now, setting up camp for her. She turned and started making her way back to the ATV.

Alison felt the weight of her bag bumping her thigh as she walked. She was glad to have her backpack and satchel. They contained everything she now owned.

Back at the scene of the battle she had managed to find her things among the spilled contents of a storage crate. In her satchel, she always carried a notebook with the locations of Harbinger supply caches. They'd set off together to access a cache that she'd hoped would be close. That first stretch had been the hardest part; relying on him to help her walk as they slowly made their way across the desert. To her relief, and likely Zak's as well, they'd come upon it right where her map said it would be; an ATV and basic supplies in a thick stand of aspen trees. Now that they had the vehicle, she no longer needed him, she thought.

She turned off the flashlight and walked as quietly as she could back toward the ATV in the dim moonlight. When she could see Zak unpacking their gear, she crouched down and watched him. In the light of a small electric lantern, she saw him unrolling a sleeping bag.

While still concealed in the sagebrush, Alison set down her armload of wood and removed an old revolver from her bag. Her father had given it to her before she left her home. It was the last time she'd spoken to him. The blued steel of the barrel gleamed in the moonlight. She worked the hammer idly, the cylinder rotating smoothly each time.

Zak could have left her as soon as they reached the ATV. She knew that. He could have left her there to continue on by herself, but he hadn't. Each night so far, she walked through this mental labyrinth just to arrive in the same place. His guilt was genuine, she determined, and so was his sense of obligation to her.

Alison put the revolver back into her bag, the urge to end him dulled once again by watching him methodically prepare their campsite. She grunted as she stood, lifted the bundle of wood, and pushed her way out of the brush. She dropped the wood beside Zak.

"Thanks." He looked up at her for a moment, studying her. "We should take a look at your leg tonight. Make sure there isn't any infection or anything."

"Sure," Alison said as she lowered herself to the ground slowly. "Can't hurt."

She began to fiddle with the inflatable cast that restricted the movement of her leg and experienced a wave of both resentment and relief when Zak moved over to help her. He pulled at some of the fastenings and depressurized it. Having the cast removed was a great relief. Soon, though, she felt a renewed warm pain bloom. Zak looked at the leg and made sounds that were hard to interpret.

"Every time I look, I feel like I'm opening the hood of a car," Zak said. "I know that's a leg, you know? But I really don't know if what I'm looking at is good or bad. If we're lucky, what you've got is a sprain, but I really can't tell. You could have torn something in there for all I know. Hell, if Hartley were here, she'd be able to figure it out. 'Oh, that's a transverse femoral tear with a lateral interstitial twist,' or some shit like that."

"That's a lot of fancy words for someone who doesn't know what he's looking at," Alison said, concealing a smirk within a grimace as Zak began to move her leg.

"Uh, yeah, I guess," he said. He looked intently at the deep purple bruise where the injury was centered. "I used to catch some medical dramas when I had recreation time. Historical ones with public hospitals and stuff."

"Well, I think it's getting better," she said. "The pain isn't as intense anymore, and I can walk a little better."

"Still, you should be taking it easy," Zak said as he re-inflated the air cast around her leg. "The last thing we need is for it to get worse."

Alison didn't say anything. She chewed idly on the inside of her cheek and held back an angry retort about only resting when she was dead. Zak left her and continued setting up the campsite, finishing up with the two small tents they'd sleep in.

Alison scooted over to her bundle of firewood and began arranging it into a small pyramid with the smaller branches and twigs below. She struck a match from a small package in her bag and stared at the tiny flame in her hand. It danced in the breeze, traveling down the wooden shaft slowly. Before the flame could reach her fingertips, she reached out and placed it inside the pyramid of branches. The kindling caught and began casting wild shadows into the night. In the flickering light, she was pulled against her will into the recent past.

She could almost see the dark silhouette of her family home, before the shooting had begun. As she stared at the growing fire, the flames began to curl around the branches. She was reminded of the searing heat that had exploded from the windows and thrown her to the ground. She tried to rush in, to do anything she could to save Eva and her mother, but someone had pulled her back. If she had just remembered then about the hidden root cellar, she would have returned sooner. That wasn't entirely true, of course; she'd been a prisoner until only recently. She had thrown herself from a moving truck in order to escape. But she was close now. Just beyond the horizon, the field where she'd once pretended to fight huge unseen enemies awaited her return.

~

"You okay?" Zak asked, tending to the fire Alison started. "You look kind of far off."

"I'm fine," she said quietly.

Zak was smart enough not to press her on it and continued to feed the small fire as she watched it burn. He was still earning Alison's trust and pushing her wouldn't help. She hadn't said much during their trek across the desert so far. She merely re-layed the relevant information about what they needed to do and where they needed to go. He knew that her family home had a root cellar; one that someone could have possibly survived in during the attack. Zak had seen Eva in the doorway as he escaped, and doubted if anyone could have survived what he'd seen. Still, even if no one was left, Zak could tell she needed to see it for herself.

Her face was lit erratically by the flickering orange light of the fire, and he could tell she was back there now, reliving that terrible night. Zak envied her in a way. Her ability to go back and work through it. Whenever he felt himself slipping back into that memory, his role in all of it, he had to fight his way out of it. Zak was afraid that if he allowed himself to fully immerse himself in the memory, he would never be able to resurface.

Seeing her face now, however, made it harder than it had ever been to stay in the present. She knew he had been there, but she didn't know everything. If she found out, she might not let him continue with her. Alison might decide to use the gun she took with her out into the darkness each time she went to gather wood. There was nothing he could do to fix what happened that night, but he could try to aid Alison in whatever she needed now. In some ways, Zak knew his presence was selfish. His assistance was borne out of guilt and the hope that by helping Alison, he would somehow be absolved of responsibility.

He shared that responsibility with many others, of course. His fellow soldiers, who caused most of the damage, the enemy rebels, who surrounded the home, and Alison's father, who sent the message to the Harbinger forces. Responsibility for anything could be shared, but no matter how many people he placed in line with him, Zak still faced his own guilt. He had fired the shot into the sky to wake Lund and Manner. He had run into the house, toward the civilians inside. When he had been confronted by Brian, Zak had shot him. And, as they'd driven away, as Manner had fired blindly into the house and into the night, Zak had done nothing to stop him. He'd been paralyzed into inaction.

Zak wiped his face vigorously, clearing away his tears. He waved at the smoke and pretended to cough, to blame them on the fire. He sat back and closed his eyes, trying with everything he had not to stray too deeply into the past. Instead, by avoiding one memory, he was confronted with another.

He saw Mark standing in the desert with tears streaming down his face, the smoking silhouette of the destroyed command mech heaped behind him like a massive dead thing. Zak had watched confusion wash across Mark's face as he recognized Alison standing beside him. Mark's mere confusion had transformed in a moment into a grief-driven rage. He'd pointed his pistol directly at Alison.

"Why the fuck is she here?" Mark asked, his voice hoarse and quiet, like he'd used it all up. "Zak, why the fuck is she here?"

Zak hadn't known what to say. His own emotions were still sorting themselves. Grief and anger made Zak want to throw Alison at Mark's feet, to allow some form of justice to be served for the ambush he'd just witnessed. Guilt demanded that he protect Alison with his life. Those two conflicting urges had manifested as a complete lack of action.

They'd talked in brief, sharp tones as Mark continued to aim his weapon at them. In the end, Zak chose to protect Alison. He'd left Mark alone among the burning wreckage of the battle. Mark's screams, as they had fled back up the dune toward the scattered supplies, still came to Zak in his dreams.

He opened his eyes and saw Alison had shifted her gaze away from the fire. She stared out into the approaching night, toward whatever remained of her home among the trees.

As the sun slipped beneath the horizon, Mark ended another day of travel. He lowered the kickstand of the off-road motorcycle he'd taken from the ruins of the Maratus, and savored a stretch that popped joints in his back. He stepped off the vehicle and removed the saddlebags strapped to the sides of the motorcycle, setting them in the dry grass he'd selected for that night's camp. The loose desert sand had given way to hard packed earth that day. It was more suitable for plant life, making the search for firewood easier. He gathered a small pile and made a fire as the light left the sky.

After this, he took out a piece of scrap metal the size of a clipboard and a white piece of chalk. The scrap had markings on it from the night before; rough calculations keeping track of his progress as he made his way toward Ember Springs. Mark used his sleeve to wipe away the chalk from the previous night and stared at the blank space.

When he left the wreckage of his mech, he'd been about two hundred miles from Ember Springs. There wasn't anything obviously important about the small mining town, but it was where the enemy mechs had clearly been headed. It was also Brooke's hometown, the reason she'd been with the advance scout party when…Mark shook his head and pushed that memory aside.

The town itself likely wasn't all that important anyway. What he was really headed toward was an enemy camp or stronghold, possibly inside a fabled complex of tunnels and chambers known to local urban myths and conspiracy theorists as the Hollows. What he would do if he found it, he still wasn't sure.

Mark finished his quick calculations, finding that he would be getting close to the town tomorrow if he made good enough time. He returned the piece of chalk to his breast pocket and the scrap of metal to his pack. As he busied himself with setting up a small tent, he imagined where he would have been if the Harbingers hadn't intervened and thrown his life off course.

He should have been in a broad gray room sleeping soundly right now, waiting for the morning commotion to rouse him for another day at the United Entities Mechanized Warfare Academy. He should have been learning about tactics, moving from lecture to exercise until his scheduled free time at the end of the day. He should have been seeing Brooke in Rec. 5 and kissing her in the darkness before heading their separate ways for the night.

Mark picked up a stone and pounded a stake into the ground to secure his tent against a cool wind coming in from the east.

Even that fantasy wasn't strictly true, though. Brooke would have shipped out with her new unit already. She would have been thousands of miles away if this nightmare hadn't begun. He'd have lost her one way or another, but this dark path was so much worse. She was not simply gone in some abstract sense, wandering the world, fighting for Stability. No. She was dead, and it was the fault of the Harbingers. Their actions had started this. He set another stake and hammered it into the earth. The stone slipped on the last swing and struck his hand as he held the stake in place. He pulled his hand back sharply and swore under his breath as a memory sprang forward in his mind.

Brooke had held his hand in hers, inspecting an injury on one of his fingers. He'd snagged it on the metal ladder they had used to get up on the roof of the vehicle garage. It was built into the high base wall and offered a truly spectacular view. Plus, it was very off limits, and therefore very private. The sun had set hours ago, and the stars were awake above them.

"Don't suppose you brought a med kit with you on this little adventure?" she asked.

"Didn't expect it to be this perilous," Mark smiled. "I'm fine, anyway."

He wiped the blood off on his gray uniform, instantly regretting it. He made a mental note to pre-treat the stain before the next laundry shift. He guided her to the edge of the roof where he'd left a blanket and two beers the previous night. They sat with their legs dangling over the edge, watching as the stars slowly rotated above them. He opened the beers and handed one of them to Brooke.

"This is nice," she said in a whisper. She took a drink and rested her head on his shoulder.

"Yeah," Mark said quietly. It was all he could think to say. He couldn't remember ever feeling this at peace.

"Why are we whispering?" Brooke asked. He could tell she was smiling.

"Because we're trespassing?" Mark said. "And I didn't want to spoil the mood."

"And what mood is that, cadet?" Brooke lifted her head and looked at him with mock reproach.

"Hey, you're a cadet too. And it's a mood where I get to kiss you on a rooftop under a sky full of stars. Romantic, right?"

"Very romantic. It was Zak's idea, wasn't it?"

"Well, yes, of course. But it's still romantic."

He leaned down to kiss her, and she leaned in as well. Her lips were soft but cool, from sitting in the night air and breeze. He reached up and put one hand on her cheek and felt something wet there. He pulled away and looked at her face.

She stared up at him, her lips still lightly parted. A small smear of blood glittered red in the starlight on her cheek. He was confused for a moment but then remembered the cut on his hand.

The thought of blood and cold lips brought him back to the desert. He looked down at his hand, the same one he'd snagged on a ladder what felt like years ago. A fresh gouge beaded with blood. He pushed back against the rooftop memory, not wanting to have it spoiled by his current mood. Leaving that memory brought him up against other thoughts he'd been trying to avoid.

Mark was as much to blame for her death as the Harbingers were. He sent her and the rest of her team into the storm. He'd decided to place a value on information above her life. He wiped the blood from his hand onto his pants and got back to work setting up his tent. The chain of accountability traced circles in his mind as he tried to force it to a close.

He'd needed to send someone. This was a fact that Brooke would have been keen on reminding him. They had desperately needed to know what the enemy had for them. Mark was left, then, with only the Harbingers to blame. They were the enemy, shadowy monsters destroying everything they could before they would eventually be stopped.

He focused on holding onto this conviction. All these things, the blame and the excuses, were true, but brought him no closer to closing the hole inside him. He reached into his pocket and pulled out the penny dangling from its chain. It glimmered in the firelight as it had every night since he'd left the battlefield. He stared at it for a long time, as the sky deepened from maroon to purple. The clasp on the chain opened easily enough. He put it around his neck and secured it. Mark lifted the penny to his face and kissed the cool metal. Its scent was metallic, like blood, and he tucked it inside his shirt.

A brief chill spread through his body as the necklace laid against his skin. Very quickly, it warmed, and then he could only sense it when he moved. He lay down on his bedroll beside the fire, abandoning the tent, and gazed up at the stars.

These same points of light had looked down on humanity for thousands of years, he thought. Every war, every birth and death. Every story ever told had happened here, in a single place. Why, then, did his own pain feel so unique? If it was just one drop in an infinite sea of pain, he should be able to lose it there somehow. Cast it into the darkness and walk on, unburdened.

Tears slid down his face and into the ground below him. The stars hanging above winked back at him. Their light fluctuated from warm to frigid as he watched them pass slowly by. He found himself trying to trace the pattern of Brooke's face among them before he eventually fell asleep.

CHAPTER 6

Katherine woke when someone knocked on her door. She wondered how long she'd been there. It was hard to gauge time without any windows or even a clock, but she guessed it was early morning.

There were two more knocks at the door, and she got up. She was wearing the same set of clothes she'd arrived in. A wardrobe in the corner was stocked with crisp grey uniforms, but she didn't feel like it was the right time to put one on yet.

"Come in," she called at the door as she began putting on her boots.

The door opened, and two stocky soldiers entered the room. Their frames and features were similar enough that they could have been brothers. It felt strange not knowing who these men were. At the Academy, she had committed more faces and names to memory than she thought possible. The thought that many of those names now belonged to the dead was unsettling. It felt to her like they would begin to drift in her mind like ghosts. She shook her head to clear it. One of the men had asked her something, and she'd missed it.

"I'm sorry, what was that?" she asked.

"Katherine Scholl, are you ready?" One of the soldiers asked. His uniform carried no insignia or marks of rank, but he was just a little taller than the other one.

"Yes, I'm ready." She finished lacing up one boot and started on the other. "Where are we going?"

The two soldiers looked at each other, seeming to decide whether they were allowed to tell her. The symmetry of the movement made Katherine smile a little. They might actually be brothers, she thought.

"You're scheduled for a meeting," the taller man said. "We're not authorized to tell you more than that."

She closed her eyes and took a deep breath as she finished lacing her second boot. The loss of authority was something else she needed to get used to. When she was done with her boot, she made a gesture at the door, and they all stepped out into the hall. The tall soldier walked in front of her while the other walked behind. Katherine noted that they were following the red line on the wall and wondered what each color meant. She was new to the Hollows and scheduled for a meeting, so red might correspond to a security wing.

After a surprising number of turns, they stopped in front of a door painted neatly with a red circle. Her escorts conversed briefly with another set of guards on either side of the door. Then she was ushered into the new room, and the door was pulled shut behind her. There was no click of a lock turning, but the swiftness of the door as it closed was warning enough to stay where she was.

The room was a painful white, like they'd used the reflective white paint normally reserved for lettering on ships to coat the entire room. The lights were also a brilliant white, balanced to mimic daylight deep within this stony labyrinth. There was a desk in the middle of the room and another door across from the one she'd entered through. In front of the desk were two green chairs that would have been at home in an ancient airport lounge.

Katherine approached the chairs, noting the carpet also looked old. It wasn't worn, but it was outdated. She sat in one of the chairs and continued to examine the room. It must have been part of the original underground complex. The huge garage she and her crew had entered through had been more rough-hewn, a recent addition to accommodate the mech fleet they were keeping inside.

Just as she turned her attention to a mess of papers and folders on the desk in front of her, the door behind her creaked open.

"Katherine Scholl." The voice was familiar. "Excuse me. Vice Admiral Katherine Scholl. It's been a long time."

She knew it was him, but she turned anyway, just to be sure. Garrin Kingston strode toward the desk with his hand outstretched, as if they were just at another officer's ball celebrating someone's promotion. She took his offered hand in a distant way, searching herself for the correct response to the situation. Should she run away? Should she take the stapler on the edge of the desk and use it to beat his face in?

"It has been a while," was all she managed to say.

"Thank you for bringing my mech back in one piece. I specifically requested that the Anansi be brought back to me. I wanted to brief you myself. I hope that's all right," he said. "The rest of your team will be briefed and held while we assess their allegiance. You warrant some extra attention, of course."

He withdrew his hand, and she remembered to breathe. He sat down opposite her, behind the desk, and took a few moments to clear a space on it for a folder she hadn't noticed he was holding. He let the folder drop with a dull thud.

"That's your file." He poked at it, seeming to simultaneously accuse her and praise her for the size of it. He leaned forward in his chair, and she could hear it creak under his weight. He wasn't overweight so much as he was generally large. "There's more information here than we have on most people. You've been busy."

For a moment, Katherine began to panic. Had this all been a trap? No, the attack at Taycher had been real. The Harbingers were real.

"Sure. I've been active with the Harbingers for a while." She felt the urge to scratch her forearms, a nervous tic she had picked up when she'd joined the military. She'd made a specific effort to rid herself of the habit when a colleague had commented on it. She focused on relaxing her hands and continued. "We've dispatched a lot of good information and supplies through the years."

"Exactly. That's what I'm saying." He flashed her a grin and leaned back. Katherine couldn't tell if he was toying with her or was really this bad at communication. "You've done absolutely outstanding work in the field. Because of you, we have our own home-built mechs you saw in the garage. Not to mention the ones you brought with you. I see the login credentials you forged were effective. That's all great, but the device you secured during the operation is what we were really after. It's going to change everything."

He gave her a conspiratorial look, like he'd said something he wasn't supposed to, and continued.

"We've also been able to train a few of our own pilots with the information you've provided over the years. You and John, I should say."

Here it was, the real reason she'd been afforded this private briefing. John, the Voice of the Fall, was supposed to be with them, and he wasn't.

"Where is Phillips?" Garrin asked coldly. "We had a team sent in specifically to extract him. Of the targets in the base, he was our secondary extraction goal."

"He disembarked…" She paused, taking a moment to construct the words before saying them. "His priorities shifted while on board, and I thought it best to let him disembark. Rather than try to restrain him, I thought it would be better to let him go."

"That's a pretty bold decision, you know," Garrin said while patting her file, almost caressing it. "That decision almost makes some of the leadership here want to disregard this service record. I told them you must have had a good reason to let him go."

"I told you, his priorities shifted and his dedication to the cause had become secondary to him."

"Yes, you did say that. What you haven't told me is where his priorities have shifted," he said, his friendly tone gone now. "You haven't told me where the man whose words helped shape the Harbingers of the Fall has gone off to. You haven't explained why the man whose mind contains so much of our structure and strategic operation was allowed to simply leave."

Katherine hadn't looked at it that way when she'd let him go. John had been intent on trying to correct some very specific damage he felt he had done.

"I let him go because he wanted to rescue an operative we lost track of in the field," Katherine said. "He treated her like a daughter. I thought we owed him the freedom to make his own decisions."

For a long time, Garrin stared across his desk at her. She felt like she was back in the classroom again, back in training and completely unprotected from his power and influence. She looked back at him, hoping what she projected was sincerity and not fear.

"I believe you," he said at last, his light tone suddenly returning. "The others left it to me to decide what to do with you, and I'm inclined to let you join us here where you belong."

"Thank you," she said, though this was all becoming too familiar. "Where do I belong here, exactly?"

"That's a great question," Garrin said. "I thought you might fit in well on our Central Advisory Board, actually. I sit on the board myself, and we need someone like you. Someone who's been on the ground, putting in the work."

He didn't wait for her to accept, and extended his hand out to her over the file. She took it. The way he squeezed made her skin crawl.

The remains of Mark's fire were cold. He opened his eyes as the sun began to brighten the sky in the east. He could reach Ember Springs by the end of the day, if he wasn't intercepted first. It might be time to finalize a plan. Once he walked into their patrol range, he'd need a story.

He could claim to be a defector. That was probably common enough now that it might even work. If he could manage to pass into their ranks, he might be able to do some damage, maybe even sabotage whatever tech they'd stolen from Taycher. He could also attempt to evade patrols and work his way toward whatever base of operations they'd set up in the mountain complexes. He could infiltrate the base and plant explosives, or find their leadership and bring the entire organization down.

Mark closed his eyes and sighed. He knew the second option was just a fantasy, something that might work in one of the films he'd watched on his optics when he should have been studying. If he tried to avoid patrols and got caught, the only future he'd have was inside a cell or in a grave. No, he'd have to allow them to find him. No matter how much it might hurt, his best chance of getting revenge, of closing the hole inside him, would be to find a way to do as much damage as he could by joining their ranks.

The thought of being around members of the Harbingers of the Fall and pretending to sympathize with their cause made him feel sick. Even having the rebel woman captive in their camp had been hard for him. Her eyes had always been searching for some weakness she could exploit. Mark's anger flashed as he remembered seeing her with Zak after the ambush had ended. Among the burning debris of Brooke's mech, Zak helped the rebel woman walk. She had managed to find the weakness in their core, and it turned out to be his closest friend.

The loss of Brooke had robbed him of something vital, and Zak's betrayal only deepened that hole. They'd been by his side for so long that it seemed like he was missing significant pieces of himself now. He couldn't help imagining another series of events that would have at least placed Zak with him now, plotting their revenge together. The image was comforting, but only momentarily. A cool breeze washed across the landscape, and he was painfully reminded of his solitude.

CHAPTER 7

Repairs on the mechs Turner and the others had brought were underway, with everyone pitching in where they could. Only three armor technicians remained at the base, and they couldn't do all the work necessary to maintain the mechs and vehicles by themselves.

He and the other cadets had managed to be surprisingly useful so far, having recently completed the repair of the Cronus. No, Turner thought, not cadets. He had to correct his thinking almost hourly. Those on his team weren't cadets anymore. After he'd received a field promotion to Lieutenant, everyone else had been promoted to Ensign. They were no longer students, but soldiers. Among the survivors inside Taycher Mechanized Armor Base, mech pilots were also in short supply.

The Harbinger forces had detonated or sabotaged all of the mechs they hadn't been able to take with them during the attack. The five units Turner and his team had brought with them effectively tripled their forces. The two that Banks and the others managed to salvage were pieced together from five separate units with varying degrees of damage.

Turner walked through the shattered central garage as work continued on the mechs inside. They'd moved all the units inside to keep them from being seen by anyone wandering by or above the base.

"Could you give us some help with this?" Ensign Payne asked. "We could use an extra hand."

"Even if it is your precious lieutenant hands," Kalen said, sliding out from beneath a heavily damaged mech. "I think I got it loose. Just grab over there."

Turner thought about flexing his rank and chastising Kalen for this remark but decided to let it go. Rank was important, but he suspected that respect would go further than anything else in this small group. Plus, he was happy to see Payne coming out of the shell he'd been in and didn't want to spoil the atmosphere. The three of them lifted a large section of reinforced armor plating off the crumpled mech's leg. This would have once been a pristine Ursidae class mech, based on the four powerful limbs. It would have been able to rear up onto its back legs to engage in bipedal combat and seamlessly drop back down onto four when it needed a burst of speed or the added stability. Based on the amount of damage to the cockpit, however, the most it could do now was donate parts to other mechs.

They set the large piece of armor on the cement floor. The sound of it clanging down echoed in the vast space. The echo died quickly, however, finding exits in the multiple holes blown into the walls and ceiling. The armor was valuable, of course, but they'd been stripping it from the destroyed mechs for two days to get at the more valuable components underneath.

"That should be all we need, sir," Kalen said. "You can go about your stroll."

He had another impulse to scold Kalen but pushed this one aside as well. Turner had somewhere he needed to be, anyway. He'd been invited to one of the officer briefings and didn't want to be late.

The only remaining habitable cadet barrack had become the central meeting space for everyone still on the base. Turner headed to a bunk room they had converted into a makeshift conference room. When he arrived, Lieutenant Vesnina was setting notepads in front of seven folding chairs arranged around a wooden table.

"You're early," Vesnina said without looking up.

"Didn't want to be late," Turner said. "Should I come back?"

"Just sit down over there." She pointed to a chair along the long side of the rectangular table. "Doesn't really matter which, just don't take the ones on the end."

Turner sat down and looked at the notepad. "Any idea what this is all about? I don't have anything prepared, if I'm supposed to."

"Not sure," she said as she placed pens next to the notebooks. "These have become more of a formality lately. No communications from anyone, no enemy sightings, rations slowly depleting. It's more about looking like we're doing something in here, I think. So everyone outside of the room feels like something is being done.

"I do think you'll be asked to speak, though. You've been out past the walls, and therefore have some information the rest of us don't. We've got information you don't have, though, too. Who knows? Maybe we'll actually accomplish something today."

"What's the deal with Banks?" Turner asked. He wasn't sure what he meant by the question, and mostly hoped that Vesnina would take the question and tell him a little about the Captain.

"No deal, really. He's just the highest-ranking officer who didn't die in the attack." Vesnina looked troubled for a moment and then continued. "The highest-ranking officer who didn't die or defect to the other side, actually."

Before Turner could ask her what she meant, Captain Banks entered the room. Reflexively, Turner stood up at attention.

"Sit down," Banks said. "Never do that again. I'm not a general or anything. I'm just the guy who didn't die." He spared a glance toward Vesnina and smiled briefly.

"Heard that, did you?" she asked, and went back to her notes.

Turner sat down, trying to figure out if Banks was angry or not. "We didn't mean anything, sir."

Banks made a sort of grunting sound. He sat in the chair at the end of the table and looked toward the door. Captain Barkley walked in with a woman Turner didn't recognize, and they sat opposite him. Vesnina sat next to Banks and began to take notes, listing those in attendance.

One of the mechanics Turner had worked with entered next and sat at the other end of the table. The last chair was taken by another woman Turner had only met briefly.

"In order to acquaint ourselves with Lieutenant Turner, I'd like everyone to introduce themselves briefly," Banks said once everyone was seated.

"Lieutenant Vesnina. But you knew that," Vesnina said, then dropped her head back down to her notes. She attempted to push her dark hair behind her ears, but it fell again.

"Captain Barkley, United Entities Aerospace Force," Barkley said with a wink.

The woman he didn't recognize said, "Commander Sarah Black, United Entities Military Research." She was older than anyone in the room by about twenty years and had a distant look about her. It was as if she were thinking about five different things, all of them more important than this meeting.

"I'm Hank," the mechanic said, leaning back in his chair and adjusting a baseball hat. "Fixer of broken things with the United Whatever."

Banks sent a glare across to the man but said nothing. Instead, he gestured to the last person.

"Specialist Camilla Plime," the woman said, tapping nervously on the table. "Also with Research."

"Now that we're all introduced," Banks said, "our newest arrival is Lieutenant Hiroki Turner. He's in charge of the small contingent of mech pilots that arrived a couple days ago. He's seen the device in action, and from what I've heard, it works better than you could have imagined. Why don't you tell them about it?"

"Excuse me?" Turner asked. "What device, sir?"

"He means whatever it is that took out my plane," Barkley said. "I've told them about it from my perspective, but I only have about two seconds of memory about the damned thing."

"Oh. Well, shit," Turner said, then flushed a little. He didn't have much experience in rooms filled with important people. "I mean, I'm not sure anything I have to say is going to be useful. We knew it was important. It's one of the main reasons we kept after them, but I don't know anything about it."

When no one spoke, Turner paused to try to remember any details from the event. It should have been easy. It hadn't been that long ago, after all. But, after everything that had happened, it felt like a lifetime ago.

"Well, we heard some jets coming in from the east." He looked at Barkley. "Your jets, Barkley. They came in fast, and I thought we'd been saved. The enemy mechs were pretty far out by the time you showed up, but I was expecting to see flashes on the ground as you dropped payloads onto their units. I didn't, though. Instead, I saw your planes hit something that wasn't there. It looked like a shield or bubble or something. One or two of them managed to pull up at the last second. One jet came back at the base and hit one of our barracks just outside here. Another one—yours, I guess, Barkley—crashed in a field way out.

"But the rest of them just exploded midair. I didn't see any of the mechs fire at the planes. From what I could see, it was just a passive protective barrier or something."

"Good. This is useful," Commander Black said, continuing to work on something in her head while she talked. "It's working just like it was supposed to. I'm surprised it was able to handle that many targets at once. We'd hoped it might be possible but never got the chance to test it."

"The chance to test what?" Turner asked. "What the hell was it?"

"You're sure we can talk about this?" Plime asked. "It's an Opal class research project. We're not even supposed to be talking about it outside of the lab."

"It's a bit goddamned late for secrecy now, isn't it?" the mechanic quipped. "Just tell him. He needs to know just how fucked we are in all this."

"That's enough, Hank," Banks said. "Yes, Plime. Just tell him."

"Well, okay." She reached down to a bag at her side, pulled out a sheet of paper, and slid it over to Turner. On it was a schematic for an egg-shaped device with technical specifications Turner couldn't parse. "The project was codenamed Project Ston, after the ancient fortress in what used to be Croatia. It's widely considered to be one of the greatest physical barriers ever constructed. But you don't need to know that. Sorry. It began as an experiment to see if we could use directed gravitational waves to tear apart incoming projectiles. The idea was that we'd be able to scale it however we wanted, to protect anything we wanted."

Turner let the words rattle around in his head, but they didn't seem to fall into place anywhere. He looked at Plime, hoping she would give him more to work with.

"It didn't work, at first," she continued. "We couldn't get the frequencies to converge in the right place at the right time. Our targeting just wasn't fast enough. That's when Commander Black discovered we didn't need to target the incoming projectiles. All we needed was sufficient power and we could project the field in a perfect hemisphere around an object. We managed to make a prototype that was large enough to protect a small sphere of carbon from incoming projectiles fired at certain velocities. With some adjustments to the frequency, you can extend or shorten the range of the dome and the velocities that can be stopped.

"We had just finished building the up-scaled prototype, with enough power to theoretically cover an entire Enclave if necessary. We hadn't even managed to test it in the field before the Harbinger attack. The idea was to eventually have one of them in each Enclaved zone in the U.E. to protect them."

"You built a force field," Turner said. "I mean, that's what it looked like."

"A force field, sure," Black said, coming out of her internal calculations for a moment. "But it's more than that. Adjusted improperly, one could theoretically extend a field *into* a structure and tear people and objects apart, at a molecular level. The distortions we were able to create even on a small scale were unimaginably strong. Our second prototype, if it's working as well as you say it is, should be able to level an entire city just as easily as it can protect one."

The room was silent, and Black went back to staring blankly into space. Turner looked from face to face around the table again, expecting to see surprise, outrage, or fear on any of them. He didn't. Instead, he saw curiosity and anticipation.

"I'm not sure what else you want me to tell you," Turner said. "It sounds like they've got the power to destroy or protect anything they want, and all we've got is a half dozen mechs and limited ammunition."

"Exactly," Banks said. "That's the most important part. The field breaks up naturally near the ground due to interference from the uneven surface of the terrain. The field shouldn't affect anything below about fifty feet or so. Ground forces are the only hope to get in and take this thing out. That's where your pilots and your mechs are going to come in. If we can get within whatever perimeter they have the Ston set to, we could launch a barrage from inside the hemisphere."

Turner felt Banks' words coming before he said them and slumped backward in his chair.

"I know you just got here," Banks said, "but we're going to need you to start preparing your team to head back out."

~

John and Eva drove through the tattered city streets back toward the downed mech. When they arrived, Conrad had the entire power core out and in the street. How he'd managed to get it out without a winch, John could only speculate.

"Hey, that's not cheap, you know," John called out. He brought the truck to a stop and backed toward the power core. "What are you going to use it for, anyway?"

"I don't got a mech or anything, if that's what you're asking," Conrad said, directing John with his hands as he continued backing up. "Stop there. Mind giving me a hand getting this in?"

John looked down at Eva, who he'd told to sit on the floorboards again, and gave her a reassuring pat on the head. As an answer, John opened the door and walked around to the power core.

"Find what you were lookin' for?" Conrad asked as they leaned down to pick up the large metal object. "Guess you wouldn't be back if ya didn't. One, two, three."

Together, with effort, they managed to lift the power core into the back of the truck. John winced as his leg threatened to buckle.

"Yeah, your information was good," John said as he rubbed his knee. "Where do you need this thing taken?"

"Mind if I ride with ya?" Conrad asked as he caught his breath. "Just me. Bee already started back a while ago. It'll be easier than trying to give you directions."

John chanced a glance at the cab of the truck and thought on the offer. The fuel Conrad had offered would be valuable on the road ahead. "Yeah, sure. Just give me a minute to rearrange some stuff."

John walked over to the passenger door and opened it. "It's all right, Eva. Come on out for a minute. We're going to give this man a ride." Slowly, she stepped out into the street and cast a distrustful glance at Conrad.

"Ah, knew there was a reason you were a bit jumpy." Conrad extended his hand toward Eva. "Name's Conrad. I'll be outta your hair soon enough. Might have something for you back at the yard, too."

Eva squeezed her stuffed whale, then looked down at the ground and took a step backward.

"Wouldn't shake my own hand myself, actually, now I think on it," he said, looking at his oil-blackened fingers. He wiped absently at his shirt and turned his attention back to John. "On the south side of town, on the way out toward Taycher. Won't take more than an hour if the roads are still cleared. Don't need to ride up front with you. I'll get in with my own precious cargo in the back. I can direct you if you open that back window."

Conrad didn't wait for an answer and scrambled nimbly into the back of the truck. He lifted the tailgate closed while John got Eva back into the cab. John slid open the back window, and Conrad called out that he was ready. They drove south, veering slightly east as Conrad directed them to his scrap yard.

They traveled along a series of roads that were clearer of debris than others John had managed in Tonopah. Conrad and Bee may have cleared them themselves, or Conrad may have just been familiar enough with the roads to know which route was best. It took only an hour for them to get out of the main heart of the city and into the more suburban sprawl. A seemingly endless expanse of identical derelict housing units surrounded them. People probably still lived in some of them, avoiding the United Entities security forces the way they had since the Decline. Outside sanctioned housing and enclaved zones, people tended to move from one home to another frequently enough to avoid arrest.

Most people who avoided being swept into the machinations of the United Entities in this way weren't revolutionary types. They were just living out their lives the way they wanted, as best they could. Often, when people drew work assignments they didn't want, they disappeared into these suburban expanses. Conrad probably found a place in a sort of gray zone where he'd been allowed to operate his scrap yard as long as he paid off the patrols with something they wanted. Much like Alison's father, he probably held another job as well to remain technically within the structure of the U.E.

Gusts of wind pulled up a thick haze of dust that robbed the landscape of detail. As John drove past another housing tract, he saw that the homes here looked different. The entire area was more than just abandoned, it looked like it had been bombed. Perhaps it had been marked as a threat and eliminated at some point. Whether this was new damage or a scar from the Decline, he couldn't tell. They traveled a few miles into more desolate land. Ahead, John saw the vague outline of a building standing among the dust and sage around them.

"That it up there?" he called out to Conrad in the back.

"Yep, that's the castle."

John pulled up to a tall fence that went around the property, and Conrad climbed from the back of the truck. He approached the fence, unlocked a series of sturdy-looking locks, opening the gate for John to drive through. Once they were in, he locked it back up and hopped back in with the power core. They continued the rest of the distance to a large white building up the drive. All around them as they drove, John could see the shapes of machines. Some were obscured by bright blue tarps, but others had been left to weather in the sun. From what he could tell, Conrad and Bee were avid collectors of all broken things. Most of the machines were agricultural in nature, but he could spot among the wreckage some armored troop carriers and utility vehicles.

None of them appeared to be in working condition, but John had learned during his time at the Academy that looks were often deceiving when it came to machinery. Some of the combat armor units his students had turned in at the end of a semester looked like these beasts. All of them had ultimately performed quite well.

"Any of these work?" John called back to Conrad.

"Not as many as I'd like, I'm afraid," he said. "Just pull into that open garage there and we'll get this out of your truck. We'll get you fueled up after, too."

The garage was a two-story corrugated metal building with a rolling door almost as tall. The open door was dark, and John hesitated to pull in, realizing suddenly how vulnerable he and Eva were at the moment. Instead of pulling into the garage immediately, he took the time to turn his truck around and back in. This had the benefit of allowing for a quick getaway, but John also decided to park the truck just outside the doorway.

If Conrad noted this, he didn't say anything. He climbed back out of the truck just as quickly as he had at the main gate and lowered the tailgate. John remained in the cab with his hand on the gun in the center console. When he heard Conrad struggling with the core, John relaxed his grip on the gun and turned around to look into the garage. Conrad had turned on some fluorescent overhead lights, and he could see more clearly what was inside.

The large open space was filled with an assortment of more well-kept machinery. Along the walls, he could see the gleaming metal of countless organized parts. In the center of the garage, John saw a bright yellow car, and he laughed. It was a sleek sport model with the hood up. A large red rolling toolbox beside it marked it as the current project.

"Just hang tight for a minute. I'll help him with the core and then we'll get on our way." John patted Eva's head and exited the truck.

"Yeah, I guess it'd be pretty hard to haul anything with that." John gestured at the yellow car. "Want some help?"

Conrad looked up from the mech's core and smiled at the car. "She's gorgeous, isn't she? One of the last gasoline-powered commercial vehicles ever sold."

"It looks new." John began pulling the core out of the truck with Conrad. "I'm surprised you've been able to keep it in such good condition."

"It's not very hard if you never drive it," Conrad grunted as they lowered the core onto the concrete floor. "It's been in here since before the Decline. I only ever looked at it before things went to shit, and I suppose it's a bit too late to cruise around in it now."

"Anything else I can help with?" John asked, looking to get on the road.

"No. Bee should be along sometime, and we can get this where I want it." Conrad looked back at the truck. "You or your little girl want to get out and take a restroom break? Something to eat? I promised her a treat back in Tonopah, I think."

"We've got a pretty tight schedule to keep, actually," John said. "You mentioned you'd be able to fuel us up. That still a possibility?"

"Oh, yes, of course." Conrad waved his hand toward the main building. "Out front, there's a pump that should still have some fuel in it, if the pressure's held. I haven't used it in a while, but the gas should still be good."

John had just reached out his hand to Conrad when he noticed a shift in the shadows. He was just able to move a few inches before something hard hit his shoulder. Whatever it was had been intended for his head.

He fell to the ground and rolled back toward the truck. He reached for his gun out of instinct but found his holster empty. He cursed himself for leaving it in the truck. Bee stood above him now, readying her pipe for another blow. Eva began screaming from the cab of the truck. Conrad looked on with a face like he was watching something particularly unsettling on television but made no attempt to stop Bee. She brought her weapon down again. This time, John had the advantage of knowing where she was, and managed to deflect most of her strike toward the concrete with one forearm. With his other hand, he reached up and struck Bee across the head, causing her to lose her balance and stumble.

A gunshot rang out in the open garage. Bee jolted forward as the bullet ripped through her. The pipe she'd been holding fell to the floor, ringing in the empty space. Behind her, John saw Eva holding his gun out in front of her, tears coursing down her face even as she continued holding the weapon steadily.

John managed to get to his feet just as Conrad grabbed for the pipe. As Conrad lurched for it, John brought his fist down firmly across the back of his neck. Conrad's forward momentum carried him down into the floor, where his head connected with the concrete with a sharp smack. He stayed motionless. Bee fell and writhed on the ground, holding her shoulder tightly. Her entire right side was now coated in blood. John moved over to Eva, quickly removed the gun from her small hands, and aimed it at Bee.

"How many more?" John asked, kicking the pipe away from them, further into the garage.

"Uh, I don't know what you mean." She blinked and looked up at him, grimacing with pain as she tried to focus. "None. No one. It's just us, I swear."

John contemplated pulling the trigger, felt the resistance of it behind his finger. Then he felt Eva pull gently on his coat. He released the pressure on the trigger and stepped back cautiously toward the cab of the truck, pulling her along with him. As he opened the door and slid Eva inside, Bee managed to get to her knees and shake Conrad, trying to rouse him. A slowly spreading pool of blood told John he might not be waking up.

John started the truck and sped back toward the main gate. As he did, he watched the main building in his rear-view mirror. When they got around the front, there actually was a fuel pump, just as Conrad had said there would be. Without wasting a moment, he swung the truck close to it and got out, leaving the engine running. Eva began to quietly whimper in the passenger's seat, but John couldn't stop to comfort her now.

He lifted the fuel pump handle and squeezed the trigger. Clear gasoline began flowing out, and it smelled right. John fueled the truck, watching for any approaching vehicles or people, but no one came. He filled the two empty fuel containers in the back of the truck as well.

When the last container was full, he removed the pump handle, tossed it to the ground, and got back behind the wheel. They reached the perimeter fence, and John cursed. The gate was still locked and looked strong. Trying to ram it would only damage the truck.

John looked down at Eva and saw that she looked terrified. "Hey, hey. It's going to be okay. They can't hurt you."

He reached out a hand to comfort her, but she withdrew from him. He followed her gaze and saw that his gun was sitting on the dashboard where he could grab it quickly if he needed it.

"Okay." He lifted the weapon and put it into the holster on his hip. He snapped it closed and lifted his hands. "All gone. It's going to be okay. There's no one coming after us. I just need to cut this fence, and we're going to be gone soon."

She didn't respond but seemed to relax a bit, breathing more evenly. John exited the truck and took a pair of bolt cutters from the toolbox in the enclosed truck bed. When he attempted to cut the first lock on the gate, he was struck with an intense pain in his shoulder. It surprised him. Bee had hit him hard, and adrenaline had done a lot to cover it up, until now. When he flexed and moved the joint, nothing felt broken. He grunted through the pain and managed to cut a total of six locks before he was able to pull the gate open.

When he got back into the truck, Eva was still curled in the passenger seat with her arms around her knees. She stared blankly out the windshield.

"Never point a gun at anything you don't want to kill," Eva said quietly.

John had put his hand on the ignition to start the truck but paused now. "What did you say?"

"That's the first rule," Eva said. "My daddy always told me never to point my gun at anything I didn't want to kill. Is she going to be okay?"

John hadn't considered that Eva might already be familiar with firearms and realized now that he'd once again underestimated her.

"You did what you had to do," he said in a tone he hoped was reassuring. He fixed his eyes on the mountain range to the south, turned the key in the ignition, and pulled through the opened gate into the desert once again. They still had a schedule to keep.

CHAPTER 8

Katherine sat at the desk in her spacious quarters. She hadn't been told where to go after her meeting with Garrin, and so she'd found her way back here. According to various insignias and placards in the hallways, this had once been a fallout shelter built before the United Entities formed. From the looks of it, it was designed to house scores of high-ranking government officials and their families in the event of a nuclear event. Whatever government branch had maintained this facility before the Decline must have been destroyed during that chaotic period. Or perhaps its location had been obscured by agents of the Harbingers. Whatever the case, the fact that it was now being used to bring down the very organization that had built it was an irony she enjoyed.

Her room was large enough for at least a family of five, if not more. The openness of the room disguised the oppressive nature of the installation. It tried to obscure the fact that millions of tons of rock lay above and below the room. Indeed, that immense pressure was being held at bay by the clever architecture employed by the initial designers of the base. Every time she shut her eyes, though, she felt the weight of the mountain above her, hovering and waiting to slip down the mere ten feet to crush her.

So, instead of resting, she pulled all the furniture away from the walls and created a path to run laps. She could have probably run in the halls, but she'd been escorted to and from everything so far and wasn't sure if she was allowed to wander. Plus, she preferred exercising alone. She ran for a while, counting off the laps in her head. Once she was so tired her legs wanted to give out, she allowed herself to sit at the desk in the corner farthest from the door. She felt like a caged animal, and was well aware she was acting like one as well.

A knock came at the door. She gingerly got to her feet and stood in the center of the room. "Come in," she called.

She expected to see the familiar faces of the probably related men who had come for her last time. Instead, a well-dressed man opened the door and looked at her in a disapproving way. She recognized him as the same man who had greeted her group when they first arrived. He was pale, like he'd spent his entire life inside the mountain. He wore a crisp black suit. It was something she would have expected to see on the streets of one of the Enclaves, not inside a commandeered military installation.

"Please feel free to change into some of the clothing we've provided you." He gestured to the wardrobe she'd pulled away from the wall. "I will wait for you in the officers' mess hall."

He hadn't introduced himself, or even bothered to shake her hand. Katherine waited until she heard the sound of the man's black leather shoes receding down the hall. She spent some time pushing the furniture back against the walls of the room, then turned her attention to the wardrobe. The uniforms inside had a distinct military cut, though not one she was familiar with. They were gray and angular, with empty spots for patches and other adornments. If these uniforms ever had any, they'd been stripped, leaving her a blank slate like everyone else in the Hollows. She put a uniform on, finding it a bit snug but enjoying the methodical procedure of getting dressed.

She fastened the last button on the gray jacket, walked to the door, and pulled it open. The hallway was empty, save for the colored lines on the wall. She stared at them, trying to discern what departments they corresponded to, then decided to walk in the direction she'd heard the man's shoes go. By the time she reached the next turn in the broad white hallway, she could already hear the familiar clinking and shuffling of people eating. The sounds echoed in the stony corridors, but she was able to locate the officers' mess hall. When she entered, a few of the occupants turned to look at her, but none of their stares lingered for very long. A new face didn't seem to be surprising for them. They must have been taking in new people every day then, she noted.

At a small table for two, she found the man in the black suit going over documents and sipping a coffee. When she approached, he gestured with one hand for her to sit in front of him. Keeping his eyes on the documents, he signaled to some unseen waitstaff to come to the table. Katherine had barely taken her seat when a cup of coffee was placed in front of her. A small carafe of cream and two small packets of sugar were placed beside it, and the server drifted off.

Katherine looked at the coffee for a long time, trying to figure out why something about it felt wrong to her. A simple but crisp blue design was painted on the outside of the cup. It was a design someone must have spent time crafting and replicating. Slowly, the strangeness of the situation revealed itself, as if from behind a curtain. Mere days ago, she had been in a similar officers' mess, with a similar cup of coffee in front of her. In the intervening time, that room had been rendered useless, had perhaps even been leveled completely, by an attack she helped orchestrate. Countless lives had been lost, and she somehow found herself in another sterile room drinking coffee from a cup with a tasteful, inoffensive pattern painted onto it.

"Drink it or don't," the man said. "We have a schedule to keep."

"Yeah?" Katherine pushed the coffee a few inches away with her fingertips. "What would that schedule be?"

As an answer, the man slid a thin piece of paper in front of her. The letterhead of the document was simple but featured a symbol she didn't recognize. It was an open pinecone. Below that was her name, then a series of bulleted items with times beside them. Each stop looked to be a mere five minutes, culminating in the final item: "*Board Induction.*"

She carefully folded the paper and tucked it into a pocket she found inside her jacket. The first item on the itinerary had said they would be touring the research facilities.

"Lead the way," she said to the man. "What should I call you?"

"Chester Breaks." He offered his hand. "Mr. Breaks will do fine."

The man's demeanor was short, with no frills. She suspected it wasn't a reflection of his assessment of her, but rather an opinion he held of people in general. When she shook his hand, he released after two measured pumps. He gathered his papers into a metal combination clipboard and document box and stood up.

"Follow me, if you please," he said.

They walked in silence down a series of corridors. Katherine managed to learn, based on which turns they made—and didn't make—that they were following the green line. Occasionally they passed by other people moving from one part of the installation to another. The uniforms she saw changed from the military style to the more relaxed outfits of what must be the research staff when they got closer to their destination. They all wore gray lab coats with identification cards, but the clothes they wore underneath were varied, even personal in nature.

"This is the heart of our research operation," Breaks said suddenly, as if a switch had been tripped in his mind. He pointed at a set of double doors with a keycard lock on the handle. "Some of the most brilliant minds of the Harbingers of the Fall are centered here, working on finding the solutions to problems that have never even been attempted before. As I'm sure you are aware, the device you brought us is taking up a large amount of their time now."

As he spoke, someone exited the lab, and Katherine got a glimpse of a brightly lit pure white room. Inside, an egg-shaped device sat in the center, a myriad of wires snaking off it in all directions. People moved around the room working on the device. She managed only this quick glance before Breaks began to move on to the next stop on the tour. "I wish we had more time, but I'm afraid we're already behind. Your tour of the research lab will have to wait."

As they walked down another long and barren hallway, Katherine asked, "When will I get to see my crew?"

"They're not your crew any longer," he said. "But I'm sure you will run across some of them as they perform their new duties. All of them have been released from the intake assessments."

"Where is Jim?" She asked this question more forcefully. She hadn't realized until now that Jim had become so important to her.

"I'm not sure, but I will have someone look into that." He raised one hand slightly and someone Katherine hadn't noticed approached them. It was Sima, the woman who'd given them the passcode on the command deck of the Anansi. She was wearing one of the grey uniforms everyone else was but had managed to find a way to wear it differently. The jacket was tied around her waist and the sleeves of her shirt were rolled up, exposing forearms covered in tattoos. Breaks gave Sima a quick order and then continued forward, pulling Katherine in his wake.

They made a few turns and before she knew it, Breaks stopped again. She nearly ran into his back.

"These are our recruitment and education suites." He indicated a series of doors at regular intervals. Each one had a somewhat bored looking guard posted outside. "New members of the Harbingers are brought here for group orientation sessions and individual assessments. We have extremely effective vetting techniques that have allowed us to cultivate an exceptionally low incursion rate. Additional courses are also taught here when necessary."

Breaks didn't ask for questions and walked away along the row of doors. As they passed the first room, she could see into it briefly through a small window in the door. The scene was so reminiscent of the classrooms back at Taycher that she felt her heart skip a beat. A uniformed instructor was going over something, and the students inside were taking notes.

They toured a few more departments, never staying long enough for her to interact with anyone. Trying to remember her path through the vast underground facility gave her a headache, and she decided to give up trying to keep a mental map. They were climbing a claustrophobic winding metal staircase. She was wondering if they were headed to the surface when the stairs suddenly ended, and they stepped out onto a metal walkway above a rough-hewn cavern. Mechs of all shapes and sizes were being worked on below. This too reminded her of the Academy. The sounds of the welding torches and impact wrenches brought back memories so clear, they threatened to take her. Along the walkway were the familiar shapes of mech pilot training simulators.

"As you've no doubt noticed, this area is newer than the rest of the facility." Breaks ran a hand along a deep scar in the wall, sending a puff of dust and debris clinking down to the ground floor. "What was initially a meager two-story airplane hangar set into the mountain has been expanded to what you see now. You'll note that your mechs are already being repaired and upgraded as we speak."

She looked down and saw the Anansi, its legs pulled in tightly to conserve space. Sparks rained down from multiple points where it was being fitted with an even heavier grade of armor. She felt a momentary pang of something approaching betrayal that she hadn't been consulted on any changes to the command

mech. But, of course, she was no longer in command of the Anansi. Now it was just another piece in the menagerie of mechs
the Harbingers had brought together here. She turned away
from the garage and looked to Breaks for what was next. He
turned and began to descend the stairwell without a word, and
Katherine followed.

~

John set up camp as far as they could get from Conrad's junk-
yard. There was still daylight left, but he was exhausted. He'd
forgotten how drained he always felt after adrenaline worked its
way out of his system. Eva was quiet and didn't seem to mind
stopping either. During dinner, two cans of beans heated on the
fire, John decided to ask her about the events back at the
scrapyard.

"You did good back there," he said, not knowing how to
begin. He'd never talked to someone this young about shooting
someone before. "Thank you for…" He wasn't sure how to end
that sentence and grew silent again.

"Is that a full moon?" Eva asked, as if he hadn't said anything.

John looked. "Not quite full, but close."

They sat for a while, looking up at the disc of the moon as
clouds slipped by. "If you need to talk about anything," he said
softly. "I'm here. I've dealt with what you're feeling. You're not
alone."

She didn't respond, but her shoulders seemed to relax a little.
John figured that was good enough for now and let the subject

drop. "Time for bed. Go get set up in the truck and I'll wash the dishes."

Eva smiled and tossed her empty can into the fire. Then she licked the metal spoon clean and handed it to him. "All clean!"

Her resilience in the face of the horrors she'd seen left him speechless. She was definitely still processing everything that had happened, but somehow, she managed to continue being herself. She retreated to the backseat of the truck where she'd set up a sleeping bag and an assortment of other things. A lantern hung from a hook in the ceiling, and a special, smaller, bed for her stuffed whale Meeple was set up near the folded blanket she used as a pillow. She settled in by herself and was quickly asleep. His own daughter had never been a big sleeper. Eva, however, was of the type that could fall asleep at any moment she wanted.

John broke up the larger chunks of wood to let the fire die. He listened to it crackle and watched the last wisps of flame. Eva whimpered from the truck and called out a muffled word that could have been a cry for her mother. John picked up his canteen and poured it out onto the remains of their fire. The embers hissed and white smoke billowed out into the night, rising slowly and fading into the stars above.

~

"Next on your itinerary will be your Board Induction." Breaks stopped abruptly in a corridor. Katherine had begun to anticipate his sudden stops and managed not to run into him this time. "I'll leave you here. You have about ten minutes to get something to eat, if you like. I will collect you shortly to be taken to the Council Chambers."

Katherine started to thank the man, but he had already walked off toward whatever next stop was on his own itinerary. She turned in a slow circle, surprised to find that she was back outside the officers' mess.

She walked into the room and found it much calmer now. The base must have been between shift changes. She entered the line for food and picked through what remained from the last meal service. She took cold eggs and potatoes and added a bagel, then looked for somewhere to sit. Instead of one of the tables in the middle of the room, she took a small booth against one of the walls. She ate for a few minutes, trying to gather her thoughts. When she heard cups being put down on the table, she was surprised to see Jim sitting across from her. He pushed a cup of black coffee over to her and took a sip of his own.

"A robot man came and told me you requested my presence." Jim laughed.

"That's Breaks," Katherine said. "He's an acquired taste. I mean, he must be. I'm not quite there yet."

"What's up with the suit?" Jim asked.

"I'm not really sure. Seems like he's the only one wearing one in here," Katherine said.

"Oh, yeah. I thought that was a little weird. But I meant yours." He reached across the table and used a finger to flick at one of her freshly pressed lapels.

"Oh, this." She looked down. "It's what they had me change into."

"Pretty dull, if you ask me." Jim took a gulp from his cup of coffee. His uniform was a grey jumpsuit, heavily stained with grease and grime. It matched his hands and face. "For a revolution, things are pretty dull in here."

Katherine drank some of her coffee and thought on that for a moment, going back through the tour she'd just taken. The whole facility had a rigid structure she also had not expected. She found herself wondering about the final item on her itinerary when Breaks walked back into the room. He looked at his watch, an ancient-looking thing, then glanced over at her.

"Speaking of dull." Katherine inclined her head toward Breaks. "My escort is waiting."

"Where you headed off to already?" Jim asked.

"An Advisory Board meeting, apparently." She pulled the folded piece of paper from her inside pocket and looked at it. "Excuse me, it says 'Induction' here."

Jim took the piece of paper from her and inspected the itinerary.

"Hell, it's like they've got an entire government working down here." He frowned and handed the paper back to her. "I've said this already, but I don't think we've been told the whole truth about any of this."

"Guess I'll find out when I'm inducted," Katherine said, forcing a smile. "Let's meet here again tomorrow and I can read you in on anything I learn."

"Sure. I'll stop in for an early lunch," he said as he stood up. "I have my own new duties to attend to, anyway."

Katherine wanted to ask him what those duties were, but he'd already gotten up and left the table. As she watched him leave the room, she saw Breaks check his watch again. She closed her eyes and took a deep breath to gather her thoughts. Maybe she should have brought John with them, forced him to stay on board the Anansi. He would have been able to reassure her with some words about a rigid structure being necessary to push back against another structure. The core idea, she imagined him lecturing her, was that both entities would dissolve simultaneously, leaving nothing but rubble behind. The Hollows, however, didn't seem easily disbanded. Something as established as the mountain base felt wrong.

She opened her eyes and saw Breaks take yet another look at his watch. She laughed, despite her mood, and wondered how many times he would do it if she stayed at her table. Instead, she stood and met him at the door.

"You're going to be late," Breaks said. This was said as a statement of fact, without the drippings of annoyance she would have expected.

"Lead the way," she said. "I'm still not sure where anything is in this place."

Together, they made their way, this time following the purple lines on the walls. They walked for a while, occasionally passing landmarks she remembered, and she finally began to piece together a mental map of the facility. They passed by the door to Research and came to a set of large wooden doors further down the hall that were completely anachronistic to the clean white walls of the corridor. The wood was such a dark brown that it was almost black. There wasn't even a placard next to the doors to say what was inside.

"Do I knock or what?" she asked. When she turned, however, Breaks had already walked away, just as he had earlier. "Okay, then."

She approached the doors, listening for any sound from the room beyond. The muffled conversation of a group of people inside could be heard if she pressed her ear to the door. From some of the tones she was able to discern, the conversation was heated. She waited for the sound to die down, and then knocked on the door.

~

As they drove down the familiar back roads toward her childhood home, Alison felt herself fading in and out of the present with each passing turn. So much of this landscape had remained unchanged for so long that if she thought hard enough, she could almost imagine herself returning home from some youthful quest or other. She might have had rabbits—or even a deer—slung across the front of her ATV. She'd only been lucky enough to kill a deer twice. Each time, they'd been thin, but they had fed her family and others for longer than she'd imagined was possible. They'd kept the meat in the hidden root cellar below the house. How had she forgotten about the cellar?

Alison was back in the present again, on a different ATV, traveling with a man and meager supplies instead of a deer. Zak held onto the trail box on the back of the vehicle as they worked their way through the labyrinth of back roads in the hills. Soon, they emerged on a main road. It may have once been paved but was now merely a slightly more compacted dirt road with darker stones. They passed by a house with a huge, weathered sculpture of a bear in the front yard. The house looked abandoned, as all the houses in the area did.

Alison wondered if they might actually be empty now. How many of her former neighbors were now inside one of the slums that had sprouted up around the Enclaves? How many would be dead from hunger, disease, or something else?

As they approached the long driveway that led to her home, she brought the ATV to a stop. A line of densely packed trees obscured the turn, but she would have known it even by a single bump in the road she'd driven over hundreds of times before. Her father had tried to get rid of that bump a few times, and each time, it had eventually come back. Something about the natural flow of the road seemed to demand it be there. Here it was again, a bump in the road, innocuous to anyone but her.

Alison dared herself to look away from the defect in the road, to look up the drive toward her home, or what remained of it. It would just be visible through a tunnel of trees. It had always been the color of faded blue jeans, with a roof patched together from a hundred different materials. It hadn't leaked, though; her father had seen to that.

She looked up, and her breath stopped. Her eyes filled with tears almost immediately, and she gripped the handlebars of the ATV fiercely. Just beyond the tunnel of trees was the black skeleton of a home. The strong frame remained intact in some areas, like the ribcage of a decayed whale. The trees surrounding the home stood tall and cold.

Alison stepped off the ATV, momentarily forgetting about her injury, and fell to the dirt. Zak leaped from the vehicle and grabbed her arm to help her up. She turned on him quickly, not saying a word, and fended off his touch with the malice in her eyes. Zak let go of her and stepped away with his hands up.

"I'm so sorry, Alison," he said. "I'm so sorry."

He was also staring up the lane, no doubt remembering the night of the attack. He'd watched her home bloom into flame and smoke as he and his fellow soldiers fled into the night.

Alison stood, with effort, and made her way slowly down the drive. Zak stayed back with the ATV and pushed it off the road to find a spot to conceal it.

As she reached the end of the lane, the trees around her opened up. The familiar glade she'd called home for so long was quiet and still. There, the same broad cottonwood tree she had climbed as a child still stood. The branches nearest the house were blackened and cleared of leaves, but it had survived. Below it, she could see three mounds of freshly turned earth. She stopped for a moment, contemplating the number. Three graves, not four.

She covered the distance as quickly as she could and fell to her knees before them, her leg searing with pain. The three graves were all of adult size. She let out a scream that seemed to shake the leaves of the surrounding aspen trees and fell forward onto the center grave. She lay there for what felt like only a short time. Her hands worked the dirt of the grave before her, and her tears seeped into the ground below. She kept her head turned to the side, looking at the remains of her home.

Zak crouched down and put his hand on top of one of hers. She recoiled instantly and brought both hands to her chest. Her fingertips were raw and bloodied.

"I checked the house," he said. "There's no one in the cellar."

Alison remained on the ground, facing toward the house with her hands clutched to her chest. Zak left her again and she heard him start preparing their campsite behind her a ways. She waited until she could hear the familiar sounds of a crackling fire, then sat up. Its flickering orange light illuminated the charred bones of the home. Before she turned toward Zak, she wiped her face. The camp was a few yards away. Her tent and pack were laid out for her already.

She went to the fire and sat down on a blanket. Without words, Zak gathered a bundle of things and brought them to her. He set them beside her on the blanket, then disappeared into his tent.

When he zipped his tent, she looked down at what he'd assembled for her. A meal of bread, one of their vacuum-packed meat rations, and a canteen of water. Beside these were some bandages, a bottle of antiseptic, and a bowl of water. Alison reached out and slid the metal bowl toward her, the water inside rippling with the reflection of the fire and the stars above. She dipped her raw fingertips into the bowl and felt it sting. Zak must have mixed some antiseptic into the water already. She used one of the cloth bandages to clean the numerous small cuts on her fingers, then dressed them with the adhesive bandages. The damage was minor, but treating them was important to avoid infection.

Once she was done, she looked at the food, but decided against it. Her stomach felt uneasy from her bout of grief. Instead, she picked up the canteen, and drank the fresh water slowly, allowing it to soothe her dry and aching throat. She didn't remember screaming, but she must have been at some point.

Alison sat for a long time, taking small drinks of water. Eventually, she set the canteen aside, crawled into her tent, and allowed herself to be pulled into sleep.

~

The broad wooden doors in front of Katherine opened after just a few seconds. The inside of the room was also a stark contrast to the sterile corridors she'd walked through to get here. Wood paneling adorned the walls, complete with large, heavy bookcases laden with equally large and heavy texts. A patterned, vaulted ceiling was broken in the center by a bright rectangle of light that shone down. The light, she thought, seemed like actual daylight. Throughout the compound so far, she'd only seen daylight-balanced light fixtures, calibrated to emit the precise wavelength of light that the sun poured down at midday all over the globe. The light here, however, was slightly different, seemingly changed by real atmospheric conditions. She wondered if the skylight went straight up to the surface but thought it was more likely that a series of mirrors and shafts created the effect.

A long, ornate table beneath the skylight looked like it had been stolen from an ancient college library. It was heavy and well used, but still elegant and cared for. At each of the twenty or more chairs, there was a lamp, a leather pad, a pen, and a stack of papers. The people she'd heard engaged in conversation were standing in a far corner of the room, staring at her. There were about ten people, all of them wearing the same dull uniform she was. As was her experience with rooms of this type, most of the occupants were men. They all seemed to be military types, most of them around her age or older. She found this unsettling. The Harbingers were concerned with the destabilization of society itself, and seeing the same kinds of people who comprised the current ruling class also filling these seats felt wrong. There should be youth in the room as well. The fate of the world had been decided too many times by people like this for it to be changed by the same. She thought that even someone like Sima, the woman with more ambition than experience, would have been preferable.

As Katherine was about to introduce herself, a hand came down on her back just below her neck. She tensed her shoulders but didn't move away.

"So, you've made it after all!" Garrin said from beside her. "Please take a seat. We've been waiting."

He directed her to a chair near the middle of the table, and she could see that her name had been pressed into the soft leather of the desk mat there. The small stack of paper was blank, evidently intended for note taking. As she sat down, the rest of the people in the room shifted around and found their own seats. Garrin took his seat, naturally, at the head of the table. He grandly leaned back in the chair with his arms behind his head as he waited for everyone to settle in.

"All right," he called out to the room. "First order of business is our newest member. Katherine Scholl comes to us from the United Entities Mechanized Armor Corps. She was instrumental in the operation at Taycher, and a primary reason we managed to secure the Ston."

Some of the people around the table looked at her approvingly, while others only afforded her a cursory nod to acknowledge they'd heard him introduce her.

"Normally, we'd have a big production for you." He gave Katherine a mock frown. "Hoods and candles and the like, but I think we can skip the formalities and say you've been formally accepted onto the Advisory Board for the Serotiny."

Katherine wasn't sure if he was joking or not and made an effort to conceal her confusion. None of this had been in any of John's writings; not any that she'd seen, at least. Garrin smiled and nodded to a tall man sitting across from her.

"Give her the short version, Tom." He made a flippant gesture with his hands, then laced his fingers back behind his head and leaned back. "She's got all the first-level stuff, so just start in with the rest."

"Ah, um. Okay." The man pushed up a pair of reading glasses and shuffled some pages off a pile in front of him. He would have been at home in any high-ceilinged meeting room of the United Entities Military. A details man, concerned with the minutiae of order and procedures, perhaps even excited by them. "So, the Harbingers of the Fall. You're familiar, I know. Every power structure currently in place worldwide is now being dismantled and destroyed. Use of activated civilian networks of operatives has increased our forces by orders of magnitude. Operatives like yourself, working within existing power structures, have all been activated as well, and a worldwide collapse is imminent. This information is nothing new to you, but we do want to assure you that the process is proceeding with exceedingly high fidelity to our predictions. Within the week, we believe that we will have disrupted over ninety percent of all government operations worldwide. The resulting chaos, according to our models, should continue for years without any external intervention."

"External intervention?" Katherine couldn't help asking, but she could already tell where Tom was going.

Tom held up his hand. He was getting into a rhythm and seemed to be enjoying his role. "Yes, okay. You'll see. Just wait. So, when a forest burns, everything is destroyed. Flora, any fauna that doesn't manage to escape, everything. And what we're left with is a wasteland. But, as I'm sure you know, forests do eventually come back rejuvenated and cleared of many of the invasive species and other ills that existed before the fire."

Katherine looked at the man and did nothing to disguise her confusion. He was obviously equating the current worldwide actions very specifically with a forest fire, but why?

"Now, there are some species of trees that produce cones that are specifically designed for this exact situation. They're not just made to *survive* a fire, they're made explicitly for the *inevitability* of a fire. These types of cones are called serotinous cones. They bloom when heated and release seeds locked within."

He paused and looked at his paper, perhaps for effect, but Katherine thought that he just needed to take a breath. She glanced up the table toward Garrin, who was smiling broadly. That smile did nothing to reassure her.

"Across the globe, there are facilities," Tom continued. "Just like this one, that have been hardened and protected from the Fall going on outside. This facility is known as Cone Alpha. We don't actually know how many other Cones exist, but even if we were the only one to survive, we will be all that's left to direct the regrowth of civilization in an organized and beneficial way.

"We are reasonably confident that we have the only existing prototype of the Ston device you brought us. Our intelligence on that, we suspect, is what triggered the Fall to begin. So, in a way, you could count yourself as one of the primary heroes of the Harbingers of the Fall. And, now that you've been inducted, of the Serotiny as well."

Silence followed Tom's speech. Katherine stared at the man, not wanting to turn back toward Garrin. She pressed her palms onto the table, willing them not to tremble. An unpleasant feeling in her stomach threatened to bring up the coffee she'd had in the officer's mess. She looked down at the leather pad in front of her and examined her name, neatly pressed into it in the lower left corner. In the upper right was the same symbol she'd seen on her printed itinerary earlier that day—a simple opened pinecone. She reached out one finger to touch it.

The people in the room expected her to say something in response to what she'd just learned, but at first, she couldn't figure out what she was supposed to say. She took a deep breath, stalling for a few more moments to gather herself, then looked at each of the faces around her. They were as dull as their uniforms. Each one could have been replaced with any number of people she'd encountered during her career. She settled on what they needed her to say.

"Thank you for your generous invitation," she said. She was borrowing, almost verbatim, from the remarks she'd offered when she was offered her leadership role at the Academy. "I am honored to accept, and I hope I will be as useful here as I have endeavored to be in my previous roles. Your trust in me is humbling, and I know it does not come easily. I don't have much more to say, only that I hope to begin learning my new role as soon as possible. If I had a drink, I'd offer a toast."

At this, she smiled in a way that she hoped conveyed a sense of humility instead of the overwhelming unease she felt.

CHAPTER 9

The lights of the small mountain town glittered in the distance. Mark had decided to ride on the main highway in order to make sure he was picked up by the Harbingers of the Fall. Claiming to be a defector should allow him access to the lowest echelon of the organization. A terrorist cause had to bring in new people somehow, and it's not like they had recruitment centers. How much damage he would be able to inflict would correspond to how much time he was willing to spend working his way into their ranks. Like a metal splinter working its way through the skin and into more vital organs, he hoped to do as much damage as he could.

He could reach town by midnight if he continued. The thought of resting and coming into town in the daylight occurred to him. It would give credibility to his story if he arrived without even the cover of darkness. The opportunity to get a sense of the landscape before attempting his first contact was too alluring, however. He revved the engine of his motorcycle and pressed on.

Ahead of him was a worn green road sign, standing tall against the dark sky, that told him the town was only twenty miles away. He brought his motorcycle to a stop beneath it, leaning it against the metal post and stretching his neck and back. He took an inventory of his belongings. His pack consisted mostly of the travel tent and meager provisions he'd brought from the collapsed command mech. He also had his pistol and ammunition.

Mark made the decision not to abandon his uniform before going into town. He did, however, pack it into his bag. What he wore now, a black hooded sweatshirt adorned with the image of two wolves howling at the moon and a pair of thick gray sweatpants, he'd salvaged from the shattered remains of a gas station convenience store during one of his breaks.

He wouldn't be able to deny his military background. It might even be his only way to convince the Harbingers to allow him entry. His skills made him valuable. There were already military defectors among their ranks, he knew. He would confirm that he had been a cadet at the Academy, and that he'd been training to be a mech pilot. Based on what he'd seen so far, there was nothing he knew that they didn't already. Holding anything back would only cast doubt on his intentions.

Mark left his motorcycle and continued toward Ember Springs on foot, expecting to be stopped by someone asking him what he was doing there sometime soon. He was able to make it to within five miles of the town before he encountered the first roadblock. Two large pickup trucks were parked under a streetlight in the road, blocking both lanes. They would have been holding up traffic, if there had been any. A man and a woman leaned against one of the trucks, smoking and having an animated discussion about something. Mark was still far enough out that he hadn't been noticed, and he stepped off the road into the ditch to watch the rebels.

They were both armed, the woman with a pistol in a holster, and the man with some kind of rifle slung across his back. Mark wondered how an organization this careless about defense had been able to mount the attack at Taycher. If this was the first line of defense for the Harbingers of the Fall, they should have been overtaken already. He was about to walk back out onto the road when he heard movement behind him.

"Hands where we can see them," a voice said from the shadows. The moonlight was stark, but still, Mark couldn't locate the source of the command. "Hands where we can see them, or we'll end you right here."

Mark slowly put his hands in the air and turned in a circle, searching for whoever was talking to him. He spotted movement coming from the trees and bushes on the far side of the ditch, away from the road.

"Are you a traveling man?" the figure asked, moonlight glinting off the end of a rifle barrel.

"I'm a cadet from a military base." He kept his eyes fixed on the barrel of the gun that continued to approach. When he didn't see a muzzle flash, he continued. "I'm here to join you, to join the Harbingers of the Fall. I followed the group from Taycher."

"On your knees," the voice said, calm but firm.

"Did you get him?" the man by the roadblock called out. "You guys still out there? You get the dude?"

Mark heard more movement, this time from behind him, and was suddenly on his stomach in the ditch. His arms were

116

wrenched behind him, his pack ripped from his back, and restraints snapped into place on his wrists.

"Shut the fuck up, man," the first voice called out toward the roadblock. "You're gonna get us killed one of these times."

"Just trying to keep things interesting," the man said as the woman laughed. "I'll take him into town for processing. I need a break anyway."

Mark was lifted roughly from the ground and hauled out of the ditch back onto the road. The man who'd been smoking by the truck approached and waved off the two camouflaged men leading Mark.

"Sorry about the warm welcome," the man said, taking Mark's pack from one of the others. "Can't be too careful and all that. My name is Benny, by the way, welcome to Ember Springs."

~

Turner headed for the daily briefing before most people at the base were up and moving. Repairs and preparations for their coming exodus were going well, and the meetings served as a daily progress check for everyone involved. He liked to arrive early so he could talk with Vesnina. He found her easier to talk to than the other people around.

As he opened the door this time, however, he saw that other people had arrived early as well. Captain Banks was already sitting at the head of the table, deep in conversation with Black. They both stopped talking as he entered and took his seat.

Vesnina was also in her seat looking through a stack of papers intently.

"Were you talking about me?" Turner asked with a smile. "Should I step back out into the hallway?"

No one laughed, and he sat down in awkward silence as he waited for someone to say anything at all. When no one did, he looked down at the printed sheets of paper Vesnina had arranged for everyone to read. Typically, it would have been a simple agenda with any action items from the previous meeting carried over for further discussion. The regularity and structure of these meetings served to normalize what was, in reality, a completely ludicrous situation. They were planning an assault on a heavily fortified mountain base with the leftovers of mechs that had just weeks ago been used exclusively to train the youngest mech pilots in the Mechanized Armor Corps.

On top of his stack of pages, maybe twenty or thirty in all, was the familiar format of an agenda. The only item on it, however, was a cryptic entry: "*Update on Project Ston.*"

He lifted the agenda page to look at what was below it. What he found were dense blocks of incredibly complex text with figures and diagrams he didn't understand spaced throughout. The title read: "*Weaponized Gravitational Waves: Risk Analysis.*"

Turner looked up from the page and started to think about what to ask, but he was interrupted by Plime, the other woman from United Entities Research, entering the room. She looked awful. Her hair was greasy and unkempt, tied up in a loose, haphazard bun. Her eyes were shot red, and dark circles under them betrayed a distinct lack of sleep. She sat down and rested her head on the table with her arms cradling it. Turner couldn't tell, but she might have been crying.

"This is everyone for today," Banks said. "We'll be meeting with Barkley and Hank separately. We have some new information to share with you."

He gestured to Black, and she rose from her chair.

"Before you is the culmination of three days and nights of work," she said. "We've run the numbers as many times and as many ways as we can. Perhaps even too many times." She looked at Plime, still collapsed on the table. "I'm going to say this plainly and simply, not to scare you, or for effect. I just want you to understand the severity of the situation at hand."

Turner looked at Vesnina, who seemed like she was going into shock already. The pages of technical text must have made more sense to her.

"The Ston device," Black continued. "Based on the reports of its efficacy and range, is operating well beyond what we thought would be possible with this first scaled prototype. Our initial thoughts were that it would only be possible to encapsulate or destroy an entire city. While this fact alone is quite alarming, our new understanding is more dire. The damage it is capable of inflicting is orders of magnitude larger than what we predicted. We're still not completely sure what the upper limits of potential destruction are, but the damage may only be limited by the hand that wields it."

Turner looked up at Black and saw, for the first time, a sense of fear in her eyes. That scared him more than any of the words she'd spoken. For a long time, he looked into her eyes, wanting her to wink at him and tell him it was all a joke. She broke his gaze and looked down at the table in front of her, resting her hands on it for support.

"Okay," Turner said, trying to stay calm. "When can we be ready to move out? If what you're saying is true, we need to leave now. We need to get this thing back before they use it or figure out how to duplicate the tech. We need to bombard the hell out of them with anything we have before it's too late."

"I agree," Banks said. "We've got most of the force ready to go. Hank has crews working in continuous shifts on the rest. But this is too important. It wouldn't make sense to send only what we have finished now. As it is, we're going to be grossly outnumbered. The best plan of attack will be to move when we have the strongest force possible."

Turner wasn't sure he agreed and looked to Black for support, but she was already packing up to leave. Vesnina, too, was already shifting and readying herself to go.

"The research in front of you is new," Black said. "That's the only good news here. The Harbingers likely do not even know what they have yet. Hopefully the only use they've found is for protection."

Turner nodded, as if this helped somehow, but nothing she said could erase what he'd seen in her eyes.

"No one can know about this." Banks looked directly at Turner. "This is the most dangerous intelligence on the planet right now. Absolutely no one is to know."

"Yes, sir," was all he could manage. He looked at the research paper, trying again to make sense of the figures and equations in front of him.

"Vesnina," Banks said as he stood up. When she didn't respond, he knocked lightly on the table with his knuckles. "Oksana, be sure to destroy the printed copies of this report as soon as Lieutenant Turner has finished."

Banks exited the room with Black. As they left, Plime seemed to slide away from the table and followed them out. Then the room was silent. Vesnina stayed in her chair and stared blankly at the report in front of her.

"Did you know this is what we were going to talk about?" Turner asked.

"No," she said simply.

"I get the sense this thing can really mess shit up." Turner flipped through the pages in front of him. His mind still didn't want to grasp the scope of what he'd learned. "How much damage are they talking about?"

"They call themselves the Harbingers of the Fall." She talked in flat tones. "They're going to bring it all down. They're going to kill us all."

Turner pulled his eyes away from a graph in the report, one that showed a line curving upward until it was a straight line. "Black said they might not even know what they have yet."

Vesnina still hadn't taken her eyes off the report, and Turner reached out and placed a hand on hers. She blinked and shook her head, seeming to come out of a daze.

"It looks like you understand this more than I do," Turner patted the pages in front of her. "To me, it's just a bunch of numbers and words I don't recognize."

She squeezed his hand and then pulled away. "Sure. I had some coursework on nuclear energy cores. This isn't the same,

121

but some of the wording and graphs make some sense to me." She pointed to the graph he'd been trying to decipher. "This one here is a measure of energy output."

"Sure," Turner said. He looked at the graph and still wasn't sure what it meant. "It looks bad."

"It is." She looked up at him, her eyes brimming with tears. "With enough energy, the Ston could destroy anything, anywhere. Entire bases, cities, maybe entire regions, who knows. We can't let them have this thing. I already lost my sister. I can't lose anyone else."

Turner reached an arm around her shoulder, and she leaned into his embrace. She was tense at first, but quickly softened, and he could feel her quietly shuddering. He hadn't had a moment to think about his own family for a while, and suddenly found himself trying to remember where his brother was stationed. Karl had never been more specific than saying he was on another continent. That was some comfort at least. Turner didn't know how far all this chaos reached. Maybe Karl was still safe. His parents, on the other hand, lived in a dense government settlement on the eastern coast of the United Entities. If the Harbinger attack was as widespread as they thought, he was terrified to think about what might be happening there.

He let go of Vesnina and she wiped at her tears. He took the moment to wipe at his own eyes before he looked at her.

"We just need to get there before they figure it out." Turner tried to sound confident, but knew the odds were heavily against them. "We can do this."

CHAPTER 10

It was just before sunrise as Alison opened her eyes. She un-zipped her tent and looked outside. A soft mist covered the glade, as it had on many mornings when she'd lived here. Tiny drops of dew covered her tent and the dry grass surrounding the broken home, each one glittering like a tiny star. Seeing the three graves underneath the burned branches of the cottonwood tree threatened to send her back into the dark oblivion she'd experienced when she first arrived. She pulled her eyes away from the graves.

Their campfire had long since burned out. Alison stood and wrapped a blanket around herself. It would be a while longer until the sun cleared the trees around them. She walked toward the house, leaving a trail of footprints in the dew-covered grass. Standing in front of the blackened wood, she fought against the urge to collapse once more. Instead, she looked around the scene for clues as to who had been here, who had taken the time to bury her family.

She looked at the tree where she'd last seen her father alive. He'd been talking to one of the soldiers while sitting on the old bench swing. Was Zak the last person to speak to her father? A swell of anger boiled up from within her but broke against her grief, washing out and leaving her flat.

The bench swing lay on the ground, partially burned, its rope draped in the tall grass. She looked at the tree itself, examining the blackened branches closest to the home. She followed these toward the trunk, and then down toward the ground. She remembered every foothold and handhold that had been useful to her as a tree-climbing youth. At the base of the tree, she saw an exposed root, one of many that had risen over the years. She'd walked along it hundreds of times as a child, and worn it smooth as she pretended it was a tightrope or a balance beam. It pointed out toward the edge of the clearing where there was a small, obscured trail. It was a path she'd often traveled as a child, yearning to explore or escape. Alison gasped and dropped the blanket.

It was merely a small tunnel-like formation through the dense foliage, used by animals to get through the forest, but it was also the perfect size for a child. She moved as quickly as she could toward the break in the trees, her leg protesting the whole way. Alison needed to crouch to enter it, and just managed to do so without crying out in pain as her leg protested. After a few yards, the branches thinned out and she was able to walk upright. Once she was in the more open forest, she spotted her way forward. It wasn't especially obvious, but she recognized it. As she walked along this remembered path, she began to allow herself to hope. And, when she saw the clubhouse, the one she'd built so many years ago from forest debris, that hope brought tears to her eyes. In front of the earthwork clubhouse, Alison saw the remains of a campfire and she felt lightheaded.

"Eva?" she called. "Eva, are you in there?"

She reached out, lifted the crude wooden handle to unlock the door, and pulled it open. The smile faded from Alison's face. No one was inside.

"Shit!" She slammed her palm against the fragile frame of the door.

She frantically scanned inside the hut in the light of the open door and saw something in the corner. She scrambled inside, reached a small pile of stones. Then, with a swift movement, she brushed them aside to find a small white piece of paper wrapped in plastic. Underneath the clear film, she could see two words: *For Allie.*

Alison stared at the letter, afraid to open it. The two words on the front were written in a child's careful but uneven handwriting. Eva's. She ran a finger across the letters, feeling the deep impressions. Alison pulled the note from the plastic and unfolded the piece of paper. She was surprised to find the rigid formed letters of an adult's handwriting on the other side.

Alison,

If you are reading this, we have already left to try and find you at your last known location. Eva is safe, and I will do everything in my power to keep it that way. I will not jeopardize our safety by writing out the locations we will be looking for you. If you are here now, it means we've missed each other.

There is an old saying, "Passing like two ships in the night." While that may be our fate now, we will hopefully share the same port soon. There is a place we both frequented at specified intervals before the Fall. I will be there at what would have been our next scheduled meeting date. If we do not find you before then, I hope to meet you there. If we do not meet you, I will retreat to the only other place I believe you may go. I'll return to the path we once took together to the north.

Also, Eva wanted me to make sure I tell you to bring crayons, because hers are almost all gone, and you always bring crayons. And now she is asking me to ask you for candy. As you can tell, Eva is in good spirits, but I know she is suffering underneath. Reuniting with you may be her only chance to heal.

J.P.

Alison trembled, wanting to simultaneously dance and collapse on the dirt floor of the hut. Eva was alive. She looked back down at the letter and smiled, even as tears obscured her vision. John absolutely had a flair for dramatic prose, even in a short note. She folded it back up and stowed it in her pocket. Alison thought back on her routinely scheduled information pickups with John and realized that the next one would be in two days. If she couldn't make it there in time, she would have to follow their original route to the north.

Alison limped from the hut and went back to camp, determined to make the first rendezvous by any means she could.

~

Mark sat against the wall in a room with no furnishings or readily apparent use. The purpose, then, must have been to serve as a room in which to do nothing. A single fluorescent strip of light was set into the ceiling. The only door into the room wasn't metal or especially sturdy-looking. It may have even simply been hollow particle board, the kind an errant elbow or angry fist could penetrate. It might as well have been six inches of concrete, however, because he'd been led to it by armed guards. Most of the journey in from the roadblock had taken them along a dark forest path. Once they'd gotten closer, they blindfolded him and led him the rest of the way to this room. What he'd heard, however, told him that he was inside the mountain, inside the Hollows.

Before they'd left him here, they had him change into a dull grey uniform without any insignias or other features. All his possessions were put into a box along with the pack they'd seized from him at the roadblock. He fought the urge to resist them when they'd taken away the coin necklace but had let them take it.

He sat with his back against the far wall when a knock came at the door. Mark awaited whoever they'd sent to question him. Strangely, the knock came again, and his wait continued. This polite respect for his permission was disorienting and unexpected.

"Yes?" Mark called out. "Come in."

The door opened, and the man who had introduced himself as Benny out at the roadblock entered the room with two folding chairs. He opened them up and placed them on the concrete floor, facing one another. He sat down and then gestured for Mark to sit in the other. He did, and looked at Benny with unchecked confusion.

"This could all be yours," Benny said, grinning and spreading his arms to indicate the empty room. He was a tall man with dark hair and a thick beard. In another life, Mark could see them being friends, but not this one. "This is either your prison or your quarters from this point on. I mean, for some people, it's kinda both, but I think you get what I'm saying. Of course, you know that no one here has vouched for you. We also know you've never been in contact with the Harbingers before. There is no way for us to verify much of what you tell us. But we are nothing if not accepting of converts. So, let's start off with an easy one. Why are you here?"

Mark took a moment to think through his response. They knew he was military; they would have already searched his bag and found his uniform. He wondered if there was anyone in the mountain that knew him, and what they might say about him.

"I didn't think about it too much," Mark began. He *had* given this question a lot of thought and hoped the story he'd settled on would be convincing enough. "I just left. I couldn't stay with my unit anymore. I'd been thinking about it for a long time, and I knew I had to leave. Especially now that things are finally happening."

"Sure, I suppose that makes sense. We hear variations of that story a lot, but we also know a small force of soldiers followed our guys from Taycher. We have every reason to believe you were a part of that group yourself. Part of a group that downed one of our mechs in Tonopah, or one of the soldiers that escaped capture out at a home. The timing of your arrival is what makes us nervous."

Mark thought over the sequence of events and continued with his prepared lie. Mark had decided to adopt parts of Zak's story as his own. Zak had left Taycher late and had managed to catch up with the group, so he used that as his foundation, and built out his own story.

"I left Taycher after a group of other guys did, caught up with them just before everything in Tonopah," Mark said. "I did stay with them for a while. But when everything happened out at that house in the woods, I couldn't stay. I made a choice. I knew that the Harbingers—that you—might not accept me, might even kill me. But, after what happened, I couldn't stay. I had to try and make it right."

Mark used the last words Zak had spoken to him. The words felt wrong even as he said them, and he hoped his interrogator didn't detect the hate hidden in them. He used his anger now, hoping to repurpose it to lend credibility to his story. He clenched his fists and stared at the floor, thinking of the battle in the valley where Brooke had died. He took a moment to arrange his next words carefully.

"She didn't have to die." He whispered it, an almost unconscious verbal tick, causing Benny to lean in closer. Mark could have brought his knee up into Benny's face right then. He could take Benny down, steal his weapon, and figure out a plan from there. He didn't. Instead, Mark continued, "Someone I loved very much died out there because of all of this. So many people have died."

"We've killed a lot of people in our own fight." Benny said, a smug look sliding into place as he leaned back in his chair. "If death is what brought you here, you're in for another helping. What made you choose our side in this? What makes our killing justified?"

When Mark didn't respond quickly enough, Benny shook his head. "I can tell you're in pain, but I'm not sure you even know why you're here. I'll take your case to my superiors. I wouldn't hold out much hope, but maybe we can find something for you to do. Prove yourself, and maybe over time, you can make a difference in here."

Benny stood, folded his chair, and left the room. Mark stayed seated and put his face in his hands, shaking with anger but not allowing himself to break. His only hope of ever seeing justice hinged on his ability to get through this convincingly. This first test hadn't gone as well as he'd hoped, but he wasn't dead yet, and that was something.

He waited for hours in the room. Once, someone came and brought him a bowl of soup and some water. They returned after he finished his meal and took him to use a bathroom down the hall. They gave him a sleeping bag and left him there again. He was in and out of a light sleep, when another knock came at the door. This one was sharper, more authoritative. The door opened immediately, and a woman entered the room. To his surprise he recognized her.

Vice Admiral Katherine Scholl stood in front of him, her glare seeming to demand respect as it always had at the Academy. If she remembered him, she gave no indication. He had been one of her students in her *Application of Tactical Analogies* course, so there was a chance she might. She looked different here, out of place. Her hair, usually pulled back into a tight bun behind her head, was down around her shoulders now. The crisp teal officer's uniform of the United Entities

Mechanized Armor Corps had been replaced by a gray, vaguely military uniform without any rank or insignia.

"Cadet Alder." She looked down at him, her face hard to read. "What brings you so far from your barracks this morning?"

"Same reason as you, I'd suspect," Mark said, hoping that it came out as banter and not an accusation.

"I know we're not in a United Entities power structure any longer, but I will have your attention." She waited as Mark stood up, feet apart with his hands behind his back. She nodded, and then continued. "I'm here to ask you a few questions, cadet. Are you prepared to answer them truthfully?"

"Yes, sir," Mark said, his face defaulting to the neutral expression expected of him back at the Academy. He felt dizzy as he remembered to be angry at this woman, but still managed to bury it as well as he could.

"Here, you will have no rank, as the Harbingers do not assign rank. Each person is assigned duties according to their value." Mark's eyes flitted to her blank uniform again, and he wondered what Scholl's value was to the Harbingers. "Are you prepared to join the Harbingers of the Fall?"

Mark nodded, unsure if he was supposed to answer verbally, but she seemed to accept his nod and continued.

"You are not vouched for by anyone here and are therefore untrustworthy at best. Your evaluation will continue even if you leave this room. Any opportunity afforded to you will be severely limited in scope. As you can tell by my presence here, I am familiar with betrayal and the emotional strain that will put you through."

Mark felt his face change at her mention of betrayal before he could correct for it. He wasn't sure what Scholl saw, and he wasn't completely sure what he was feeling. He took a short breath and tried to become stoic once again.

"At ease, Alder." Her tone softened. She gestured for him to sit, and Mark took his seat again. "If your intentions are as pure as you claim, then what comes next won't be a problem. We'll pull out any information you may have about the strategic operations of the United Entities in a series of interviews. If you cooperate fully, we may allow you to join one of our least sensitive service roles. Are you prepared to accept these terms?"

He nodded again. The Harbingers clearly already knew more than he would ever be able to tell them. All he needed to do was answer some questions, and they'd let him join. He wasn't sure what the rest of his entry into the Harbingers would entail, but it all felt ludicrously easy so far. There was probably some other process underway he wasn't aware of. His knowledge of interrogation tactics was limited, but he did know that a lot could be learned from having the right person interview a detainee.

Why had they employed her to interview him? Having the wrong person do it could have detrimental effects. This, he knew from personal experience. He'd made the mistake of having Zak work with the rebel woman they'd captured. He blinked away tears that came suddenly and looked at his former instructor.

"I am aware that you're a trained mech pilot," she continued. "That's a valuable skillset, one that may be of particular use to us. But, until we can trust you, I'm sure you also understand that those skills are more of a liability to us than an asset. Remain in this room and await your next interview."

She turned to leave, then hesitated. Mark was worried she would ask him more about his reasons for being there. He wasn't sure he was ready to try that one again.

"I know this is frustrating. You've only just made the turn to the Harbingers. Breaking ties you've forged over many years to join our cause is admirable. But let this decision sink in. Use this time to fully explore your own reasons for joining us. Consider this a decompression. I had to endure some of this myself when I arrived, and I've been with the Harbingers for quite some time."

As she walked to the door, Mark thought back to his time in her course at Taycher. As he imagined her standing in front of his classroom, he corrected the image with the fact that she'd obviously already been a traitor. His anger flared, and he resisted the urge to lunge at her as the door clicked shut.

Katherine closed the door and nodded at the guard standing next to it. A few yards down the hallway, Garrin stood with his feet spread apart, taking up more of the walkway than necessary. Since she'd had Alder in her course at the Academy, he had sent her in to get a sense of the cadet's intent. As she approached Garrin, an instinctive apprehension made her feel for her sidearm. It was there. They'd allowed her to have it back after her induction, and it made her feel more secure to have it.

"So, what's the decision?" Garrin asked in a gruff tone, staring down the hallway toward Alder's door.

"I'm not sure," she said. "From the files we have, he was generally well behaved at the Academy. No anti-government sentiment reported in any of the siphoned psych assessments. He held a mostly ceremonial leadership title among his cadet group. Average marks in everything but intuitive strategy, where he excelled. He was on a leadership track for our command mechs, but he'd only just completed live-pilot training when the attack happened. When our attack happened."

"I'm familiar with the files," Garrin said. "You knew the kid at your Academy. What's your gut say?"

"Like I said, I'm not sure." She took a deep breath to formulate her thoughts. Garrin wanted something new to chew on. "He was a cadet from one of my classes at the academy, yes. He was a fairly adept tactician then, so he might have been hiding the urge to defect. But, he accepted my presence here in the Hollows without much surprise. Someone like him, someone who's just turned their back on everything they've been taught, should react with something more than acceptance. A sense of guilt, being faced with an authority figure from the Academy, or even a sense of relief would make a lot of sense. But what I saw in there felt calculated, like he was trying to remain calm."

"So, we don't have a new pilot." His face wrinkled up in a petulant way, and he looked away from Alder's room down the hall and back at Katherine. "Damn shame. Would have been nice to have another Academy-trained pilot in here. I'll have him assigned to the excavation project. I want you to keep your eyes and ears on him, but there's no sense wasting a good set of arms and legs."

For a moment, Katherine thought Garrin was going to invite her to whatever was next on his itinerary. Instead, he walked past her, his knuckles grazing down her arm. She brought her arm in and didn't turn around to give him any more attention as his footsteps faded down the hall.

She had some free time now and headed for the officer's mess for her meeting with Jim. She surprised herself by managing to find it without relying on the colored lines on the walls. Jim was sitting in the same booth they'd shared the day before.

He waved as she walked over and sat down. A server arrived at the table before she could even begin talking and deposited a cup of coffee in front of her. Much like the last time, it made her uneasy, and she looked at it warily.

"Sorry," Jim said. "I thought you might want some. Had it ordered before you showed up."

"No, it's fine." She eyed the cup, trying to find the words to describe her unease. "This is all just too much."

"Yeah, you had that induction or whatever." Jim leaned forward, eager for new information.

"Not here." The room was nearly empty but still too crowded for her to feel comfortable talking to Jim openly about her induction into the Serotiny. She looked down at the cup and pulled it toward her. "These cups are nice, aren't they?"

"Yeah, sure." Jim cocked his head a little and smirked. "They look like something that was already down here before the base was repurposed by the Harbingers."

"Cups like these are so fragile. It's really a wonder they survived down here for this long." She picked it up and took a sip of the coffee inside. It was good. She'd hoped it would have at

135

least been bad coffee. It tasted like it could have come directly from the same batch she'd had at the Academy.

"Someone must have made sure to keep these safe and preserved," Jim said, trying to figure out what she was trying to say.

"They would, yes." Katherine took another sip. "Someone must have tried very hard to make sure that these would last a very long time down here."

Katherine wasn't sure if the message was going through. The cups, and by extension, everything else in the mountain, weren't designed to just dissipate like John's vision for the Harbingers. She decided to continue that train of thought later.

"How is it going in the hangar?" she asked.

"It's hard work, but it keeps me busy," Jim said. "You should come by sometime. Maybe I can show you around. I don't think they included us in your grand tour the other day."

"I saw the garage, but from a catwalk up above." She took another sip of her coffee. "They've got a whole suite of pilot training pods. It's an impressive operation."

"It's a lot of firepower locked inside a mountain." Jim sat back in his chair. "It feels like we could be doing more."

"We're doing more than you think," she said, and left the conversation there.

CHAPTER 11

Zak unzipped his tent and found Alison packing their campsite vigorously. She'd managed to get most of it stowed in the trail box on the back of the ATV but was struggling with the tangled remains of her tent.

"Here, let me get that." He stepped out of his tent and stretched in the morning light.

"I've got it," she replied, breathing heavily.

"Why the rush?" he asked. "What happened?"

He could tell she'd been crying again, but what was driving her now seemed new. She was packing with purpose.

"She's alive," Alison said, the words tumbling out in short bursts between breaths. "She's alive, and she's so close. I have to leave now."

Zak rubbed his eyes. He wanted to ask why she thought that, but Alison had already returned to her task. As he was rolling up his own sleeping bag, a note landed on the ground next to him. He looked up and saw Alison with a blanket roughly bundled in her arms.

"Read it and give it back to me," she said, then returned to packing.

Zak read the note. Someone had Eva, someone Alison knew well. His eyes widened as he reached the end.

"Where are we going?" he asked. "How long do we have?"

"It's at a ridge back near Taycher, if we can make it." Alison continued strapping the last of her supplies onto the vehicle, putting far too much strain on her injured leg. He worried what it might look like the next time he took her cast off to have a look. "It's a drop point I used to exchange intel with an operative inside the base. They're going to be there in less than two days."

Zak stopped packing his own things momentarily. The prospect of going back to Taycher and the Academy did something to him. He hadn't thought about much more than helping Alison for days, but the idea of seeing the destroyed base again was unsettling. He wanted to ask who her contact was, who had been selling secrets to the Harbingers. He looked over at Alison, sweating and struggling with the supplies on the back of the ATV, and pushed the question aside for now. He could ask later when they stopped to rest.

He quickly finished packing up his own tent and supplies and found room for them on the back of the ATV. As he strapped down some of the more haphazard items, Alison busied herself by putting gasoline into the fuel tank. Before he had another moment to think about what was ahead, they were pulling away from the destroyed house and the graves beneath the tree. The mist trapped in the glade swirled as they made their exit.

Zak held on tightly as they flew down the dirt roads. When they crested a small hill, all four tires left the ground momentarily and he gripped the sides of the trail box. They were going much faster than they'd managed before. They traveled for hours, with Alison making decisions at forks in the road as if she had an internal guidance system. Zak knew by now, however, that her knowledge of the landscape was extensive. She'd been a courier, running information between various rebel encampments and drop points across the southwestern deserts of the United Entities for years.

If they maintained this pace, they would make it back to Taycher with plenty of time to spare. He was about to shout this mental calculation when Alison let off the gas. They slowed to a crawl, then came to a stop at the top of a rocky overlook. She got off the ATV and limped away, muttering something about a main road.

Zak thought about going after her, but instead dismounted and walked to the edge of the overlook. A few twisted, ancient, pines provided some shade. He took a deep breath as he looked out over the desert. Looking for where the base should be, he found a bright spot on the desert valley, just beyond the next ridge of low mountains. It looked like it could be the dry basin the base was located inside. A cool wind pushed up over the ridge, and the sound of it running through the pines calmed him. As far as he could see, mountain ranges rose and fell like waves on a sagebrush ocean, gradually overlaying one another to the horizon. As he stood there, he could almost imagine he was there for no other purpose than the view.

The engine on the ATV fired up again and he was pulled from his moment of peace. Alison called for him to hurry, and he jogged back to the vehicle. They drove at dangerous speeds, this time aided by the downward grade of the mountain. Then, as they crested a smaller set of foothills, he saw the definitive shape of the base's central tower far in the distance. He smiled. They were close.

As he turned his attention back to the road ahead, gravity seemed to shift. The wheels of the ATV dug into a rut that cut across the road like a wound, wrenching the entire vehicle sideways. For a brief moment, Zak saw the ground approaching, and then the ATV was above them.

He landed hard on his side and rolled off the narrow dirt road into a thick tangle of sagebrush. He saw Alison land and roll to the opposite side of the road. Even as he struggled to get up himself, he saw Alison claw her way back onto the road.

"Fuck!" she screamed as she tried to stand. She collapsed as her leg refused to take her weight.

He got to her before she tried to stand again and tried to calm her down. She fought him to try and get to the ATV which had landed upside down a few yards up the road.

"We have to get it turned over!" she managed to say as she pushed at him again. He looked at the vehicle again. Clear fluid was leaking from it, gasoline. The large red jug had landed even further up the road and was cracked open, seeping fuel into the dust.

Zak left her and sprinted for the ATV. He heaved all his weight onto it. It rocked, toppled onto its side, then flipped completely back onto its wheels. He was out of breath and hadn't even inspected himself for injuries yet. Before he could take the time to do that, he covered the rest of the distance to the ruptured fuel jug. He managed to get it tilted up, saving what little was left inside.

"Just hold on, I'll be right there!" he called back to Alison, who had gotten to her feet and was limping up the road.

She was crying, but not from fear or pain, he knew. They were so close, but the ATV was in no state to continue. The handlebars were bent at an awkward angle, and the front tires had come free from the rims. She reached the vehicle and began hitting it with her fists. Zak leaned the broken fuel jug against it, making sure not to spill any more of it. He went to Alison and pulled her away.

"Stop," he tried to say calmly, but his voice came out with panic around the edges. "Stop or you're going to hurt yourself."

She sank away from him and into the dirt, furious tears streaming down her face. Zak put his hands out, a wordless plea for her to stay where she was. He left her and then walked around picking up the supplies that had scattered in the crash. As he bent down to pick up a small first aid kit, he finally remembered to check himself for injury.

He felt a general soreness that would likely become a full body ache before too long, but didn't feel like he had any broken bones. He brought the first aid kit over to Alison and began checking her for new injuries. She let him check, taking in deep breaths as she attempted to calm herself. After finding no major new injuries, he turned to inspect her leg. He was worried about what he might find and wasn't sure if he should even take the cast off. After a moment, he decided to make sure nothing else had happened to it.

She didn't try to mask a cry of pain when he deflated the air cast and pulled it off. He set it to one side. Her leg looked bad but still wasn't broken. Maybe the cast had protected the leg during the crash. It was more swollen than before, and he decided his first instinct was right. He reapplied the air cast and doled out some of the anti-inflammatory pills they had. She took them without protest, seeming to be deep in thought. He left her and started the task of getting the ATV off the road. Daylight would be gone soon, and he needed to get their camp set up.

While he did this, Alison seemed to be working through what to do next. He started a fire and prepared a small meal from what was left of their provisions. They ate this in silence for a while as the fire crackled and spit occasionally.

"I'm sorry," Zak said after he finished, unable to think of anything else to break the silence. He was afraid she wouldn't respond when she sighed and looked at him.

"We're not going to make it," she said flatly. She picked up a piece of stale bread from her plate and tossed it at the ATV. "I fucked up, and now Eva…"

"How far is it?" he asked, not willing to accept defeat. "If we leave now, can we make it?"

"No. I don't know." She looked down at her cast in anger and something approaching shame. "I'm not going anywhere on this fucking leg. I hate when I can't do things."

"I can see that." Zak had a fleeting urge to smile. Alison and Eva shared the same tendency toward blunt statements. "What if I went ahead? Tried to get John to stop and wait for you."

She shook her head. "No, he won't trust anyone but me. And even with a flashlight you might end up with an injury like mine walking around in the dark."

"Can we fix the ATV?" Zak asked.

"The damage probably isn't as bad as it looks. These things can take a beating." She looked at the ATV and frowned. "But it's also not going anywhere soon. I can fix it, but not in time to get to Eva."

"Well, we have to try something." He didn't like the defeated tone Alison was using. "You can't just give up."

"Give up?" Alison looked at Zak furiously for a moment and then looked down. "Maybe she'll be better off without me anyway."

"Fuck that," Zak said. "Don't do that. You're all she has left."

She nodded, and new tears fell from her eyes into the dirt. Zak thought for a moment, and then had an idea. "What if I take the note with me? I can use it to prove I'm telling the truth."

Alison looked back up and seemed to consider it. "Yeah, that might work."

"I'll leave when it's bright enough to see." He smiled at her, hoping it might reassure her that it was still possible.

There was a silence, and Zak took the opportunity to ask what he hadn't earlier. "Who are we supposed to be meeting there, anyway?"

"I don't see why it should be a secret anymore." Alison tossed another piece of stale bread out into the darkness. "His last name is Phillips. He's a teacher or something. Or at least he used to be."

Zak tried not to let his shock show on his face. He must not have done a good enough job of it, because Alison blinked at him and cocked her head to the side. "You know him, then?"

"Thought I did." Zak jabbed the fire with a stick, sending a plume of embers into the night air. "He taught me how to pilot. Taught all of us how to…" He didn't finish the sentence.

Zak wondered if he should feel hurt to discover that Phillips was a traitor. He wondered if that word even meant anything anymore; if there was anything left to betray. Zak wasn't even sure about his own place in line for judgement, after deserting his friend to help this rebel woman. Memories of eagerly taking in lessons from Phillips came back to him, and he had a sinking feeling in his chest as his admiration for the man instantly crumbled. They'd all become a well-oiled unit under his guidance. What was the worth of that knowledge, now that he knew it had come from a traitor?

"I think we're all just trying to find our place in this," Alison said with a tone of understanding that was soft and unexpected. "We're all just pieces on a board that was set before we ever knew we were playing."

"We still make choices," Zak said. What she said was true, sure. The world was set long before he'd ever even thought about his own place in it. But that didn't excuse him, or anyone else, of their mistakes.

Alison reached out and placed her hand on Zak's shoulder, pulling him back from the edge of another descent into memory. He looked at her, trying to figure out what she was thinking. Tears forming in her eyes glittered in the firelight, and he realized she was crying for him.

"I forgive you," she said.

Zak didn't respond; he had no words. He felt like he was falling, and so he turned his gaze to the fire so he would have something to ground him. What she'd said echoed through him but wouldn't settle. She still didn't know everything, so she couldn't truly forgive him.

Alison removed her hand from his shoulder and left him alone to stare into the fire. He heard her try to contain a moan of pain as she hobbled to her tent, and then she was gone.

He placed his branch onto the fire pit. New flames curled around it, the smooth bark first becoming black and then cracking apart. The edges of these tiny fissures began to glow, and slowly the branch joined the rest of the embers in a uniform rippling orange light.

As he listened to the soft crackle of the spent fire, he heard another sound coming from just beyond their campsite. Zak looked over to the ATV and saw a small kit fox dart into the low pulsing light. About the size of a small cat, it gingerly lifted one of the discarded pieces of bread with its tiny jaws. For a moment, the fox stared at Zak, trying to decide if he posed a threat. When Zak didn't move, the fox slowly retreated beneath the ATV and disappeared into the dark murk of the night. As he peered into that darkness, he realized that he could see detail now. The moon had risen and given definition to what had previously been only void.

Alison had said he might be able to make it to the rendezvous if he left in the morning. She wasn't going to ask him to leave now, had even told him it was a bad idea. But leaving now made sense. Any advantage they could get was worth the risk. Zak looked for Alison's bag and found it. He opened it to find the note from John. It was there, neatly folded and bright in the moonlight. On the front, written in a child's hand, were the words "For Allie." He put the note into his pocket. He also took out Alison's notebook.

A feather marked the page she'd been using most recently, and he opened to it. Spread across the two pages was a hand-drawn map of the area with dozens of routes and details marked out with tiny and precise lettering. He found where they were on the map easily. She'd added a new marker with the current date beside it. Off in the direction of the Academy was another point along a ridge marked with the letters "JP." Beside this, a series of dates were written. Most of them had already passed, likely previous times she'd visited the rendezvous point. There were a few more dates, however. The next one was for the following day. As John's note had said, he would be there at the time and place they would have met next.

Zak shut the notebook and added it to his own pack. While taking a flashlight from his bag, he also saw a piece of white chalk rolling around near the bottom.

He took out the chalk and flashlight and stood in the moonlight. He'd taken the chalk piece from Mark's bunk after the attack. The bunk, and the entire room, had been burned beyond recognition, but the chalk had remained. So much had happened since then. He didn't even know if Mark was still alive.

Zak shook his head and shouldered his pack. He scribbled a quick note onto the top of a small toolbox with the chalk and put it into his pocket. After making sure he had everything he would need, he clicked on his flashlight, and set off toward the ridge.

Mark lay on a cot that had been brought into the room earlier with one of his meals. It was a significant upgrade to the single folding chair he'd been afforded up to that point. Right then, it could have been his childhood bed, for all he knew, because bandages on his eyes blotted out all but the most brilliant light. A woman in a long grey lab coat and a man with a long rifle had come into his room shortly after his meeting with Katherine Scholl. They'd asked him if he was ready to have his optics removed.

When he hadn't answered, the woman began unpacking a shockingly simple toolset. She'd arranged an assortment of delicate tweezers and scalpels on a soft velvet cloth. In the end, she only needed one blade and one set of tweezers for the job. While he was lying down, she'd numbed his face and then performed the extraction with him awake. It was painless up until the last step.

"You're going to feel a tug when I disconnect it from your optic nerve," the woman said seconds before sending a white-hot shock of pain ricocheting through his skull. "Of course, if there's any scar tissue built up, there may also be a sting."

The man with the long gun laughed a little but regained his composure quickly.

The second eye had been significantly less severe, but Mark was left feeling more helpless than ever. He'd grown accustomed to his optical implants, even if he hadn't used them as often as some people did.

"You understand," the woman said. "We can't have people walking around with government-registered communications optics."

"Sure." That was the only word Mark said during the whole process.

She bandaged him up and told him not to move around too much. He'd spent most of the time since lying in the cot. Once, someone came and guided him to a bathroom, then returned him to the bed. He'd just begun to wonder if they'd forgotten him when there was a knock on the door.

"Come in," Mark said. "I'm sure it's open."

The door opened, and unfamiliar heavy footsteps filled the room. Mark heard the folding chair beside his cot creak as the person sat down. His instinct was to try to get away. Something about this new presence was alarming, but in his current state that was impossible.

"I don't know what you think you're doing here." The voice was gruff and angry. Dangerous. "If you pull any bullshit, I'll have you shot. I don't trust anyone until they've proven to me why they're here." The man paused, as if expecting Mark to respond.

"I don't know why I'm here," Mark said. It was a risk, but he could tell his change-of-heart story wasn't working the way he'd hoped. "I knew I couldn't do it anymore. I didn't know where to go, so I just kept going." Mark remembered something from one of his counterterrorism courses at the academy and decided to use it. "Stability is a lie."

The man next to him grunted and stood up. Mark heard the door open, and the footsteps continued out into the hall. After he could no longer hear them, Mark took a deep breath and let it out.

"Mr. Kingston can be a little intense," a new voice said. Mark flinched and felt the blood drain from his face. He hadn't known there was anyone else in the room. A new, lighter, set of footsteps approached him and he felt his body tense up. He was worried they'd decided to kill him rather than risk keeping him around.

"He means well." The new, slick voice sounded vaguely robotic. "You've been assigned to the excavation site while we evaluate your usefulness to the Harbingers. It's hard work, but it will get you out of this room. Our doctor said you should be cleared to start in the morning. Rest up. I'll be back in the morning to escort you."

"Thank you." Mark scratched at the skin around his bandages. "Do you know when I can take these off?"

"Doctor said nine hours. From what I understand, it's more about making sure you don't rub your eyes in your sleep. Wouldn't want to rupture anything."

Mark stopped scratching and returned his hand to his side.

"I'll see you in the morning," the man said. "I will be your Acclimation Specialist. I've worked with others in your circumstances, so don't fret too much."

Mark heard the door swing closed, then the faint click as a lock was put in place. Mark was left alone, wondering what kind of person used the word "fret" in everyday conversation. He had to keep reminding himself this was all for a bigger purpose. It was uncomfortably easy to become numb, and just move from one moment to the next. He was in a unique position though,

149

possibly able to do some real damage to the heart of this organization. What could the Harbingers be excavating? He filed this new information away, and hoped he wouldn't pop his eyes in his sleep.

CHAPTER 12

Alison opened her tent and looked up at a dull gray sky. The sun hadn't risen yet, but there was enough light to see. A fine coating of mist covered the tents, bags, and ATV. The vehicle was useless, she thought. She looked down at the cast on her leg, similar feelings of disdain coursing through her. She tried to stand and was devastated to find that her injury was worse than the day before. She tried again and managed to take a few steps out of her tent, but had to sit down in front of the remains of their campfire. The crash had done more damage to her than she'd realized.

Dull anger and shame welled up inside her as she prepared to rely on Zak once again. Now that she was thinking about it, she hadn't heard him at all yet. Usually, he already had the fire going for a meager breakfast. Inside the fire pit was only white ash, and the small pile of wood still remained beside it from the night before.

"Zak?" she called out, feeling even more helpless than before.

She waited, hoping that calling his name would be enough to get him out of his tent. When he didn't respond, she looked for his bag and saw that it was gone. She fought a wave of fear that chilled her skin. Being alone in the wilderness wasn't new to her, but somehow it felt different now. Maybe it was that her injury made her vulnerable, but she suspected that she'd begun to rely on Zak for more than simple assistance. And now he was gone. He'd run off on her in the middle of the night.

She looked toward the horizon and saw the top of a building poking toward the milky blue predawn sky. The central spire of the Academy. No, she knew he wouldn't just abandon her. He must have set off toward the rendezvous early, even though she'd told him it was a bad idea. It bothered her a bit that he'd gone against her advice, but a large part of her was relieved he was already moving.

Her bag was on the ground near the remnants of the fire, so she checked inside. She wasn't surprised to find John's letter missing. Her notebook was gone as well, and this made her angry for a moment. Zak would need it though. It had the precise location of the rendezvous point.

She looked at the ATV again and shook her head. Grunting with the effort, she managed to stand up. That was her task, then, to get it working again. Meaning to get started as soon as possible she decided to skip breakfast. When she went to collect her toolbox, she saw a note scrawled with chalk on top:

"Sorry I stole your stuff. I'll be back as soon as I can."

~

"Hey, wake up," Vesnina said. "Banks wants to talk to us."

Turner sat up and took a moment to remember where he was. He'd been ordered to take a break from preparations in the garage and get some rest. So, he'd climbed into the cockpit of the Nanook, their Ursidae class mech. He'd climbed aboard ostensibly to keep an eye on the final preparations, but part of him irrationally wanted to make sure no one left without him. The last thing he remembered was watching someone complete the final welds on the armor plating of the Kapu, their agile four-legged reconnaissance mech. Sparks had fallen down from above like a rain of fire.

Now, it was morning, and the activity in the garage was slower. The piles of supplies next to each mech and truck were nearly gone, stowed away in every open space available. A group of soldiers sat on the ground drinking what might be coffee, but was probably alcohol of some kind, from tin mugs.

"Everything's ready?" Turner picked up his sidearm from the darkened display panel in front of him and strapped it to his side.

"Almost," Vesnina said. "Just a few more things to zip up." She handed him a cup of coffee he hadn't seen her holding. "I let you sleep as long as I could, but Banks wants to see us."

"Another meeting." Turner took the offered drink and gulped down half of it. "Lead the way."

They exited the mech through the open hatch in the back and descended to the ground. A large canvas tent was set up in the center of the garage. Banks was already standing outside when they arrived. He ushered them in and closed the canvas flap behind them.

"We've received a message from central command," Banks said, with an air of excitement. "It's brief and fragmented, but we think we have it figured out. It's been broadcasting at low frequency for a while. We don't know how long it's been there, but it may have been running the whole time and we just didn't hear it because we were sweeping with the known ciphers. This one is hidden on the wide band."

Banks reached over to an antique-looking radio device and flipped a switch. Instantly, the tent was filled with the high chaotic sound of static. He twisted a few knobs, and a pattern began to fade in through the cloud of noise. If Banks hadn't pointed it out, it would have been easy to mistake it for just more random noise. The static had a definite pattern of bursts, though, coming every few seconds.

"What does it say?" Vesnina asked, leaning closer to the ancient radio to listen for the pattern.

"We're not completely sure, but it's simple Morse code. It's encrypted, of course, but each word they broadcast uses a different high-clearance cipher. Ideally, the only place with access to enough ciphers to decode all the words are friendly bases." He reached for a sheet of paper filled with notes. On the page were some words with their counterpart Morse code printed above them. "What we've pieced together so far are the following words, in no particular order: '*Overwhelming. Gather. Trust. United. Final. Chain. Collapse. Harbingers. Rendezvous. Offensive. Forces.*' There are a whole lot more, but what I think you need to know is that one of the words we've been able to pull is '*Taycher.*' I'm sure there's a cipher that will put the words in the right order, but I think I can already tell what the message is trying to say."

"You think Command is asking anyone who hears the message to converge here." Turner stepped closer to Banks to look at the sheet of paper. "You can't seriously be asking us to wait here until help arrives."

"No, I'm not." Banks put the sheet of paper down. Many more like it were spread across the table. "I can't risk what we've gathered here on what may not even be orders from Command. We have to get our forces out of this base by sundown. Like I said, we have no idea how long this message has been broadcasting."

"So, what are you asking us to do?" Turner asked. "We don't have room for everyone, even if we dropped every piece of cargo we've loaded up."

"I'm not asking you to take everyone. The plan will remain nearly the same, but I'm adding some additional personnel. Plime and Black, from Research. Their expertise could prove invaluable once you're able to get close to the Ston device." He turned to Vesnina. "I want you to go as well."

"That isn't necessary, sir," Vesnina said quickly. "I can help you here. I don't need special treatment."

"It's not special treatment," Banks said, brushing the argument aside. "You've proven to me that you know what you're doing. I need you to keep our research team working on how to stop their goddamn thing from being weaponized. Turner will have enough going on managing the convoy. Black and Plime have already been briefed and are gathering their essentials now. You may want to go make sure they're not bringing the entire lab with them."

"You want me to babysit the scientists?" Vesnina asked.

"I need you to make sure that what they know is put to use," Banks said. "The rest of us will stay here and see what this message is all about. Now get moving." He waved Turner and Vesnina off, and together, they exited the tent into the busy garage.

"Guess I'd better go get myself packed up." Vesnina saluted Turner and left at a brisk jog, nodding at Barkley as she passed him.

Barkley was walking much more confidently now. After his encounter with the barrier in the sky, he'd been badly hurt. But now, he had regained all the cocky charm of a fighter pilot. Turner hadn't known him before the crash, but he thought that Barkley might be even more cocky now that he'd cheated death.

"So, we're saluting you now?" Barkley asked.

"It's just command structure." Turner felt blood rush to his cheeks and clenched his jaw. "Where do they have you set up?"

"No need to account for me in your convoy. I've got my own ride outta here, groundhog." He stepped back and gestured to something in the garage beneath a wind-torn tarp. "It's just a cargo lift fitted with some weapons. She won't be winning any dogfights, but at least I won't be stuck on the ground with you assholes. Banks has me making some reconnaissance flights of the area today."

"Good luck not breaking up on takeoff," Turner said. "It will be good to have a set of eyes in the sky. Just watch out for invisible walls."

~

Eva ran toward John along the ridge near Taycher. They'd made it there at midday and would spend the rest of the day waiting to see if Alison would reach them. He was concerned someone might see the thin trail of dust Eva was bringing up with her footsteps and walked out to meet her. Eva should probably take a break anyway. She'd been moving around since they stopped, burning off all the nervous energy she'd been storing up while they drove.

"You should probably stop running around like that." He didn't want to scare her, but the last thing they needed was a visit from some unexpected guests from the base down below. "We have to keep a low profile while we wait to see if your mother will get here."

"You mean my sister," Eva said, catching her breath.

"Oh, yes." He felt a twinge of panic. Alison had managed to maintain the façade that they were sisters since she'd left to join the Harbingers, and he hadn't wanted to break that.

"I know she's not my sister," Eva said. "Everybody thinks I don't know, but I can hear them talking."

John didn't know what to say. Eva was always finding new ways to surprise him with her awareness. "Why didn't you say anything?" He found that talking to her reminded him of conversations with Alison.

She shrugged and reached down to pick up a rock. As she looked at it, she deemed it worthy of collecting and added it to a growing bulge in her pocket. "The first time I heard them talking about it, I just pretended I was asleep. Allie didn't want to stay with me, so I just pretended like the rest of them."

"That's not true," John said reflexively. "The world isn't the way she wanted it to be for you. Going and doing the work she did was the only way she knew how to fix it. Alison wanted to stay with you, she just felt like she couldn't."

Eva shrugged again and looked down, apparently hunting for another rock to add to her collection. He saw a wet spot appear in the dirt, quickly followed by another. Eva was crying.

"What's wrong?" He knelt down and lifted her chin.

"What if she doesn't want me?" Eva asked, her eyes averting his as new tears formed and ran down her cheeks.

He wrapped her in his arms, and she collapsed into sobs.

"Your mother loves you more than anything. If she can, I know she'll do everything in her power to get to us." He looked out beyond the ridge, hoping to see Alison approaching. The desert was still, however, and so they would wait.

CHAPTER 13

Chester Breaks walked ahead of Mark through a maze of corridors. Another person, armed but not actively threatening, followed behind them. Breaks, Mark noted, didn't carry a sidearm on him like many of the people in the Hollows. He filed this away in his mind and returned his focus to the turns they made. They'd come and escorted him from his room at what felt like an early hour, but inside the mountain, he couldn't be sure. They hadn't exactly given him a schedule, and he hadn't seen a clock in any of the hallways yet. It made him feel like he was separated from the world outside by more than just stone and steel.

Breaks pointed at things as they moved along, and Mark tried to commit as much to memory as possible. Even small details might be useful if he could get the information out to someone.

"If you turned left here, you would reach the common showers and lockers. We'll get you assigned one of those eventually. You'll be working a five-hour shift today." Breaks turned his head briefly and looked back at Mark. "Like I said, you're not the only person to come to us unvouched. We'll get you up to speed on what's expected. It's a good thing you came when you

159

did. Mr. Kingston has just given the order to shut down our new acceptances."

"Why would you shut down recruitment?" Mark asked, genuinely interested.

"Need-to-know, I'm afraid." Breaks slowed a bit and fell into step with Mark. "I will tell you that there are things moving. Exciting times are ahead."

Mark got the impression Breaks had been a salesman before joining the Harbingers. The man even insisted on wearing a traditional suit instead of the standard utilitarian garments worn by most people he had seen so far. Mark looked down at his own clothes. The uniform they'd given him definitely wasn't new, but it also wasn't tattered or torn. It implied a certain level of resource maintenance. They clearly had an abundance of what they needed to survive, but they were still looking to make sure everything lasted.

"Well, I've got some other things to take care of," Breaks said in his unsettling and sudden way. "I'll leave you here, and your escort will take you the rest of the way." He gestured forward with a flourish. The soldier behind him nudged his back with the butt of her rifle to remind him she was there, and Mark continued on.

"I wish you the best, and feel free to say hello if you see me around the Hollows," Breaks said. "I'll be tracking your progress myself." He gave a short wave, turned on his heel, and disappeared down another hallway.

"That guy is a fucking weirdo," the soldier behind Mark said after Breaks was gone. "Seems like he's everywhere."

Mark didn't respond, unsure of whether the woman was being friendly or just speaking to herself.

"Slow down, will you," she said. "As soon as I drop you off at the excavation site, I've got laundry duty."

Mark slowed, and the woman fell into step with him. "Where were you stationed?" She asked this casually, as if they were meeting in a market.

"Taycher," Mark said. "South of here a few hundred miles."

"A grounder, eh?" She slung her rifle on her back. "I made my way here from Sheppard, the Air Force base up north of here. But I've been with the Harbingers for years. How'd you find this place? After everything started, I got brought here in a convoy with a bunch of defectors. When we got here, there was just a skeleton crew running the place."

"Just followed the crew that ran up through Taycher," Mark said, trying his best to hide a bubbling anger. "Decided I didn't want to be there anymore. Thought I might join up with the Harbingers."

Mark became aware of the soldier's gaze and thought she might be attempting to pry new information from him for her superiors. Another test.

"What'd you do at Taycher?" she asked.

"Pilot. Well, I was a cadet." Mark reached up to rub his right eye. "I was at the end of my live piloting training when everything happened."

"The itching stops eventually. I promise." She tapped beside her own eye. "I had my optics removed when I got here too. Kind of a shame to see them go. They were pretty useful. Name's

161

Carmine Gonzales, by the way." She reached a hand over to Mark.

"Mark Alder," he said as he shook her hand. "All that training and they've got you running laundry inside a mountain?"

"Yeah, pretty small stuff, I guess." She shrugged. "But whatever it takes to bring it all down. I'm technically assigned to a tactical ground support squad, if they ever need me. But we've all got jobs in here. Try to keep your uniform clean. The ones that come out of the hole are always the worst."

"The hole?" Mark asked.

"Oh, yeah, sorry. The excavation site is what the bigwigs like to call it. But it's just a big hole." She laughed and waved at a guard as they passed by. "Turn here. We're almost there. You'll see."

Ahead of them was a large metal blast door. Two guards stood in front of it. They nodded as Mark and Gonzales approached, then both guards put keys into slots on either side of the door and turned them simultaneously.

"Oh, it's gonna be bright." As Gonzales spoke, the door began to rise. The light from outside was blinding. "They keep the lights pretty low inside the Hollows. Saves energy, I guess. The only places you're gonna find bright light from now on will be in the medical or science wings or outside. Guess that's a perk of working in the hole; you get to see the sun a bit more than the rest of us."

The door opened only high enough for Mark and Gonzales to duck underneath it. Once outside, Mark blinked as his eyes adjusted to the sunlight. They were standing in a small clearing with tall pine trees ringing it. Paths led to the left and the right, but there were no signs to direct him to the excavation site.

"This way." Gonzales unslung her rifle and now had it in a more ready position. She pointed to the path on the right. "We're not too far from the gate."

As they walked along the path, Mark took a deep, exaggerated breath. While inside the mountain, he hadn't realized how stifling the air was. He took another breath and looked over at Gonzales.

"Yeah, I guess there are a few perks to your assignment." She took a deep breath of her own. "The air in the mountain is a closed system. Some people think they're even lowering the amount of oxygen in the mix to keep our lungs working, or something. I think it's bullshit, but whatever."

They reached another checkpoint, an electronic rolling gate set in a huge fence, and stopped in front of it.

"Knock, knock, guys," Gonzales called out. She waved at a camera mounted on a fence post. "Got a fresh one for the hole."

The gate buzzed and slid open. Just like the blast doors at the mountain entrance, it opened just enough to let them through. Mark heard the sounds of a construction site ahead. After a hundred yards or so, they came around a bend in the path and found a clearing much larger than the one near the mountain base entrance. In the middle was a huge circular depression in the earth that dropped down for at least a hundred feet. At the bottom of the sunken area sat a large industrial building with three conveyor belts reaching out of it. They extended all the way to the natural surface level. A constant stream of material poured from each of them, adding steadily to large piles of rock being tended by bulldozers and other earth moving machines.

A middle-aged man covered in dirt approached Mark and Gonzales, holding a hard hat and gloves in one hand. His other arm was immobilized by a sling and rested on a round gut.

"You've got a fresh one for me, eh?" the man asked.

"Treat this one nice. He's from a base down south." Gonzales nudged Mark with her elbow. "Go on, now. Have fun with your new friends."

"Perk up. You look like we're gonna throw you in or something," the man said with a grin. "My name is Henry. Put these on and follow me. I'll take you down and give you the grand tour."

Mark put on the hard hat and started with the gloves as they walked,

"Oh, they grow up so fast." Gonzales pretended to wipe away some tears. "You be good and don't get into any trouble. I'll be back at the end of your shift to escort you back into the Hollows."

"I've got a cart over here." Henry gestured to an orange electric cart with two seats. "They paired you up with me because I tore something in my shoulder a couple weeks back. Guess they figured I'd do some good and train a new hand."

They got into the cart, and Henry drove down an earthen ramp toward the building at the bottom.

"This used to be a gold mine," he said. "Long time ago. When we started, this big pit was already dug out. Must not have found much here, because it didn't go very deep. Now we've got a more vertical process going on. Big elevator in the building down there, takes ya deep underground. We're just digging away down there every day, hauling shit to the surface, and the transport team takes it all somewhere else. Not sure what happens to it after that. Maybe nothin'.

"Made a lot of progress for a bunch of guys with primitive tools. Jackhammers, picks, shovels. You get it. We're already down about a quarter mile. Not claustrophobic, are you?"

"Not that I'm aware of," Mark said. "What are we mining? Gold?"

"Not mining anything," Henry said. "Orders are to dig a shaft as deep as we can. A waste of effort, if you ask me, but I don't do the decisions around here."

"We're just digging a hole?" Mark asked, confused.

"Yep." Henry looked amused. "Lotta the guys are calling it the Grave of Civilization."

"You haven't asked anyone what it's for?" Mark asked. "It's a lot of work if you're not even processing the material you're excavating."

"Asked a lot of those questions myself at the beginning. Why this? Why that? Nobody knows. If they do, they're not telling. I think it's just to keep us busy. You'd have a lot of people just sitting around twiddling their thumbs in the mountain if they didn't find something for us to do. Hold on."

Henry jerked the wheel of the cart and turned down off the long spiral ramp leading to the bottom of the pit, plummeting down the steep edge. The cart gathered speed, and Henry flashed a wide grin. When they got to the bottom, he slammed on the brakes, sending the cart into a slide toward the building in the center of the open pit. They finally stopped, and Henry slapped the steering wheel with his good hand.

"Ha! Great, right?" He smiled at Mark broadly, then drove the final yards to where the other carts were parked. "Gotta get my thrills somehow."

Mark nodded and stepped out of the cart, making a mental note to hold on the next time someone said, "hold on."

"All right, let's get downstairs." Henry opened a door to the building. "Don't worry about the darkness. Your eyes will adjust soon. Just follow me."

He led Mark through what sounded like a workshop but only looked like a murky series of poorly exposed photographs to Mark's unadjusted eyes. By the time they reached a large elevator cage, things had become a bit clearer. He could just make out some of the details of the space. The three conveyor belts he'd seen pulling material out of the building all reached in toward a central shaft. The shaft itself was big enough to swallow a couple of mechs if they'd somehow stumbled in here. The vast, open darkness of that hole frightened Mark more than he thought it would. The elevator was nothing more than a cage suspended by wires and anchored to the edge of the hole with a metal frame. Around the shaft's perimeter was a fence made out of rebar poles in the ground with orange plastic netting strung between them.

"It's a bit of a shock, I know." Henry opened a small gate on the elevator cage. "Once you're downstairs, you won't even realize how deep you are. I mean, or you might. Some guys do have a bit of trouble with it, but it passes."

"Sure," Mark said as he stepped into the elevator cage.

Henry followed him in, flipped a switch on the inside of the cage, and they began to sink into the earth. Mark thought for a moment that this might be a good time to enact a small measure of revenge on the Harbingers. The railing around the elevator cage was below hip level and it would take very little effort to send Henry plummeting to the ground. It could even be passed off as an accident. He shook off the thought. The idea that he would somehow get away with that was ludicrous, and he needed to focus on reality.

Also, the thought of actually pushing this man from the elevator felt wrong. On some level, he knew that Henry and everyone else he'd encountered were rebels that deserved whatever came for them. But it was getting harder to see it that way.

It was probably just his mind helping him acclimate to his new environment, he reassured himself. It made sense. If he hoped to stay alive long enough to do some real damage to this organization, he needed to blend in, to become part of whatever was happening here.

~

Zak's lungs worked to move the dry desert air in and out of him as he ran toward the ridge. The sun radiated above him mercilessly. He kept his eyes moving, looking out for his next footfall while still trying to keep himself oriented in the right direction. Weaving through the sagebrush wasn't easy, and at times, he had to force himself through a narrow passage between the dry bushes. His hands were already scratched and bleeding. He'd have to spend his next break looking for the gloves in his pack.

After a few more turns he came to a stop at a cracked two-lane blacktop highway. It was one of the main roads into the base. He looked in both directions before attempting to cross. There were no vehicles on the road, but he did spot the weathered sign for a gas station, probably the one Alison had mentioned. It beckoned him with promises of shade and rest, but he couldn't stop now. In just a few hours, the sun would go down, and Phillips would disappear with Eva back out into the desert, headed north.

He pulled out his canteen and took a long draught while sizing up the remaining distance to the rendezvous marked on Alison's map. The ridge wasn't too far, but he felt unsteady. He'd been moving since before daybreak, stopping only briefly for water and food when he knew he needed it. After returning the canteen to his pack, he rummaged for his gloves. Once he found them, he stood back up and walked across the road, pulling them on as he went.

Once he was on the other side he resumed his faster pace. It wasn't a run exactly. He took care to slow down when he reached particularly rough terrain. Soon he was back in a rhythm and felt his mind drifting, as if it were trying to protect him from the growing weariness and pain in his legs. Instead of the increasingly difficult path ahead, he found himself thinking back on what had caused him to join the military, what had put him on the path that had led him here.

He'd been in the communal bedroom at a state-run house for older wards of the state. His record with foster placement wasn't good, and so they'd pretty much given up trying to place him anymore. He was almost an adult anyway.

He sat on his bunk looking down at a slip of paper. Everyone in his age group had undergone their final assessments that day to determine their work paths. Zak had no real friends, and so when he hadn't shared his results with anyone, they hadn't thought anything of it. It was odd to think that someone's entire future could be summed up with a single slip of paper. He read the words again:

Subject: Zakary Lockwood

Control Number: 031522

Determination: Acceptable

Recommendation: Military Service (Suitability rating for all branches: Acceptable)

When the test proctor had given him the results, Zak hadn't understood what they meant. The woman had taken his slip and made a sound like she was looking at a winning lottery ticket. Evidently, his scores on the various assessments were high enough that he had multiple choices for his future.

"Basically, any branch of the military might want you," she'd said. "There are some branches that are more selective than others, of course. But, scores like this mean that if you make it through basic training, you can probably go into whichever one you want."

He'd left for training the very next day, much to the confusion of his peers. When they'd asked where he was going, many of them had scoffed at his being given such an assignment.

"Ghost kid can't even reach the top shelf in the pantry," one of the larger and pushier children said. "What the fuck is he gonna do, climb inside the guns and clean the barrels?"

"Maybe they'll just use him for target practice," another kid had said.

The training he underwent had been tough, but he'd managed to get through it just like everyone else. Grueling hikes had been but one of the myriad challenges he'd faced. As a smaller cadet, the training often required more effort. He'd made it through by sheer force of will. Then, when faced with the decision of which branch he wanted to put as his first choice, he'd selected the Mechanized Armor Corps.

The machines themselves had fascinated him, of course, but he also saw that the acceptance rate was lower than any of the other branches. He'd struggled through so much in his life already, that he figured he may as well continue taking whichever was the most difficult path forward. Whenever he managed to overcome some obstacle that seemed impossible, he felt more in control of his life. If he could do the impossible, he could survive anything.

Zak stepped on a loose rock and stumbled, bringing him back from his memory. The ridge was closer, but the sun was going down. He would beat this desert, he had to.

CHAPTER 14

Katherine ran along her improvised track in her room again. She'd pulled the furniture back away from the walls after she returned from her meeting with the new recruit. Garrin told her there was an indoor track and gym available to her, but she preferred the solitude of running by herself. Even back at the Academy she'd had a treadmill in her quarters so she could run alone.

She'd been read in on the grandest secret of the Harbingers of the Fall, and she felt lost. She now knew that the Harbingers were meant to bring down the structure of society only so the Serotiny could assert its own framework over the foundation of the world. She still believed in the cause of bringing down the existing systems, but perhaps it had been naïve of her to believe that the ultimate goal was an organic regrowth. The future she'd envisioned was green and gradual. What the Serotiny proposed, though, was artificial, manufactured.

She stopped running and caught her breath. She needed to talk to Jim about this, but she still couldn't be sure who was listening and when. If John were there, maybe she would have been able to talk to him as well. Hell, maybe he would have been able to convince the Serotiny to allow for some of the organic growth she had hoped for. John had written about that natural regrowth of civilization so eloquently in his prose. There was no way he would approve of an endgame like the Serotiny.

Her breathing became more regular as she rested, and she resolved to find out where Jim was as soon as she was able. She grabbed a towel from the wardrobe and walked to her shower in the corner of the room. A personal shower was a luxury bestowed on only some of the people in the Hollows. Why she'd managed to obtain one wasn't entirely clear to her, but she assumed it had something to do with Garrin. He was never one to shirk the benefits of, if not rank, status.

She wondered what the power structure really looked like inside Cone Alpha, as they'd called it. The organization of the Hollows was more complex than it appeared on the surface. There weren't any traditional ranks or hierarchies in place that she could discern. Instead, there was an intricate web of responsibility that kept everyone and everything flowing in a particular direction. She wondered what direction that was, exactly. If she followed the threads upstream, would she find one person tugging on them? It was possible, but Katherine didn't think that level of organization was feasible for a single person. And what if there was no head? What if the Harbingers of the Fall was only the collective will of the people that comprised it? The idea gave her chills as she undressed. If that was true, her own intent must be reflected in the workings of this place somewhere.

She showered quickly, donned one of her gray uniforms, and left the room. The faded purple line along the walls led her to Chester Breaks' room. He was also housed in the cluster of rooms with personal amenities. She knocked on the door, and he opened it almost too quickly. He stepped back from the doorway to allow her to enter.

"Oh, I don't need to stay long." She stayed out in the hall. His quarters were much like hers, but there was a distinctly clerical feeling to it. Along with the bed and wardrobe were a dozen or so aluminum filing cabinets and at least four separate information terminals.

"Nonsense," Breaks said. "I've been asked to check up with you periodically, anyway. I had you scheduled for a meeting later today. Have you reviewed your schedule?"

"Oh, yes." Katherine had forgotten entirely about her schedule. She was supposed to be headed out to the excavation site to check up on Alder at the end of his shift. "I just wondered if you might be able to tell me where they...where we have Jim assigned today. He and I had grown pretty close on our journey here, and I'd like to make sure he's doing all right."

"Of course," Breaks said. "I'm not actually sure, but we assigned most of your crew from the Anansi to fleet duties. Maintenance, training, all that. You're welcome to visit any of them during your recreation time."

"Absolutely," Katherine said. She still hadn't stepped into the room, but Breaks didn't press the issue. "I'll see you later for our meeting."

"Until then." Breaks extended a hand, and she shook it. "Mr. Kingston expects an update on the Alder situation as well."

Katherine turned and left, following the yellow line that would lead her to the north exit. This walk took significantly longer, and she began to wonder if she was supposed to be following the orange line when she rounded a corner and spotted the exit door. The two guards nodded at her as she approached. They turned keys in boxes on the walls, and the door opened just enough to let her through. After being inside the mountain, she was eager for the opportunity to get outside.

~

"Okay, where is she?" Eva asked, suddenly poking her head up from the back seat of the truck.

"I already told you, I'm not sure if she will be here." John rubbed his eyes and pulled the plastic lever beside his seat to bring it back up. They'd been at the top of the ridge all day as the sun slowly worked across the sky, and he was losing hope. "If she's not here soon, we'll have to keep going and see if she can meet us at our next stop."

Eva kicked the back of his chair. "I'm tired of driving."

"Hey, I'm tired of driving too," John said, a little more sternly than he'd meant. "Besides, you're not driving. I am. Would you like to give it a try?"

"Yes." She gave his chair one more kick and crossed her arms in front of her.

"If you drive, how do you plan to reach the…" John stopped talking and grew quiet.

"I'll use my backpack and Meeple to—" Eva started to answer before John could reach back and hold his hand out for her to be quiet.

John pulled his gun from its holster and carefully opened the door of the truck. As he did, he heard the unmistakable sound of someone climbing up the loose stone slope on the other side of the ridge. He left the door of the truck open and tried to make out details of the figure as they approached. His heart soared at the possibility that Alison had found them. But, as his eyes adjusted to the approaching gloom of night, his hopes were replaced with caution.

He thought of calling out to the figure, but something stopped him. He'd watched Alison climb this very ridge dozens of times when he had information drops that also included an in-person debrief. The person below was not moving with the careful, practiced movements of an experienced desert runner and climber. John watched as whoever was approaching slipped and took a moment to regain their footing. They were wearing the faded crimson of an academy uniform.

John drew back from the ridge and almost tripped over Eva. He hadn't heard her leave the truck.

"Get back in the truck," he said quietly. "We have to go."

Eva was still trying to get a look at the approaching figure, so he picked her up and carried her back into the truck. "What if it's Allie?" she asked, clearly upset. "We can't leave!"

He placed her in the passenger's seat, then got in himself. "It's not her," John said as calmly as he could. "I don't know who it is, but it's not her. It looks like someone from the base noticed us. We can't take any chances. If she got our note, she knows where we're going next."

He put the truck in neutral and allowed it to coast backward, silently, away from the edge of the ridge. When he was far enough away, he turned the ignition on and drove away slowly, trying to bring up as little dust as possible.

Zak heard the truck at the top of the ridge start its engine, and he pushed to the top just in time to see its dim red taillights dip out of view behind a rise in the landscape.

"Shit!" He waved his arms, hoping that John would come back. When he didn't, Zak went to sit on the ground and suddenly felt his body give out. He lay there in the dust looking up at wispy orange-hued clouds, trying to collect his thoughts. It was becoming harder to think clearly as his mind started to fade. He was experiencing heat exhaustion, he knew, and managed to pull his canteen from his side and drink what little was left of his water. John and Eva were gone, and he needed to get back to Alison. They needed to get moving toward whatever the next place was that John had written about.

He rolled onto his side, intending to get up, and was greeted by a small pile of rocks. They were all very clearly gathered from around the ridge; the work of a child trying to amuse themselves no doubt. Eva was here. Zak tried to get up and found that his body felt too heavy to move. As he rolled onto his back, his vision dimmed and then there was darkness.

The Nanook was fully fitted for departure, but Turner was still checking and re-checking it. The remaining work on the other units was being taken care of by Hank and the other more tech-minded soldiers left on the base. As he tugged on the straps holding a bundle of supplies to one of the rear legs, Kalen walked up to him.

"I cinched that one pretty tight." He smiled and offered Turner a flask. "I'd pretend to be offended, but it looks like you've got something on your mind."

"Just don't want anything to go sideways like it did the last time." Turner took the flask and had a long drink from it, then nearly spit it out. "Shit, what is that?"

"Hey, that's top-shelf stuff from the bar on Rec. Five." He took the flask back and had a drink himself. "Nobody was using it, so I helped myself. You shouldn't worry so much. Everything is about as sideways as it's possible to be already."

"Sure." Turner rested his hand on the cool metal hull of the Nanook and looked up at it. "And how are you doing?"

Kalen laughed and shook his head. He took another drink as an answer.

"Really, I want to know," Turner said.

"I don't know, man." Kalen rubbed his eyes. "There are times I find myself able to just focus on the work. You know? I can just get the job done and move onto the next thing. But when there's nothing left to do, I remember him. He's in the mass fucking grave out on the training field."

Turner didn't know how to respond, but he tried anyway. "I'm so sorry. I'm sorry they did it that way."

"It's fine. They did what they had to do. I don't envy what they did while we were gone. I just wish I could have done it myself." Kalen put the flask away into an inside pocket of his jacket. "Being here has made it so much harder, too. Every damn room in this place has a memory of him hiding inside it, like a ghost. I sit at the fire sometimes and I can feel him next to me, and I'm afraid of opening my eyes to see that he's not. Some nights I can even fall asleep still believing he's there."

He put a hand on Kalen's shoulder. "We'll make sure his sacrifice—everyone's sacrifices—aren't for nothing. We'll get these bastards."

Turner looked out over the small core of mechs they had, and wondered how he was supposed to follow through on those words. But they would try, he thought, and that would have to be enough.

CHAPTER 15

The late afternoon light was overwhelming, compared to what she'd been used to in the mountain. Katherine allowed herself to stand in the clearing outside the mountain blast door for a few moments while she got used to it. The first thing she noticed when she had adjusted was the greenery. It was shocking just how much grew here. Then she felt the breeze, and it sent a chill down her back. This was what she wanted the future to look like, she thought. Not whatever stale preservation was happening inside the Hollows. She looked for a path and was surprised to find someone waiting for her along the one that headed to her right.

"Hello, ma'am. Carmine Gonzales," the woman said. "Honored to meet you, ma'am."

"Katherine will do. From what I understand, there's not much of a rank system here."

Gonzales laughed. "Sure, but some of us sit on a Council and some of us wash laundry." The woman flushed and covered her mouth with one hand. "I'm sorry. I don't know why I said that. I was just saying that some people are, uh, burdened with more responsibility than others."

"Relax. It was funny." Katherine rested a hand on Gonzales' arm briefly to calm her down. "Besides, you're right. There is some level of organization. Were you supposed to be taking me to the excavation site?"

"Oh yeah!" Gonzales gestured down the path. "This way. They've got me picking up Mark from his first-ever trip into the hole. I can't wait to see how dirty he's got his uniform."

"Hard work down there?" Katherine asked, noting that Gonzales had called Alder by his first name.

"I've never done any of it down there, but from the look of the uniforms I clean, yeah, it's pretty hard work."

"Do you do a lot of escort missions?" Katherine asked.

"Hey, I guess maybe that's why I keep getting these." Gonzales smacked her head lightly with her palm. "I was in a tactical unit that specialized in asset protection. Dignitaries, generals, spoiled kids of dignitaries and generals. It was always a bit more complicated than that, of course. We'd need to get someone from one enclaved zone to another. Or, occasionally, we had to go into some of the dead zones and extract someone suspected of being a member of the Harbingers."

"Ironic," Katherine said.

"Oh, you don't know how many times I actually found whoever I was supposed to be tracking down and just sort of pretended they weren't there." Gonzales looked up and squinted, as if trying to count, then gave up. "Some of the people I was supposed to bring in are here in the Hollows."

"Must feel pretty good, knowing you're the reason they can keep contributing," Katherine said.

"Yeah, sure." Her eyes darkened. "Those are the ones I encountered without my team. Some we found as a team and…"

"We all make sacrifices for the Harbingers."

"Someday we will all fall," Gonzales said quietly.

"Fall with grace," Katherine finished the catechism.

They reached a tall gate and waited until it opened enough for them to walk through.

"So, you checking up on Mark, too?" Gonzales asked.

"I've been tasked to make sure he is who he says he is. We don't have anyone here to vouch for his intentions."

"Seemed like a pretty good dude." Gonzales shrugged as they walked toward an electric cart. "Really seems like he wants to know how everything works. Start contributing."

Katherine nodded and added that to her mental report on Alder.

They took a cart and drove down the earthen ramp that led to a large white building below. Katherine was able to close her eyes and enjoy the wind on her face before they reached the bottom of the pit.

Once they parked and went inside, the overwhelming din of the mining equipment and workshop washed away any serenity she'd cultivated on the journey. The rickety elevator that carried them down below did even more to tip the scales toward unease.

"It's just a big hole, is what I tell myself when I have to come down here." Gonzales leaned out over the gate of the elevator cage and peered down into the darkness. Katherine fought the urge to pull her back in. "We're about halfway down, I'd say. But they could've made more progress since I've been down here. It's been a few weeks."

181

"You didn't bring Alder all the way here?" Katherine asked, alarmed he'd changed hands so many times.

"Dropped him off with Henry. They paired Mark up with him because he fucked up his shoulder. I think he's milking the injury to get himself into a foreman spot. But don't tell him I said that."

Katherine added another note to her growing report. When the cage finally touched down on solid ground, she took a deep breath. The air was thick with dust. She looked around and found two massive yellow pipes pumping air down from the surface. One of the workers was standing directly beneath one of them, evidently taking a break. The worker's long hair blew around in the downdraft, her hard hat beside her.

Katherine pointed at the hard hat. "Shouldn't we have one of those?"

"Oh, shit. Yes. Wait here."

As Gonzales scampered off to locate hard hats, Katherine wandered around the excavation site looking for Alder. It was gloomy at the bottom of the hole, but they'd managed to light the area pretty well. Strings of work lights crisscrossing overhead, like a spider web with lightning bugs trapped inside it. Several workers were operating the conveyor buckets, filling them with the dislodged material to be taken to the surface. Some were crowded around a medium-sized construction vehicle fitted with a jackhammer on the front. A thin wisp of smoke came from the engine at the back of the unit, indicating something was wrong.

She spotted Alder wrestling with a handheld jackhammer near one wall of the shaft, breaking apart an area as other workers used shovels to remove the dislodged rock and earth. He was working hard: breaking up an area, lifting the jackhammer, then moving on to repeat the process. He seemed to be doing well, and when a horn sounded from above, the workers around him all smacked him on the back or helmet. A man wearing a sling on one arm punched Alder lightly on the shoulder.

"Here you go," Gonzales said, returning with a hard hat for Katherine. "I suppose you don't really need it anymore, though. Shift's over. That's Alder over there. Do you want me to go collect him?"

Katherine thought for a moment and decided to limit her direct interaction with Alder. He seemed to be fitting in well with the people he'd been in contact with. "You go ahead and take him back up to the surface. I'll talk with the man who's been training him today. Henry, right?"

"Whatever you say, boss," Gonzales said. "Mark's got a group orientation session in one of the classrooms after he gets cleaned up, if you want to catch him then."

She walked toward Alder's group as they stored their shovels and equipment against the wall. Alder lowered the jackhammer to the ground and stretched his back and shoulders.

"Didn't I ask you to keep that uniform clean?" Gonzales asked as she reached him. "All of you need to take better care of these things."

The group laughed and joined the queue for the lift. Alder noticed Katherine watching him and gave her a nod. She nodded back but didn't move in to speak. Instead, she found Henry by looking for the man with his arm in a sling. She tapped him on the shoulder and directed him out of line.

"Aw, man," Henry said. "What'd I do now?"

"Nothing that I'm aware of," Katherine said. "I just wanted to talk about Alder's progress. It looks like he's coming along."

"Oh, yeah. Taught him everything he knows." Henry smiled. "Hard worker, but they all are on the first day. It's day twenty that really shows you who the real heroes are down here."

"How is he getting along with the other workers?" she asked.

"Oh, fine. The guys like him because he takes direction well. That's because he's a military type. We don't see a lot of them down here. Speaking of, why *is* he down here with us, anyway?"

"I'm not at liberty to discuss Alder's situation," Katherine said. "But if he's doing well here, I'll be happy to report that back upstairs."

"Yeah, he's doing great. Eager to work. Curious about the whole scope of the excavation." Henry looked around the site, taking it all in. "You don't realize how big an undertaking this is until someone new points it out to you."

"Is there anything in particular he's shown an interest in?" Katherine asked, noting that this was the second person to mention Alder's curiosity.

"Anything and everything, really." Henry looked over as Alder boarded the elevator. "I think he's aiming to work his way up. I think he's used to having more responsibility."

"That could be it." Katherine watched as Alder rose in the elevator. They made eye contact, and a shiver went down her spine. She couldn't tell for sure in the gloom, with all the dust in the air, but she felt malice in his stare. He rubbed at his face and shook his head, appearing to be dislodging some dirt from his day of work, then turned and talked to someone next to him on the lift. As he passed beyond the net of lights, he was lost from sight.

Katherine and Henry boarded the next lift, and she found it much easier to breathe once they began their ascent. At the surface, Katherine made small talk with Henry as they walked with the crowd back into the mountain. She immediately found the colored path toward the mech hangar and followed it. The walk took a long time since the hangar was all the way on the south side of the facility. As she made her way there, she thought about what she would tell Jim. She hadn't been able to fully process everything herself yet.

Jim was also finishing up his day of work when she arrived, stowing a welding hood in a locker. She headed over and caught him just as he closed the door.

"Well, if it isn't our fearless leader," Jim said. "Down here to mix with us common folk."

"It's not like that," Katherine said.

"Hey, I know. I was just kidding. You look worried. What's up?"

"I'm fine," she lied. "I just want to catch up."

She spotted someone doing some work on a large plate of mech armor and directed Jim toward it. The sound was constant and loud. Probably enough to hinder anyone attempting to listen in on their conversation.

"Something about this place doesn't feel right," Jim said, recognizing their newfound privacy. He leaned against a workbench and picked up a welding torch. While they talked, he pointed at the various parts of it, like he was explaining what he'd been doing before she arrived. "This place is too well stocked and way too organized. Listen, I'm glad they've got their shit together, but this doesn't feel like the Harbingers I know. And wouldn't all of this be more useful out there in the field right now?"

"You're right," Katherine said. She took the welding torch from Jim and pretended to inspect it. "I've learned something about this place. There's another organization buried within the Harbingers of the Fall. This place isn't meant to just bring down the current order, it's also been built to survive it. They don't just want to bring everything down; they want to replace it. That's why we've got so much support. That's why it seems so well organized."

"I guess it shouldn't surprise me." He took the torch from her and feigned a laugh. "Power has always been a great motivator for people. I should have known the Harbingers wouldn't be able to resist."

"Would it be so bad to have a head start when things start over?" Katherine asked, trying to convince herself it was true.

"The Harbingers were never meant to form the new foundation, only to clear the land," Jim said. He was reciting some of the words that John had written. "An organization that succeeds in bringing down the tower of civilization cannot be trusted with building it again. The Harbingers were engineered to do one thing, and it's up to someone else to build out of the ashes."

"You're right." Katherine sighed. She reached over and took the torch back. "I don't know what to do. The Serotiny, that's what they call themselves, is established in multiple locations. I don't even know how many there are. But if they're all being led by the kinds of people leading this one, what they build won't be any better than what we fought to bring down."

Jim perked up suddenly, "You know what? We could just leave. I've already heard other people worried about the purpose of this place. This kind of planning for the future is hard to hide. We wouldn't be alone if we decided to just go somewhere else and start a community."

The idea immediately seemed to crack the shell she'd been building around herself. It also felt a little like surrender. But she couldn't deny that it would be better than sitting inside the mountain while the Serotiny made the same mistakes they'd seen throughout history.

"Okay, so maybe we leave," She couldn't commit to leaving yet, of course. There was still a chance the Serotiny could be stopped or guided out of its plan. The allure of leaving was strong though, and so she indulged in it. "We could leave and start our own community somewhere else. Live our own lives and let them play with their little group. I could gather as much information about their plan as possible before we left. That could give us an edge we'd need."

"Meet me here after your Council meeting, or whatever it's called, tomorrow," Jim said. Katherine saw that he was serious, and felt the pull to give in too. "I'll put out some feelers, see what some of the other people in here are thinking."

Katherine looked at him for a moment, worry sparring with relief inside her. His warm smile reassured her. She tossed the welding torch back onto the workbench, surrendering to the fantasy they were building. If they did do this, they'd have to be careful and discreet. It was lucky, then, that's he'd spent years perfecting those very skills.

~

Zak opened his eyes and saw a different sky above him. It had only felt like a minute, but now the first stars were beginning to shine. He'd been too late. John would be well on his way to the next rendezvous, and Zak still had to get back to Alison. The thought of telling her that he'd failed made him wince with an almost physical pain. They had been so close.

Zak felt fingers of panic creeping from the back of his mind and took a deep breath to calm himself. Every moment he spent lying on the ground feeling sorry for himself, John was moving farther away.

He managed to stand up. The cool air felt good, but he was still dehydrated and exhausted. He needed to find shelter and rest, or he wouldn't be telling Alison anything. Before going back the way he'd come, he bent down and selected a rock from the pile Eva had left behind. It was a small dark stone, about as big as a shirt button. When he held it up to the fading light in the west, he saw that it was actually a deep translucent red, like blood made solid. He put the stone into his pocket where it joined the piece of chalk.

As he walked and slid down the ridge back the way he'd come, he thought about what he would say to Alison when he reached her. The thought of returning without good news made him want to give up altogether. Alison knew the next place to check, at least. And John *had* been at this rendezvous, even if

Zak hadn't been able to catch him. There wasn't anyone else who would be up on this particular ridge right now. And the stone in his pocket was proof that Eva was still okay, at least that's what he'd decided to believe.

He reached the bottom of the ridge and set off for the gas station where he would get some rest. The map also promised a cache of supplies that might be useful. As soon as he was able, he'd get back to Alison and work on what they needed to do next.

CHAPTER 16

Alison drove the ATV onto the cracked highway and stopped. After working on it throughout the previous day, she'd eventually gotten it working properly. They'd lost most of their fuel in the crash, but she had enough left to get to the gas station. When Zak hadn't shown up the next morning, she'd set off toward the rendezvous point. She hoped to intercept someone along the way. Her hope was waning now that she was close to the station and still hadn't come across anyone.

She would fuel up at the station and press on. Zak might even be resting at the station. The journey to the rendezvous couldn't have been easy on foot. She was eager to continue, and even though it left her vulnerable, she decided to stay on the road. It wasn't far.

She'd used the station often in her travels, most frequently when she was meeting with John for his intelligence drops. The station was also the same place she'd been when Jim had told her about the beginning of the Fall. She saw the sign first, a sun-faded green and white rectangle against the cool blue of the morning sky. Soon, she came up to a green cement dinosaur in front of the station, its paint chipping from neglect. In the years when this station was active, she imagined children must have climbed on the statue.

She pulled in and parked near a deceptively old fueling pump. The Harbingers regularly stocked the station with fuel, but the pump switch was inside the convenience store. She and Jim had filled up a lot of vehicles the last time she was here, but there should still be enough for her to fill up the ATV. She might even find a replacement for the red fuel container that had broken in the crash. As she gingerly dismounted the ATV, she was pleased to find that her leg held her weight. Spending all day at camp had forced her to rest it.

As she approached the open doors of the convenience store, she peered into the deep shadows within. She crossed the threshold and stepped on a piece of glass. The crack was sharp in the silence. A shadow at the back of the store shifted suddenly and Alison saw a gun pointed in her direction.

"It's me!" Alison shouted instinctively. It could be Zak, but she really had no idea.

"Shit!" said Zak's voice. "I almost shot you."

"No, you didn't," Alison said. Her heart was racing, but a smile came to her face involuntarily. "Just doing a little shopping."

She realized, then, that she hadn't heard Eva or John. Her smile faded. It meant that Zak hadn't made it in time.

"Why didn't you wait for me at the ATV?" Zak asked.

She was alone, and had no guarantee that Zak would come back for her. It was better to rely on herself whenever possible. She didn't convey any of this to him, but he probably understood. As her eyes adjusted, she could see that Zak looked awful.

"You look like shit," she said. "Are you okay?"

"I can't find water," he said. "I thought there were supplies."

Alison waved him over to a large rack of old magazines. She pushed on it, and it didn't budge. Zak managed to help her and together they pushed it far enough to reveal a plastic bin with a yellow lid in a rough-cut hole in the wall.

Alison had made sure to leave the cache stocked the last time she was there, and she hoped it still was. Zak leaned against the wall as Alison pulled the bin out. When she opened it, everything was still there. She took out two water bottles and handed Zak one.

She drank some of hers as Zak gulped his greedily. This seemed to steady him somewhat, and he looked at her with sorrow in his eyes.

"I couldn't stop him," Zak said. "I tried, but he must have spotted me and gotten spooked."

"I know," she said. The two words said a lot. They said that she knew he'd tried, and they said she appreciated it.

"Do you know where he's going next?" Zak asked after another gulp of water.

She nodded. John would follow the Harbingers of the Fall now, and hope that she also made it there eventually. She worried Zak might not want to continue with her if he knew, but she pushed that thought aside for now. Zak had put everything into trying to reach John and Eva.

"They were there, though." Zak said firmly. "I don't think anyone else would have been in that exact spot. And I found this…" He pulled the red stone from his pocket and handed it to Alison. "There was a little pile of rocks up on top of the ridge, like someone had gathered them up. It had to be Eva, right?"

Alison held the stone, red reflections visible along the edges in the gloom of the convenience store. Yes, Eva had held this stone. She closed her hand around it and clutched it to her chest. Then, almost without meaning to, she leaned her head on Zak's shoulder. He stiffened for a moment, but relaxed and let his head to tilt over hers. He was asleep before she could get up. She was comfortable, though, and so she allowed herself to sleep as well.

~

"You don't look particularly inspired," Gonzales said as Mark walked out of a morning group orientation session, something like a cross between a church sermon and a history class. "I know it can be a bit hokey, but the sentiment behind everything is what counts. It keeps us united."

"Yeah." Mark made a mental note to watch himself around Gonzales. She was more perceptive than he'd initially given her credit for. "It's all just a lot. I mean, I just spent however many years of my life being taught the exact opposite of what they're saying in there."

"I get that." She signaled for him to make a left turn. The next item on his itinerary was a meal in the mess hall, and since he still hadn't been deemed trustworthy, he would be dining with Gonzales. "I remember feeling like there was this voice inside me screaming back at everything they were teaching me.

Stability this, Stability that. It can get confusing trying to deprogram yourself."

Mark nodded and kept walking. He needed to get away from this conversation as quickly as possible. He'd barely been able to hold this façade through the class and was worried it would rupture with any more pressure.

"So, what brought you here?" he asked, hoping the change in subject was gentle enough not to be noticed.

"Same things most people will tell you, I guess," she said. "Making the world a better place for everyone, distrust of the government, family stuff. Everyone's got their own unique blend of crap that got them to look into the Harbingers."

They walked into a large room with rows of metal tables. Along one wall there was a line of people serving themselves from a buffet-style offering. The scene was so reminiscent of his time at the Academy that he felt an uneasy sense of vertigo. Things inside the Hollows were so organized that he was having a lot of moments like this. He wondered if the similarities were intentional, meant to help people like him adapt to the new ideology.

Gonzales led him to the line and handed him a tray with little compartments for each item. He continued down the service line, the uneasy sense of familiarity continuing to grow. At the end, he grabbed his silverware and followed Gonzales to a table. As he sat down, he saw two of the people he'd been working with inside the hole the day before. They gave a short nod and a smile as a greeting, but evidently saw his escort and didn't invite him over to their table.

"What's up?" Gonzales asked as she sat down in an empty chair.

"This all just feels so…" Mark didn't know how to explain it. He put his tray down and took another look around.

"Everything seems a bit too normal, doesn't it?" Gonzales smiled and aimed her fork up at him. "It feels like you're back on your base. Yeah, I felt the same way early on. I still do sometimes."

"I guess I didn't really know what to expect." He sat down. "The movies and stuff always show rebel bases as dark and dirty. I figured the Harbingers would be a little more organized than that, but I didn't expect this."

"You know, I think it has a lot to do with who we all are." Gonzales speared a potato wedge with her fork and waved it around as she spoke. "There are a lot of military types in here. I'd say at least a quarter of our ranks come directly from United Entities active-duty soldiers who saw action up close."

Mark nodded and bent over his tray to eat. He didn't like feeling comfortable inside the Hollows. This place should elicit feelings of rage inside him at every turn. Part of him did still want to inflict violence on everyone in the room. He could take his metal tray and beat Gonzales over the head with it, then take her weapon and use it to inflict some damage. But another part of him saw these people as wayward brothers and sisters. They'd all betrayed Stability in the name of some chaotic ideal, but maybe they had their reasons.

"You asked me why I'm here," she said, seeming to read his mind. "And my answer is kind of personal. But if I tell you mine, will you tell me yours?"

Mark hesitated. He wondered if he'd be able to deliver the most recent iteration of his lie without cracking. Thinking it would look suspicious if he didn't, he nodded.

"My brother joined the Air Force right out of preselection school." She smiled at this memory. "Tested high on all the right stuff and landed a sweet gig as a pilot. He was so proud. Anyway, he goes and gets himself blown up on his first combat mission. And I got all patriotic and said I'd go and avenge his death. Take out some terrorists. Defend Stability, rah rah."

Mark had heard similar stories from other cadets at the Academy. Revenge made a good motivator, he knew, on either side.

"My scores weren't as good as his, so I ended up in a tactical unit doing extractions and personnel transfers. One night, though, we go to extract a guy from an off-grid camp who was using a RogueNET to disrupt CorNET financial transactions. I kick in this dude's door and he's just a kid. I froze up. I'd been expecting some slob behind a terminal covered in food crumbs. But it was this kid, and he looked so scared. My unit came into the room behind me and one of them hit the kid across the head with the butt of their rifle."

Mark nodded. Raids like the one she was describing were a standard tactic for neutralizing radical elements. They could be messy, he knew, but they were a necessary part of the main objective.

"The kid died right there," Gonzales put her fork down and wiped at her eyes. "Just a twelve-year-old kid, a brilliant one at that, working from his bedroom to take on an entire government. Anyway, I soured from there. During every mission I'd be looking for ways to undermine the success of the operation.

Eventually, I took a huge risk and reached out to the Harbingers and started doing what I could."

Mark didn't have a response. He'd never heard directly from a member of the Harbingers why they'd turned. His prepared lie felt insufficient, having heard Gonzales speak.

"I showed you mine, now show me yours." Gonzales put on a weak smile and sniffed away her tears.

"I guess it really comes down to losing my girlfriend in a fire-fight," he began. Perhaps he could use the same trick of using his very real anger to convince her. "It was just this completely unnecessary thing. We shouldn't have even been there." Mark was surprised by some of the words but continued. "Someone should have been there to help us, and it shouldn't have been our responsibility. We didn't start this goddamn fight."

It was all he was able to say. He felt a truth buried in it some-where, burning like a hidden coal in the hollow of his chest. An-ger wanted to flow in two separate directions. It threatened to spark a fire within him again, and he let out an unintentional groan.

"Hey," Gonzales reached across the table and grabbed his hand. "You don't have to say any more. I've had a lot of time to process why I'm here. It sounds like you've got a ways to go still. Take all the time you need."

～

Turner was inside the Nanook again, this time getting ready to pilot it out of the garage. Kalen took the weapons station and Vesnina was taking care of sensor sweeps and communications.

It was tight, but they all fit into their posts. They had decided to use the Ursidae as their command mech in this core. Without a Nieth class, the Nanook had the broadest range of communications and sensor equipment on board. They'd also outfitted it with some sensor modifications to make it better suited for the task, at the expense of some of its defensive capabilities.

"All right, let's give this a shot," Turner said over the radio as he engaged the startup sequence for his mech. He keyed in his optics to the navigation display and eased the mech out of the blasted garage. Vital statistics about his mech and the others in his core were displayed on his retinas and the screen in front of him. "When we've powered up, we'll be headed north along the route plotted in your navigation. Maintain radio silence for all but essential communication. And if you do need to talk, make sure you've got everything set to our tactical frequencies."

"They don't need a first-year comms speech," Kalen said from the weapons station.

"I'd rather give a pointless speech now than have someone blast our location out later," Turner said, frustrated. "Get your station up and running."

"Yes, captain," Kalen said with a smirk.

"Get formed up in the parade yard, and we'll leave once everyone has their systems running." Turner nodded down to Vesnina at the sensor and communications array as she brought them online.

Once their core was assembled, Turner gave the signal to head out. Seven heavily armed and fully crewed mechs, with six support trucks down below, left the base on a northern bearing. It was the same path they'd taken not long ago, but they were armed with more information now. They now knew that the enemy had a weapon with capabilities far beyond anything seen before. Turner, Vesnina, and the two scientists in one of the support vehicles were the only ones that knew the true nature of their mission. They needed to do whatever they could to infiltrate the Hollows and destroy the Ston device. The rest of the soldiers under his command believed they were only setting up a forward camp for future actions. He'd need to tell them eventually, but for now he needed to get them there intact.

"I want a sweep of the area as soon as possible," Turner said to Vesnina. "I don't want any surprises, especially this early."

"Preliminary scans show nothing of interest," Vesnina said. "But I should have something clearer for you soon."

"Weapons systems are fully operational," Kalen said. "I can't believe you let them take the main cannon off this thing just to put a goddamn radio antenna on top."

Turner ignored him and focused on the tactical display they'd managed to rig into the pilot controls. It showed the positions of the other six mechs around the Nanook. The Iris and the Icarus, two lightweight Aves class mechs, were out front. As he looked at his screen, he thought about their formation and made a last-minute change. He sent orders to the Remus, a Lupine class mech, to fall back to a more distant trail position. He had put Black and Plime into the truck shadowing that unit, and he wanted them as far from any danger they might encounter as possible. He watched out the windshield as that mech and truck complied with the order and fell back.

"I've got our first full sweep," Vesnina said. "There's something out to the northwest. Pretty far. Could be nothing, but we might want to steer clear. Looks like it could be a small vehicle."

"Does it have a heat signature, or are you just getting that on geometrics?" Turner asked.

"It's got a weak heat signature." Vesnina read the information as it came across their screen.

"We can't spare a unit to chase them down," Turner said. "Keep an eye on them as we move. If they turn back or anything, let me know."

He looked at the edge of the map at the red dot representing the vehicle when a new green dot appeared on the tactical display. The dot flew past the others on Turner's map, then began to circle at the edge of their sensor range. Turner leaned forward in his seat against the harness and looked up through the thick glass into the sky. A small black shape darted through the air and did a series of complicated maneuvers. Barkley was testing the capabilities of his new wings.

"You picking up Barkley out there?" Turner asked Vesnina. "He's practicing for his fancy flying badge."

"Yeah, I've got him," Vesnina said. "Looks like he's circling the base."

Turner nodded and sat back in his chair. He took a deep breath and closed his eyes. The next few hours would be simple. He'd rotate the mechs occasionally to give the two units up front a break, but most of the systems would operate on their own, unless something changed dramatically.

"You're doing fine," Kalen said. "You haven't screwed up once!"

"Thank you, Kalen. Your vote of confidence is noted." Turner opened his eyes and checked his displays to make sure he'd been right.

"Oh, there's still time for you to fuck up," Kalen said. He shifted quickly out of range as Turner sent a kick down in his direction. "Careful, or you'll hit the button that fires our warning flares or something."

"Just shut up, Kalen," Turner said, trying to withhold a smile. Any positive reinforcement, and Kalen would keep talking. "Let's just take this thing as it comes. We've got a lot of desert to cover."

~

Alison walked unsteadily down the bare shelves of the convenience store. She'd remembered Eva's request from the letter and didn't want to disappoint her. Next to a pile of dried-out glue sticks and faded construction paper, she spotted a small box of crayons with a thick layer of dust on it. She reached down and picked it up, inspecting it to make sure all colors were accounted for. As she slipped it into her pocket, she heard Zak drop something outside.

She went out and saw him collecting spilled food rations back into a canvas bag. The cache of supplies in the convenience store would allow them to eat for at least another week. Alison hoped they wouldn't need that long, but it didn't hurt to be prepared.

She was about to help Zak collect the scattered food when a brief unnatural sound drifted across the desert. It was so low that it was hard to pinpoint the source, but Zak immediately turned toward the base.

"Shit," Zak said as he finished grabbing the spilled supplies. "That was a mech cycling up. The older power cores do that when they haven't been fired in a while. We have to get out ahead of them to stay out of range of their sensors. If we look like a threat, they'll send someone to intercept us."

They quickly finished strapping the fuel and supplies to the ATV and headed north into the desert. Mountain ranges rose up on either side of the main road that went through the valley. Alison veered off the road and drove up the range to the west. She needed to know what they were up against. Riding blindly forward kept giving her the feeling that something was right behind them.

When they had gained sufficient elevation, she coasted to a stop and turned back to look. Behind them, she could see the mechs only as a cloud of dust leaving Taycher.

She got off the ATV and winced. Her leg was getting better, but still limited her mobility. She was finding it harder to ignore Zak's constant pleas for her to take it easy. She got around to the back of the ATV and opened a container she kept things she might need quick access to. A lighter, flashlight, tissues, their small supply of pain pills. She pulled a spotting scope from the box and aimed it toward the mechs in the distance.

"Looks like seven mechs," she said. "They're not working with one of those huge spider things, though, so I don't think we need to worry as much about them seeing us." She'd ridden in one of the big ones for a while with John, and knew they were typically used as the command center for a group of mechs. She handed Zak the scope to verify what she'd seen.

"The one in the middle has been modified." Zak took a moment to steady his hold on the scope, leaning against the ATV for more stability. "Looks like they removed the main gun and added an antenna off a command mech to the top of it. I'd say the range they're working with is right around fifty miles with line of sight. They probably know we're here."

Just as Zak handed the scope back to her, a jet flew by overhead. It banked toward the mechs and did a close flyby before pulling up and heading back toward Taycher.

"Shit," Alison said and pulled out her notebook. She flipped through it and stopped on a hand-drawn map of the mountain range they were in. Tracing a path with her finger to the north, Alison looked back down toward the core of mechs. "We're not going to be able to stay out of range on this thing. At least John left already. He should be okay. You said he was in a truck, so he'll probably stick to the paved or good dirt roads. That would put him about here." She touched a spot on the map nearer to Tonopah, then waved out ahead of them vaguely. "Over there, probably following the 84. It's a pretty beat-up old road, but he'll make good time if it's still clear. He should be able to keep pace ahead of your fucking pals out there. We need to get out ahead too, and we're going to need a truck if we want any chance of catching John before he gets to Ember Springs."

"Where do you think you're going to find a truck?" Zak asked.

She looked at him, nodded toward the mechs in the distance, and smirked.

"No way," Zak said. "They'll see us coming a mile away. Strike that, they'll see us coming *fifty* miles away. And they are not going to take kindly to me helping you."

"Not if we stay low," Alison said. "Let them come to us. Look at the map. You said their sensors are good for line of sight. We're in the Great Basin. This area has *hundreds* of mountain ranges running north-south. They'll probably stop for the night around here. It's the last good position to defend for a while. If we drop down into the basin on the other side of this range, we can outpace them by using this road here. It's shorter." She touched another part of the map. "If I'm right, we'll be within a mile of their camp, and they won't have any idea we're there."

"Even if they do stop there, you can't keep walking on that leg or its going to keep getting worse." Zak looked out at the mechs bringing up dust in the distance.

"Let me worry about my fucking leg," she snapped. Again, he was right, but that didn't matter. Eva was alive and they needed a truck. There were trucks headed their way. She'd figure it out. "I can make it."

~

John had chanced using the main road when he left the ridge. He wanted to put some distance in before stopping for the night. Eventually, he'd pulled off the road near a vertical face of sandstone cliffs. They'd slept in the truck and left in the morning when the heat in the cab became stifling.

With the gasoline he'd managed to take from Conrad's junk-yard, he could make it all the way to Ember Springs without a resupply. The relatively smooth roads were a welcome break from the rough and sometimes unpredictable dirt roads and trails they'd been using for most of their journey. With a long way left to go, main roads were really the only option. He would break away near towns and other obstacles but always return to the highway.

Eva seemed relieved to be on the even roads as well. She was asleep in the backseat under a blanket. John reached up and angled the rearview mirror so he could see her. An active rebel installation might not be the best place for a child, but it was a place both Alison and John would be welcomed. And if the Harbingers managed to continue following the plans he'd laid out, it would be one of the safest places in the world as everything fell apart.

John twisted the mirror back into position and checked the road behind him for anyone pursuing them. The only cars he'd seen since they left the base were abandoned husks. Twice, he had to pull off the road to navigate around a blockade. Neither of them had been manned by anyone trying to stop them.

Out his windshield, John saw a long stretch of highway heading down into a broad open basin. He let off the gas, allowing the truck coast down the long gradual grade, and tried to relax a little. Out there, in the vast open desert, he could almost imagine he was just going for a drive. The turbulent clouds above moved imperceptibly as he made his own slow journey. This was a drive he might have taken with his own daughter, had things been different. Perhaps the back of the truck would have been filled with fishing gear instead of hastily packed gasoline containers and provisions.

But there wasn't anywhere to fish anymore. Any body of water stable enough to support a fishery was tightly regulated. The only people able to fish were either powerful enough to secure the privilege or cunning enough to do it without being caught.

John pulled out of the daydream and focused on the reality ahead. A dangerous landscape peppered with hostile agents of all kinds was before him. Pretending he was on some idyllic fishing jaunt would only soften his instincts.

He maneuvered his truck around the charred remains of a tour bus in the middle of the roadway. The sun burned red high in the turbid sky. A thick smoke had engulfed this end of the valley. Was it coming from a forest burning somewhere, or a city? Was what was happening now really any better than what they'd had before? John imagined that the Earth was simply ill, that humanity had grown like a cancer through to the very foundation of the world. That wasn't quite right, though. Humanity, in many ways, was worse than a cancer. It was a disease with free will: the will to continue the constant and unyielding poisoning of every system it could touch. Then, just as the host had neared death, humanity managed to stabilize its patient. And instead of trying to reverse the damage, it pushed forward at just the right pace to keep itself alive at the expense of more and more of the host.

The United Entities had adopted the phoenix as part of its logo. The phoenix and the eagle, two majestic symbols united in protecting the pulsing ruins of a grand, grotesque tower. How had they come to adopt the phoenix as their own, the bird of legend that allowed itself to be reduced to ashes and be completely reborn anew? The audacity of that choice was galling.

There was nothing new about the United Entities. It was just a further condensation of everything that had driven civilization to the heights of excess, greed, and exploitation. Even if the Fall was successful, humanity would probably spasm once more and give birth to an even more distilled and malignant version of itself.

Perhaps it would be better to allow the disease to finally die. Surely the planet deserved this small dignity; to die quickly and start fresh from the ashes.

"Are we there yet?" Eva asked from beneath her blanket in the backseat. John shook his head and tried to form a response. Before he could answer, she was back asleep.

He felt hot tears course down his face as shame overtook him. A cancer? How easy it was to sentence a whole civilization to ashes when he forgot the faces that would burn in such a blaze. He'd spent countless nights in his room above the desert writing down these kinds of thoughts. He wiped at the rivers of regret and pain, fighting an irrational fear that if he didn't manage to stop them now, he never would.

~

When Mark finished another shift in the hole, Gonzales was there to greet him. She was standing by the lift smiling at him. They boarded the lift. As always, it was crowded, but they managed to get a spot on the edge so they could face out. It occasionally made Mark feel like he was going to fall to his death, but it was preferable to being crammed somewhere in the middle of the crowd. It smelled a hell of a lot better, that was certain. He'd fallen into his new routine more easily than he'd expected.

Wake up, get escorted to breakfast, then it was off to the hole for some hard work with no discernible purpose. After that, he went with Gonzales to the mess hall, or whatever else was on his schedule. Gonzales raised her eyebrows and smiled at him again, and Mark cocked his head to the side.

"Why are you looking at me like that? Is there something on my face?" he asked.

"No. Well, yes, but that's not why." She held out a small box to him as the lift began to rise.

"What's this?" he asked.

"Just open it, I think you'll like it."

He eyed her with mock suspicion but took the box from her. It was about the size of a large book and labelled with his name in marker on the top. He cut the packing tape with a fingernail and opened the box. Inside, he found his dog tags, gloves, and an assortment of other items they'd taken from him when he first arrived. As he moved some of the items around, he saw the coin necklace shining in the low light. He nearly dropped the box.

"Thought you might want these back," she said.

His first reaction was an intense wave of grief, but that was quickly replaced by anger. These people had taken Brooke from him, and he was supposed to be grateful that they were returning his last connection to her? He stared down into the box as the elevator continued to rise through the earth. Over a dozen harbingers were with him on the lift, pressing close and making it hard for him to contain his emotion. With great effort, he closed the box and held it to his chest.

"I'm sorry," Gonzales said. "I thought that having some of your things back might help you feel more comfortable in here."

"I'm fine," he lied. "Thank you."

CHAPTER 17

A round device sat in the center of a large white room. It was connected to an impressive assortment of extremely dated computer terminals augmented with more modern equipment. Along one wall was an ancient-looking public address system with knobs and switches labeled with the names of each sector of the Hollows.

Katherine was taking an evening tour of the research labs with Breaks and Garrin. She'd requested it because her initial tour had only brought her as far as the guard station in front of the double doors. Now that she was thinking of leaving, any information she could get was extremely important. She was introduced to several scientists whose names she hadn't bothered to try and remember. They didn't seem interested in her either, and went about their work as if the visiting group wasn't there. Some of the scientists had come directly from Taycher, and that part did intrigue her. It didn't seem like any of the higher-level researchers had made it, however.

"So, this is what we brought with us from Taycher," Katherine said as she leaned in to get a closer look at the readout on one of the terminals. None of it made sense, but she acted like it did. "It's smaller than I thought it would be."

"The actual device is smaller than that," Breaks said, as if he were selling the thing. "Most of the outer shell is just to shield us from the radiation it puts off. Unshielded, it could kill us all and disable most of the equipment in the lab." He looked disconcertingly calm as he said this, and then continued. "We could make these things much more portable if we left that part off. Any units we complete will have to be shielded the same way before we can put them to use."

"You're planning to make more of them?" Katherine asked.

"We already have." Garrin stepped into the conversation. He gestured to the other stations around the room with clusters of grey lab coats around them. "This is one of the greatest tactical advancements in human history. Every Cone is going to get one of these bad boys. We'll be able to set up anything we want, anywhere we want."

Katherine must not have hidden her emotions well, because Breaks flashed her a look she couldn't quite read. It could have just been him trying to interpret her response, she thought she'd seen a conspiratorial look in his eyes.

"All right, I'm headed out," Garrin said. "This technical stuff always bores me. I'll see you at the Council meeting tomorrow." He winked at Katherine.

She shuddered but managed to smile back. "See you then."

Garrin made a show of turning his large frame around and heading for the door. Katherine thought that he looked like the proverbial bull in a china shop, liable to push over one of the intricate devices around the room at any moment. He was probably going to the recreation wing, where he would settle in at the bar and drink more than his share of the rationed alcohol there.

"He's a lot," Breaks said. "A simple piece in a complex machine. But a piece well cast and tempered for his task."

Katherine was surprised by his tone and tried to read his expression. He was looking down at his suit, brushing off some dust from a crisp lapel. When he looked back up, his dark eyes searched her face, as if looking for confirmation of something.

"Don't look so surprised," Breaks said. "You couldn't have thought Garrin capable of all this. If you did, my faith in you was misplaced."

In truth, she hadn't thought he was. Garrin was an effective influencer and mover of people, but he wasn't a tactician. He'd built a pattern of manipulation that served him well in his exploits over the years. But it was a pattern borne from trial and error. A pattern honed from early childhood, where he had no doubt used his larger frame to assert dominance over other children. Everything else had been an evolution of that one tactic.

"No, you're right," Katherine said. She needed to do a better job of hiding her emotions. Garrin suddenly being back in her life was wreaking havoc on her. Memories that she'd long since packed away had become free to roam once again. "It makes sense that someone here has some deeper influence. If I had to guess, I'd say it was more than one person. I'd also guess that those people aren't necessarily on the Advisory Board."

Breaks revealed nothing in his expression. His eyes continued to search hers, still looking for something. She began to feel like he was trying to read her mind when he finally spoke.

"I need good, loyal followers of the true nature of the Harbingers. I believe you've proven yourself to be of a similar mind to me. If you can assure me that you're committed, I can promise you that the Harbingers will succeed in their true goal."

She was concerned he was testing her allegiance to the Serotiny. After thinking on his words for a moment, she decided it was worth the risk to see where the conversation led. The Serotiny was just another power grab in a long unbroken chain of power grabs. Each one had led humanity time and time again to brutal systems of exploitation and pain. She nodded in agreement, ready to backtrack if needed.

Breaks continued his expressionless stare, then turned and walked out without another word. Katherine was left standing in the research lab, wondering what would come next.

The Ston device from Taycher sat in the center of the room like a religious object of worship. She could see now that the other stations around the room had similar-looking devices taking shape. Researchers and technicians were working on each of them, duplicating the technology. There were at least six of them in various stages of completion. The thought of Cones across the globe wielding this power over others made her feel ill.

She was torn in two directions. In one, she could pursue whatever Breaks had been talking about. He was right that she'd made a commitment to another interpretation of their purpose. If that was still possible, she felt an obligation to see that commitment through. In the other direction, breaking ties with the Harbingers entirely and starting something new with Jim and other like-minded people was tempting. She felt an unfamiliar sense of insecurity as her will turned inside her like a coin tumbling through the air.

~

Zak and Alison were tucked into a wind-worn hollow in a sandstone outcrop. It was warm and surprisingly comfortable, so Zak had been asleep until Alison woke him a few minutes ago. The ground thrummed with the rhythms of an approaching formation of mechs. The machines were moving slowly through a basin between two tall mountain ranges to the east and west. The ranges were almost close enough to make the area a canyon.

"They don't look like they're stopping any time soon." Zak squinted in the afternoon glare, trying to get a good look at the units.

"Even if they go past us a few miles, we can cover the distance at night." Alison looked at her map. "This is one of the last defensible positions for quite a ways. If they don't stop here, they're making a mistake. I would take two of those units, the light ones…"

"Those are Aves class," Zak said.

"Aves. Yeah, sure. I'd take the two smaller mechs and post them on the two ridges looking out over the surrounding area." She adjusted the focus of her scope as something changed in the formation. "You see? There they go."

Instead of two mechs, two trucks turned off from the main group and headed toward peaks on opposite sides of the main formation. The main core came to a stop, and the silence that filled the valley was startling. For a long moment, nothing happened. Then dozens of hatches and doors on every truck and mech began to open. Like ants climbing from a nest before rain, people spilled out onto the desert landscape. Preparations for a night of rest had begun. The two trucks that turned off reached the top of their respective peaks quickly.

"So, what's the plan?" Zak asked. He still didn't like the idea of stealing a truck from people he knew, but Alison was right that they wouldn't be able to catch up to Eva without one. "The lookout trucks are probably our best targets."

"I agree." She was looking at the truck to the west, which was closer to where they were hiding. "I only see three people up there with that one. How were you handling fuel distribution when you left?"

"When I was with them, each vehicle carried their own fuel, to keep our supplies spread out in the event of an attack."

Zak took the scope from her and looked at the truck on the ridge. The blood ran from his face when he got a good look at the people who were with it. Hartley, Lund, and Payne were setting up their own small camp to keep watch over the mechs below. Zak watched them for a long time without saying anything. Payne was actually talking to the others. It was nice to see him finding a place within the group. Hartley was the cadet that had bandaged his head what seemed like months ago. Zak reached back and felt the wound at the back of his head. It was mostly scabbed, but still recent enough to hurt faintly.

The person that gave him the most pause was Lund. She'd been with him the night they had taken Eva and Brian home. Had she been driving or shooting when everything went wrong? He couldn't remember.

"Old friends?" Alison asked with a sneer. "Are you sure you can do this?"

"It's just weird to see them, is all." He handed Alison the scope and turned away from the truck on the ridge. "I feel like I've betrayed everyone. I just want all of this to be over."

Alison didn't say anything, just watched as the people by the main formation continued to set up their camp.

"How can you be so sure of yourself?" Zak wasn't even sure what he meant by that. She didn't respond, so he worked to clear it up. "I mean, how do you know you're on the right side?"

"I don't have a side. Not anymore," Alison said. "The only person I'm committed to now is Eva. She's out there somewhere, and these are just people standing in my way."

"I know these people, though," Zak said. "What if they were your people? What if we had to get through your friends to get to Eva?"

Alison seemed to think about this for a moment, then looked at Zak. "It wouldn't matter. I don't care who or what it is. Anything between me and her is an enemy, and I'll do what I have to do."

Zak believed her. It would be good to adopt the same mentality, but he wasn't sure he could. As the sun slipped behind the western ridge, his friends became mere black silhouettes against a blood red sky. They could be anyone now, he thought.

As the sky darkened, Alison packed up what little she would be taking with her. They needed to leave behind everything else in order to move as quickly as possible.

"I need you to help me get this off," Alison said, as she undid the straps on her air cast. "It's only a mile or so, but I can't make it with this thing on."

"Absolutely not," Zak said, and then without thinking he added, "I'll go by myself and come back for you."

"You know that's not going to work." She continued trying to get the cast off herself, and got another strap loosened. "I don't care if my leg falls off. I'm getting that truck and I'm getting Eva back."

He thought about arguing, but gave up and helped her remove the cast. When he did, he didn't like what he saw. Her leg was more swollen than he'd ever seen it. The skin was even more bruised and looked stretched tight.

"Alison," he began. "You can't keep ignoring this."

"Watch me." She stood up and began hiking up the mountain.

He stuffed the deflated cast into his bag and then set off after her. As they climbed, he saw that she'd packed all her belongings into her bags but one. In her right hand, she held her revolver.

CHAPTER 18

A cool wind blew through the canyon, carrying the scent of a distant storm. Most of the camp was resting, save for the few other stragglers who couldn't sleep and those who were on watch. Turner sat in front of the Nanook, holding but not eating a protein bar from their rations. A tiny fire in front of him flickered in the wind. He'd tried to sleep but found his mind imagining the damage that could be unleashed if the Harbingers managed to weaponize the Ston device before they could be stopped. Only a handful of people even knew the true nature of their journey north. Almost everyone under his command believed they were part of an advance team. To them, they were heading to establish a forward base camp for future operations against the Harbingers.

He would need to tell everyone the truth, and soon, if he expected them to follow him into what was almost certainly a suicide mission. They had a solid day of travel ahead of them tomorrow, then a half day or so more before they passed Tonopah. There was still time, but he needed to draw up some sort of plan that was more developed than rushing in guns blazing once they reached the Hollows.

Turner tossed the wrapper from his protein bar into the fire, and looked up toward the stars. Someone sat next to him, but he didn't look back down.

"Making a wish or something?" Plime asked.

"No, but maybe I should." Turner closed his eyes for a moment, then looked over at her. "What are we doing out here?"

Plime smiled wearily and shook her head. "Trying to stop a rogue organization from destroying everything and everyone we've ever loved?"

"Oh, that." Turner rubbed his face and groaned. "When you put it that way, I guess it makes sense. Why'd you have to go and make a thing like that, anyway?"

The remark, meant to carry a lighthearted air, landed heavy.

"I don't really know," Plime said. "Our team hit on something truly revolutionary, and we just couldn't stop. The possibilities of an energy source like the Ston are astounding. The applications for powering our cities, spaceflight, scientific advancement. Being in the room as we developed it, we felt like we were reading the source code of the universe."

"You felt like gods," Turner said.

Plime was quiet for a moment. "I suppose that may have been part of it. I think the people who developed nuclear fission must have felt the same way."

"We weren't ready for that when it happened either," Turner said. "Nuclear stockpiles, mutually assured destruction, nuclear disasters, the attacks with dirty bombs. It was too powerful. It still is."

"Are we ever really ready for anything? Humanity, I mean. We learned to forge metal and made better swords and knives.

Developed gunpowder and dynamite, and we created guns and bombs." Plime looked into the tiny fire. The orange flames reflected on the metal hull of the Nanook as it loomed above them. "Give us fire, and we will burn things. It's in our nature. But we can do so much good with these things, too. We have done good things."

"None of that is going to matter if we can't stop the Harbingers," Turner said. "Please tell me you've found a way to locate the Ston when we get there."

Plime seemed to cheer up at this. "We have! At least, in theory. The Ston gives off a very distinct radio frequency. With forces that intense, you can only contain so much of it. Our shielding did a wonderful job of canceling out all but the highest frequencies. If you've got the right equipment, you can listen for it and follow the sound."

"What do we need? I'm sure we can take the receiver out of one of the mechs if we have to."

"That's the best part." Plime was back to smiling again. "All you need is a simple radio. A modified field radio would be enough. Hell, a handheld unit could do it."

"Could you key it into our optics?" Turner asked.

"That is a good question," Plime said. "I'll see what I can do."

"What about shutting the damn thing down?" Turner asked.

"That's a little trickier. We need to be in the room with the unit. And we can't just detonate it either, unless we want to bring the whole mountain down on top of us."

"I'd prefer we didn't," Turner said. "But if it comes to that, we might—"

A gunshot sounded from somewhere close. Turner was up before the echo of the shot returned from the east. He looked up to see a muzzle flash on the western ridge, quickly followed by the sound of the shot.

"To arms!" Turner yelled. "Western ridge. We've got enemy contact on the western ridge!"

The red taillights of the truck he had sent up there began glowing. Someone had turned it on up there. Then, before he could even get out of the camp, it disappeared from sight over the other side. He ran for the ridge but quickly realized it was pointless to try and scale it on foot. A truck came up behind him, and he hopped onto the rear bumper as it went by. Soon, they were at the top of the ridge. Turner motioned to the soldiers who had come with him to fan out and secure the area.

He approached the lookout campsite, terrified at what he might find. In the dim firelight, he saw Payne with his weapon drawn, aiming into the darkness. A smear of blood stood out across his pale face. Hartley was lying on her side with Lund hovering over her, pressing down on a gunshot wound. The other truck had already made its way to the bottom of the other side and was driving across the desert at speed, carrying whoever had attacked his people, no doubt.

"Should we go after them, sir?" someone asked.

His instinct was to say yes, but he stopped himself. "No. We could lose it too. I'll be surprised if whoever took that one doesn't wreck, driving through the desert in the dark."

Turner went to Hartley, as the rest of his team continued to search for any enemy soldiers.

"Just apply pressure." Hartley said. She was laying back on the ground grimacing in pain while she talked Lund through the steps to care for the wound. "Turner. Get something you can use to tie a tourniquet, and anything you can use to fill the hole. I can't see how much blood I've lost. I'm feeling a little dizzy, so that's not a good sign."

Turner looked around the site and found a duffel bag. He removed its carry strap, pulled out an undershirt he found inside, and rushed back. Lund had cut up the length of Hartley's pant leg to expose the wound and was still applying direct pressure.

"That's great, Turner. Tie that around my leg up high and get it as tight as you possibly can." This was all basic care, but Turner appreciated the instruction. As he pulled the strap tight, she screamed, but quickly regained composure. "Lund...Tear the shirt into strips and pack the wound with it. Fuck, you guys, I'm about to pass out. Don't let me die, all right?" Hartley winced again and closed her eyes.

"You're going to be fine," Turner said. "We're going to take care of you." He pulled the strap again and tied it off. To his relief, the bleeding slowed substantially.

Lund began handing him strips of the shirt. It felt extremely counterintuitive, but he began packing the wound full. The idea, they'd insisted during his mandatory battlefield medicine course, was that the risk with gunshots was blood loss. Infection can be treated, death can't. He got the wound filled just as the rest of his team returned. They reported that no one else seemed to be on the ridge.

"We have to get her down to the med tent," Turner said. "Manner will know what to do." He rested a hand on Hartley's forehead. She didn't respond. "You're going to be all right."

They lifted her into the back of the truck. Payne wanted to stay at the top of the ridge, but Turner ordered him into the truck as well. He pulled four others away and instructed them to take over the watch shift on the ridge. Turner headed back with the rest of the team down to the main camp.

The truck came to a stop in front of the tent where Manner had set up his bedroll. Turner was relieved to see that Manner had already taken out and arranged the medical supplies to care for any injuries. The remaining team of soldiers carried Hartley out of the truck and laid her on the ground in front of Manner, who got to work doing what he could to save her. Hartley was still unconscious. Manner waved everyone but Lund away.

His first instinct was to grab the nearest radio and call for Taycher to send Barkley in with the cargo lift he'd been flying around when they left. It had some weapons on board and could easily take out whoever had shot Hartley and stolen their truck. This instinct was wrong, he knew. A radio signal strong enough to reach Taycher from out here would be detected by someone else. They were alone in this desert.

A small group of soldiers were standing near him, waiting for orders. "Fire up the mechs and get sensors going as soon as possible. Make sure no one else is surprises us out here."

He left them to do as he'd said and went looking for Payne. Turner found him sitting with his back against the truck they'd come back with. He still had his rifle out and was looking around the campsite, nervously searching the shadows for movement.

"You can put that down now." Turner didn't wait for Payne to do it himself, and gingerly removed the rifle from his hands. He set it out of reach and joined him on the ground. "Everyone is awake, and they will keep watch. I want to go over what happened, if you can do that."

Turner thought, not for the first time, that Mark should have been the one doing this. He'd always had a disarming calm that managed to slice through tension. Small fights and disagreements at the Academy could always be undercut by a single word if Mark was around. Turner didn't have that gift.

"I need to know what happened, Payne." Turner heard his own stern tone and attempted to correct it. "It's important we know what happened, so we can go from here." It wasn't much better, but it would have to do.

"I...I don't know." Payne began rocking back and forth rhythmically. Turner hadn't seen him do that for a long time and hoped they hadn't lost Payne again. "I was watching. I know I was. Nobody came up the ridge. I was watching, and I know no one came up the ridge."

"Calm down. Payne, what happened when they did get there? How many were there? What did they look like? What did they do?"

"Zak was there," Payne said suddenly, as if he had just processed the information. "Zak Lockwood and a woman. I don't know where they came from, but the woman got into the truck first. I yelled for her to stop, and then Hartley got up. She was sleeping. She got up. And she tried to get into the truck. Zak shot her. He shot her, and he just stood there looking down at her."

"Are you sure it was Zak? The woman, did you recognize her?" Turner asked, unsure of how to process the information himself.

"The rebel woman we captured." This, too, seemed like new information just now coming through for Payne. "I thought they died. Their truck got hit, didn't it?"

"I thought so too. Keep going. What happened next?" Turner wanted to get as much from Payne as he could now, while the memories were still fresh, and he was still able to talk about it.

"Zak stood for...like, a really long time, and the woman turned the truck on. While I was trying to get my gun..." Payne stopped talking and looked up to where the truck had been. Turner was about to prompt him again when Payne continued. "Lund came out of the tent and got off a shot, maybe two. I don't know if she hit anyone. That got Zak moving. He got in the truck, and they just left. They just drove down the ridge and kept going."

"Payne. Hey, are you listening?" Turner made an effort to get Payne to look at him, but his eyes kept slipping back out into the darkness. "Soldier, look at me. Now."

It seemed to work for the moment as Payne's training asserted control over his behavior. He blinked a few times, shook his head, and managed to focus on Turner.

"I need you to keep this to yourself," Turner said. "You can't tell anyone else about who you saw. Do you understand?" He held Payne's gaze and waited for a response.

Payne nodded but didn't say anything more.

"Lie down." Turner stood and looked toward Manner's makeshift medical bay. "I'm going to go check on Hartley, okay?"

He left, making sure to take Payne's rifle with him, and walked over to where Manner was tending to Hartley. A pile of blood-soaked strips of shirt had already been removed, and Manner was looking into the wound. Lund held a flashlight over the procedure like a kid holding a light for a parent doing work in a garage. Hartley was mercifully still unconscious.

"Forceps," Manner said to Turner. "The big tweezer-looking things." He pointed to an assortment of tools laid out on a towel.

Turner knelt down and handed over the requested tool. Manner immediately plunged them into the wound and withdrew a metal slug from Hartley's leg.

"Looks like it stayed in one piece and didn't hit anything too serious." He dropped the bullet onto the towel and put the forceps down, then picked up a large syringe-like device. He inserted it into the wound and pushed down on the plunger, releasing coagulants and white spheres that immediately expanded to fill the wound cavity. He wrapped the wound with bandages, then looked up. "We'll leave the tourniquet on for a bit longer to give the filler time to seal up the wound. I think she's going to be okay, though. What the fuck happened up there?"

"Two people stole the truck and shot Hartley," Turner said before Lund had a chance to answer. "Payne is pretty messed up, but he says they just showed up and took off. Lund, if Manner doesn't need you anymore, I'd like to talk with you and get your angle on it."

"Sure," Manner said, waving them off. "There's not much left to do here but monitor her and make sure nothing changes."

"Great." Turner stood up and left with Lund. When they were far enough away, he stopped. "I know who stole the truck, and we can't let anyone else know. You can't say anything."

"What the fuck do you mean?" she asked. "That goddamn traitor shot Hartley. Hell, she could die!"

"Keep your voice down." Turner did his best to remain calm himself. "I don't want this group any more scared than they already are. If Zak can switch sides, who knows who the hell we can trust."

Lund stared intently at Turner, turning the idea over. "Fine. But if I see him or that woman, I'm not waiting for orders." She pushed past him toward her tent.

Turner had only Hartley to talk to now, but she was still unconscious. He walked back and sat on the ground next to her. Drawing circles in the dirt, he watched as Manner removed her tourniquet and checked to make sure the bleeding had stopped.

"Shit, this was a lucky shot," Manner said as he changed her bandages. "Missed the major trouble spots. She's going to be okay. I mean, she's not going to be a hundred percent for a while, but she should be able to walk with help in a day or so."

Turner looked up from his circles in the dust. "You call getting shot lucky?"

"I mean, I'd rather not ever be shot, but if I ever have to be, this is a best-case scenario." Manner pointed to her inner thigh. "Your femoral artery passes along here. That's...well, that's one of the places Shakey took shrapnel back at Taycher before we ever left. Hartley got hit with a bullet at close range on the outside of her leg. There's a lot of muscle there but a lot less stuff that'll kill you in minutes. I mean, the best place in terms of survival is a hand or a foot, but this isn't as bad as it could have been."

Hartley murmured, "It's nice to know this searing pain is all part of my good luck." Her eyes were closed, but she managed a smile that was part grimace.

"I'll go get you something for the pain." Manner stood and walked a few yards to the medical supply boxes.

The contents were in disarray, and while he was looking through them, Hartley spoke in a low whisper. "We can't tell anyone about this. They can't know it was Zak."

Turner sighed with relief. "I'm glad you feel that way. Not a word. We can't have that kind of panic now."

Hartley nodded but didn't say anything else. When Manner returned with the painkillers and a canteen of water, Turner stood and picked up Payne's rifle.

"Manner here tells me you should be running drills again in no time." Turner brushed dirt from his pants. "Try not to get shot again while I'm gone, all right?"

~

Zak looked down at his gun. The digital screen on the back showed he had nineteen rounds left in his clip. The missing round had hit Hartley. He'd tried his best to aim for the outside of her thigh, and he thought he'd done it right. He'd even brought down the power level to minimize the damage. They'd just needed the truck, and if he hadn't taken care of Hartley himself, Alison would have. But still, he had shot her. The same person who had cared for him after he'd injured himself was hurt or possibly dead because of him.

They'd almost managed to get it without any violence at all. Alison had managed to get into the truck before the first person had even seen them. No one had expected an attack coming from the camp side of the ridge. Payne had noticed them though, and then Hartley charged at Alison. Zak brought his gun up and shot her, almost without thought, but now he was consumed with the decision.

The moments he'd spent standing over Hartley as she bled into the desert ground had seemed to go on forever. The only thing that pulled him from the daze was Lund firing at him. He'd seen the look of pure fury in her eyes. A moment longer and she might have gotten off a good shot at him. The look on Lund's face was imprinted on his mind so clearly that he could see it when he closed his eyes. It hadn't just been anger he saw. There had also been betrayal, mixed with loss. He'd made a choice he would never be able to undo.

Zak looked over at Alison as she weaved through thick sagebrush. She was trying to get as far from Turner's group as possible. Her fierce eyes were focused on the path ahead. He knew that if they were fast, they might be able to catch John before he made it to Ember Springs. He wasn't sure if he could forgive himself, but it was done now. He needed to focus on what was ahead of them.

CHAPTER 19

Katherine got into the council chambers early and found Breaks there, too. He was sitting in one of the chairs against the wall instead of at the long oak table underneath the dimming skylight. The last light of day was passing through layers of smoke to finally terminate here, bathing the room in disconcerting shades of yellow and orange.

Breaks looked up from a document he was reviewing. There were red notes all over it from where he'd made corrections. "I was just making some changes to a duty roster. Every piece with a place, and every piece in its place." He put the document down and gestured for Katherine to sit next to him. "Just something my mother used to say. It's about keeping your house in order."

"I'm familiar with the saying," Katherine said as she sat in the offered chair. "Although I always saw it as kind of oppressive."

They looked at the council table in front of them in silence. No one else had arrived yet, and there weren't any agendas on the soft leather mats in front of each chair, either.

"Tonight's meeting has been canceled, I'm afraid," Breaks said. "I sent word to everyone. Everyone but you. We have some things to discuss. You can speak freely here; I have made sure our conversation won't be overheard."

Katherine said nothing, thinking that was exactly the sort of thing someone said when they were recording a private conversation. Breaks had said he had something to talk about, so she would wait for him to do the talking instead. A unique combination of excitement, fear, and unease mixed within her as she waited for him to continue.

"We have been watching you for a long time." Breaks stared out in front of him. "You've been unquestionably one of our most valuable assets in our task. We specifically brought you here to keep Garrin in check, given your history. As you've already realized, his overzealous ambitions are contrary to the correct end goal. It's nothing we can't handle, of course. I feel we owe you the small respect of bringing you in on what we're really doing here."

He looked over at Katherine and lingered there for a while. She didn't know what to say, so she nodded for him to continue.

"We who want to see the mission of the Harbingers carried through do not have a name," Breaks said. "We have no symbol, no catechisms, no embossed letterhead." He waved a hand dismissively at the table. "We simply exist, and that is enough. The very creation of objects, creeds and doctrine are irrelevant if they are to later be burned. So, the only things that need to be created are the things we require to accomplish our goal."

Katherine pieced together what he meant. There was yet another secret group within the Hollows, it seemed. This new, apparently nameless, group was trying to guide the Harbingers back toward the original vision.

"You will not know how many others are with us, but I will tell you that we are not weak." He paused, seeming to leave a space for a response.

"What exactly are you planning?" Katherine asked directly. If they wanted to disrupt the Serotiny, she needed to be sure the plan was sound. She also needed to know that this new nameless group wasn't just vying for power too. If that was the case, packing up with Jim and disappearing was beginning to sound very appealing.

Breaks was silent for a long time. Eventually, he took a deep breath, then began talking in a low monotone. "Assets have come into a serendipitous alignment. We will have a uniquely beneficial window of opportunity very soon. We've nearly reached our target depth at the excavation site. Once certain variables are arranged correctly, one of the working copies of the Ston device will be lowered into it. Our team from the Taycher research lab learned long ago that what the Ston is capable of defending, it can also destroy. They've kept that fact hidden from Garrin and his old boys' club, of course."

Katherine felt her pulse quicken at the mention of destruction. The device could protect a wide area. What could they be targeting that big?

"Our research team has been modifying their copy of the device to disrupt rather than protect. As you know, the original device creates a shield above that can be expanded and contracted to protect a given site. This modified device will be able to generate the gravitational wave underground."

"You're going to destroy the Hollows, collapse it entirely," Katherine said in awe.

Breaks spent another moment in silence, staring out at the council table. The break was appreciated. Her head was spinning. The loss of life he was talking about was colossal, but maybe they'd found a way to get out safely. The Harbingers had never shied away from casualties, but she liked to think that a general current of decency ran through their philosophies.

"Life has existed on this planet for billions of years." He said this distantly. "Our ancestors only came onto the stage in the last few hundred millennia. Life preceded us, and it will outlast us. It has always just been a matter of when."

Katherine focused on her breathing as he spoke. What happened next would depend heavily on her ability to remain stoic. What he was describing was not just the destruction of civilization, but the erasure of humanity itself.

"If we succeed in activating the Ston at our target depth, we'll shatter the crust of the Earth." He said this with a flat tone devoid of the emotion the statement should have carried. It terrified her, the cool and emotionless way he said it. "What follows will be the Fall of mankind. The destruction of every monument ever built. Every technological improvement, every work of art, every trace of our ever existing. The sacrifice of life will be great, but in the end, the Earth itself will heal. Life will eventually prevail and continue on without us. To bring down the tower of civilization, we must shatter its very foundation."

The afternoon light painted the room crimson as Chester Breaks stared out emotionlessly. Katherine forced herself to remain calm, trying her best to look both interested and approving. In truth, what he had said scared her more than anything the Serotiny could have ever accomplished. Mere minutes ago, she'd been content to run off with Jim and start a rogue colony far away from all of this. Now, though, there was a terror inside her she couldn't run from. This nameless void of an organization was going to destroy everything.

~

A sign for the Lakeview Lodge stood out against the sky. They'd been driving for a while, and it was time to find a place to stop for the day. The lodge itself wasn't open of course. It was little more than a collapsed pile of bricks and boards, but John pulled into the parking lot. The paved ground would, he hoped, lessen the amount of dust that would blow into the vehicle while they slept. He wasn't sure how the lodge had ever been successful. It was the only man-made thing other than the road for fifty miles in any direction. Two ancient gas pumps hinted at what might have allowed the establishment to exist. He imagined that whoever built the lodge had probably lived there as well. It sounded like a peaceful existence, being surrounded by nothing but endless desert and an occasional traveler.

"Where are we?" Eva asked from the backseat.

"Nowhere," John said. "Just an old hotel. We're going to sleep in the parking lot tonight."

"What's a hotel?" she asked.

John laughed. How could she not know what a hotel was?

"It's a place where people used to pay to sleep." He hadn't thought explaining it would be this hard. "It's like a house you pay to live in for just a day or two."

"Why would people do that? Why not sleep in a car or bring a tent?" She looked out the window at the sign.

"It was convenient. You could just go into your room and go to sleep in a real bed and then leave whenever you needed to."

"You sleep in the same bed as a bunch of other people?" Eva sounded disgusted. "What if it was smelly?"

"Some of them were," he laughed. "The trick was trying to forget how many people slept in the bed before you."

"Sounds weird." Eva said this with finality, as if that was the only thing that needed to be learned from the conversation.

"Maybe it is," he said. "I remember staying in little roadside places like this when I was little. It was always exciting because it meant we were going somewhere new. It was like we were exploring."

"Why is it called the Lakeview Lodge?" Eva asked. "I don't see a lake."

"I don't know," he said, growing weary of questions for the moment.

John got out of the truck and looked up at the sign. It looked familiar somehow. Had he stayed here when he was a child? He might have. The lake he and his family had gone to a few times was somewhere to the east. They might have rented a room here once, but he couldn't remember. That lake, he realized, was gone now. It had actually been a reservoir fed by a diversion from a major waterway. Extreme drought had forced officials to shut it and several others down years ago.

He pushed these thoughts aside and went to the back of the truck to get something for them to eat. They might not get to stay in roadside hotels like he had when he was a child, but he still hoped that Eva and Alison would be able explore the world together.

~

"I have it on the sensor sweep, it looks like a wall about a mile high," Jensen said. Turner had brought him in to take Vesnina's place handling communications and sensors. Vesnina was down in the truck with the research team. He wasn't really concerned about them drifting off task and had her there just to keep track of their progress. Black and Plime could often drift off into their own world and forget to report back when necessary.

"That's gotta be the same thing we saw when we left Taycher, right?" Jensen asked. "The thing that took down those jets?"

"Yeah, that's it," Turner said. He switched his comms to talk to the whole core. "We're coming up on our next stop here in a few miles. We'll set up camp for the night before we move on. I don't want to go any further with the light leaving us like this. Everyone get settled when we stop, then meet near my mech for a briefing."

Turner selected a spot with hills around it to make camp, and exited the Nanook. He sat on the hood of one of the trucks while he watched the others get set up. Out in the distance, the mountain range where the Harbingers were hiding loomed dark on the horizon. Turner wondered how Zimmer and Mark ever managed to speak in front of groups so confidently. Yet again, he felt like an imposter in his position. These people had no reason to follow him, but for some reason, they did. He knew it wasn't because of his natural leadership quality. That was something he'd seen scored as below average enough times to understand he didn't have the gift.

Kalen spotted him and walked over. "Stage fright? Don't worry about it, really. They don't need much. A couple sentences about duty and honor, and you'll have them ready to do anything. We want to be here, remember that." He smirked and patted Turner's shoulder.

"I'm not sure they'd be as eager if they knew what I'm going to ask them for," Turner said. "I'm not sure *I'm* even ready for what comes next."

"What comes next?" Kalen asked, his smile fading. "I thought we were just setting up a forward reconnaissance position. Waiting for reinforcements, or what have you."

Turner shook his head and looked out at the mountain again. "We need to make an assault on the Hollows."

"What do you mean?" Kalen laughed nervously. "Wait, you're serious, aren't you? Shit. *Are* you serious?"

"We don't have a choice," Turner said. "Well, not the way I see it. We either fight, or we die. It might not be today, but if we can't take the Hollows, they'll use the Ston device as a weapon against us."

"The shield?" Kalen had lost any semblance of his normally nonchalant manner. "How the hell would they use it as a weapon?"

"I'm not clear on the physics, but it's got a lot to do with gravitational waves. The device they stole from Taycher has the ability to destroy entire cities, maybe even more than that. Black and Plime are still doing the calculations on what the range could be. It's bad."

237

Kalen looked out at the mountain with Turner. After a moment, he put a hand on Turner's shoulder. "It's been a hell of a good time serving with you, sir."

"Fuck off," Turner said.

"It has. You might not know how to talk to people, but I have never doubted your intentions, and neither have they." Kalen looked out as people began to gather around the truck, then left to join them.

Everyone must have sensed something was different, because a hush fell over the crowd. Turner didn't stand on the truck to get above them and project his voice. Instead, he hopped off the hood and sat on the ground in front of it. He gestured for them all to sit as well. If he was going to ask them to sacrifice their lives, he would do it from a place of humility, a place of equality.

"I don't know how to do these," he began. "I'm not a talker. I give orders, and you do them. That's something I get. But I can't order you to do what we need to do tomorrow."

The crowd seemed to hold their breath, and Turner continued.

"The Harbingers have a device—I'm sure most of you are aware of it—that can shield an area from incoming aerial attacks and sensor sweeps. It's called the Ston, and they stole it from Taycher. We've picked it up on our sensors just ahead of us, a blank void on our scans that looks like a mile-high wall that isn't there. The good news is that the device does have some limitations. The field breaks up near the ground, so we should be able to move freely beneath it. Once we're inside the Ston's hemisphere of protection, we'll be able to use our sensors and weapons effectively again."

238

Everyone was looking at him intently. He averted his eyes, so he didn't have to see them.

"We're not here to set up a forward recon camp." The silence from the group was more intense than any sounds of shock or surprise would have been. "The device isn't just a shield. It's also a weapon, or it can be. The damage it can do is on a scale the world has never seen. Nuclear weapons are nothing compared to this thing. If we can't either take it from them or destroy it, this will be the end of everything we know."

Murmurs rippled through the group. He scanned their faces and continued.

"Those of you who remain here in the morning will move into enemy sensor range and begin an all-out attack on the Hollows. A smaller unit will use that assault as cover to infiltrate the mountain base. Anyone who doesn't think they can do this should leave. We will not judge you. Not for long, anyway, because in all likelihood, we will not be alive to judge you."

The eyes of every soldier were still on him. No one had made a move to leave. Turner took a moment to regain his composure, absently drawing a circle in the dirt with one finger. He was reminded of the times Mark had insisted on drawing everything out when they'd made plans.

"I am a soldier of the Mechanized Armor Corps." Kalen's voice came through the crowd. "I will fight the enemy of Stability, even if it should cost me my life."

A beat of silence was broken as another voice joined the recitation of the Armored Soldier's Creed, a passage they'd all memorized in their early days of training at the Academy. By the end, every one of them was speaking in unison,

239

"My armor is my shield, as it shields that which I love.

My armor is my weapon against the forces that would seek to destroy us.

I will fight the enemy of Stability, even if it should cost me my life.

My armor is a tool in a greater machine working to defend Stability.

I am a tool in a greater machine working to defend Stability.

I will fight the enemy of stability, even if it should cost me my life.

Stability before self.

I am a soldier of the Mechanized Armor Corps."

Turner stood and brushed the dirt from his pants. He looked over the group, trying to meet each of their gazes and project a sense of surety he didn't feel. Zimmer and Mark may not be there, but he was, and that would have to do.

"Thank you. All of you. I think we can do this. We have to. We'll move out at sunrise."

~

The suddenness of the forest had startled John. One moment, they were cresting an endless sea of hardpan desert hills, and the next, it seemed like they crossed some marker and found trees growing on both sides of the tattered road they were on. He hadn't seen this many trees in years. The change in the light had been enough to cause Eva to sit up in the backseat.

"Where are we?" she asked, her eyes wide as she took in the green scenery.

"Almost there." John thought back to the map he'd seen on the Anansi with Katherine and Jim. The beginning of the trees meant they were close. "We'll sleep here in the forest tonight, and we should make it to my friends in Ember Springs tomorrow."

"Do you think they'll be nice?" Eva asked, squeezing her stuffed whale tightly.

"I'm sure they'll be delighted to see us." John turned away from the road for a moment and smiled at her, just to put an emphasis on his reassurance.

"And Allie will be there too?" Eva asked the question in the halting way one might if they thought the answer was no.

"I don't know, hon. If she's out there, she knows where we're going." He tried to think of something to add. "You'll be safe there, though. Where we're going, people will work to make sure no one can get us. We can ride out most of what's going on and then go figure out the rest of our lives once things have calmed down."

"So, we're going to be with the good guys?" Eva asked.

John didn't know how to answer her, so he didn't. He stared out the windshield. As they drove, a canopy of trees formed overhead, making it harder to navigate. The sun had already nearly set when they'd arrived at the tree line. He needed to stop and wait for the morning light.

"One more night," he said, more for himself than for Eva. He pulled the truck off the road and into a small clearing. Once he managed to get the truck nestled behind a thick copse of aspen trees, he turned off the ignition.

241

When he stepped out of the truck, he was shocked by the chill under the trees. He leaned back against the door. Bird calls faded in and out on the wind, and a constant low rustle of leaves compelled him to stay quiet. He obeyed the impulse and listened for a few minutes. Eva must have understood as well, because she, too, was quiet. The forest seemed to go on forever. He could see, in the fading light, that the trees grew larger ahead of them, like the legs of an endless army of giants.

Their previous stops had been in the open desert. The danger on those nights had been that someone would spot them. A forest presented with the other side of that coin. The foliage provided a comforting level of cover, but could also contain any number of dangers within the shadows beneath their branches.

John patted his pocket absentmindedly, looking for a pack of cigarettes that wasn't there, and felt the reassuring shape of the photograph he kept there. He pulled it out, looked at the faces of his family for just a moment, and then returned it to his pocket. He thought about what lay ahead. The Harbingers would no doubt accept them with open arms. His self-determined mission to save Eva would be seen as one of heroism and sacrifice. John knew the truth, however. His mission hadn't been driven by some sense of duty, but by his own guilt. The act wasn't even one worth celebrating, as in many ways, it was a selfish attempt to atone for a lifetime of mistakes.

And what good would it do, in the end? He was delivering Eva into a sealed base flooded with doctrine he wasn't even sure he believed anymore. John found himself imagining heading east in the morning instead of north. He could work his way around the mountain range ahead and drive into the wilds.

Perhaps he could teach Eva how to survive on the land and let her decide what to do with her own life in a few years.

He shook his head, realizing it was impossible. He knew a bit about surviving in the wilderness, but not enough to make a life. And then there was the specter of Alison. His note had assured her that Eva would be delivered safely to the Harbingers of the Fall if their first rendezvous failed. It had failed, and he was now bound by his promise to complete the journey. And, if Alison didn't arrive, perhaps John could help Eva maintain a healthy skepticism of the Harbingers.

He patted Eva on the head and walked to the back of the truck, where he got blankets and a bag of food and tucked them under one arm. He passed a couple of blankets to Eva, who tucked them under her arm in the same way. With his free hand, he shook the gas cans. There was enough to get them the rest of the way. They would probably be intercepted before he needed to worry about fuel, anyway.

Eva got back into the truck and diligently flattened her blanket on the backseat. When she was satisfied with the flatness of her bed, she sat calmly as John prepared a meal for them. He handed her a bowl of cereal with a foil cover, a bottle of water, and some powdered milk. She ate and drank without complaint while John got into the front seat of the truck with his own rations.

"Can I have a story?" Eva asked when he was settled.

John thought about saying no, but an internal voice asked him why. He didn't have a good reason, so he nodded.

Eva smiled, pulled her blanket up to her chin, and dipped her arms underneath. "Make it one about me and Meeple saving the world from a big space monster."

John laughed. "You seem to have a good grasp on that story already. Why don't you tell it?"

"No, I want a story from you," she said with just a hint of a whine.

John sighed dramatically. "If you say so. But don't get mad when I tell it wrong."

He launched into a tale about a strong, resilient little girl and her sidekick whale. He found the act of telling her a story calming. When he saw she'd already fallen asleep before the end, he decided to finish the story anyway. He spoke out loud about how the little girl overcame the evil space monster and saved the whole world.

CHAPTER 20

Zak watched trees whip by the window as Alison drove their stolen truck along a rough forest road. The light had almost completely faded from the sky, but Alison pressed on. They'd pushed the truck to its limits all day and had only recently entered a forest of redwood trees. The trees had started out thin but had very quickly risen to meet the sky in front of them. They'd decided not to use the headlights out of fear that someone would see them, and continuing by moonlight alone was becoming impossible. Even if they could continue, they might drive right by John if he had stopped.

"Shit," Alison said as she slowed the truck and pulled off the road. "We need to get there before my people realize your friends are on their way. Once that happens, I'm not sure if I'll be able to get us inside. I hope John and Eva made it in already."

"We can leave as soon as it gets bright enough to see," he said, trying to reassure her. "You made good time today. We'll make it. We might even catch them before they go in."

Alison didn't say anything, just closed her eyes and rested her head back on the seat. Zak reached down to the floor and pulled up a pack with rations inside. He withdrew a protein bar and offered it to her. She took it absently and put it down next to the gearshift.

Zak opened his own and, though he didn't actually want it, ate it slowly. As they sat in the truck, a light patter of rain started to fall. It coated the windshield in a sheet of glistening droplets. Through each one, Zak could see the dark shape of the mountain against a backdrop of stars. Those stars were slowly overtaken by the clouds, and soon there was nothing but shadow.

"What happens when we get there?" Zak asked, breaking the silence.

"I hadn't really thought about it much," Alison said with her eyes still closed. "I guess it depends on what your privvie friends decide to do once *they* get here." There was a sharpness to her tone, and a familiarity to her argument.

She was right, of course, but there was more to it than that. Now that his usefulness in Alison's quest was running thin, Zak felt the urge to leave the truck and wander into the forest. It was the first time he'd really thought about his own future since they had walked away from the ruined remains of the command mech with Mark's hollow screams following them. Zak couldn't return to his friends, not after what he'd done, and he'd be even less welcome with the Harbingers. He felt more alone in that moment than he could ever remember feeling in any of the homes he'd been in as a child. He'd betrayed his friends, he'd betrayed his country, and he'd betrayed Mark. Would Mark ever understand the choices he'd made? Zak fought his breathing as he felt his mind begin to slip into a fog of fear and uncertainty. He closed his eyes and was surprised when he felt Alison's hand on his shoulder. He pulled away instinctively, but her hand remained.

"I'm sorry," Alison said quietly. "I didn't mean to be dismissive. I appreciate what you've done for me, for Eva."

"You don't know what I've done." He hadn't meant to say it out loud, really, but now that he had, the pressure welling up inside him was unbearable. Her comfort was misplaced, and she needed to know what he'd done that night in the woods.

"I don't," she admitted. "But I know that the game was rigged before either of us made our first move. You didn't have a choice."

"Did I?" He looked over at her. "I chose to play the game; I chose my side. We all did. And I shot him. No one pulled the trigger for me. Brian is dead because of me. You've lost everything because of decisions *I* made."

Alison's eyes flashed with rage and her hand slipped away from his shoulder. Then, almost as quickly as it had come, the anger drained from her face, and tears began to run down her cheeks.

"We all make decisions." She put both of her hands alongside his face, and he fought the urge to pull away. If she needed to speak to him directly, he would stay firm. "But there are some things that are truly out of our control. All we can do is our best. I've made choices that I'll have to live with, and you'll have to live with yours, but you don't get to choose who forgives you."

Mark lay on a cot in the room he'd been assigned to and stared at the ceiling. They hadn't moved him into one of the group barracks yet, probably because he was still being evaluated. His mind was awash with the information he'd been able to gather about how things were run in the Hollows. There wasn't a traditional power structure in place, and he found that fascinating. He wondered if orders came from some unseen figurehead, or if things ran through some complicated system of shared leadership. Though Garrin and Katherine seemed to hold more sway than people like Gonzales and Henry, no one had spoken of a grand leader.

The group education sessions hadn't been particularly useful. They'd basically spouted off the same tired lines he'd been warned against in the various briefings, trainings, and classes throughout his life. The only thing different about these offerings had been the framing. Instead of a critical analysis, he'd been expected to offer nothing but an almost religious acceptance.

Today's session had concluded with everyone in the room repeating the same catechism over and over again. The person leading the group had said, "Someday we will all fall." Then, in unison, the class had responded, "Fall with grace."

The exchange was surreal, but also surprisingly familiar. All indoctrinations, he supposed, followed a certain rhythm and course. He caught himself repeating that rebel call-and-return from the meeting and decided to override it with something from his own training. For some reason, he could only recall a single line of the creed he and his fellow cadets had recited so many times at the Academy.

He whispered the line, hoping it would be enough to push back. "My armor is my shield, as it shields that which I love."

The words did their work and cleared his mind. He reached into his shirt and felt for the penny on the end of its length of chain. The shape of it was smooth and regular. Having it back was reassuring. Brooke had sacrificed herself for the rest of them, and he needed that to mean something. They were all pieces in a larger mechanism, and his duty was to do what he could from the inside of this terrible machine. He enclosed the penny in his fist and tried to focus on why he was there, tried to stoke the anger that had been so useful to him before. To his surprise he found the flames of vengeance cool and flickering against the winds of empathy. This realization startled him.

Why should he feel anything for these people other than disgust? Just because Gonzales and Henry seemed like himself in so many ways did not excuse the dark doctrine they'd chosen to align with. Stability was the pillar upon which everything he knew was founded. It was what Brooke had died for.

He felt his rage die again as a thought drifted into his head. Brooke hadn't died for Stability. She'd died to save him. She'd sacrificed herself for love. He felt himself drawn to a memory, and surrendered to it.

They'd been tangled up in one of their secret places back at the Academy. It had been warm, and Brooke's skin was soft and slick with sweat. Her head rested on his chest, and she ran her fingers lightly along his forearm, sending shivers through him. His own hand was curled deep into her thick brown hair.

"I'd want it to be on a mountain," she said quietly. They'd always whispered when they were alone. Even though no one knew where they were, it was a way to make their conversations even more intimate. These moments were all theirs. "Somewhere green where I could take walks without ever seeing a person or a building."

"Big house or little house?" he'd asked.

"Big enough." She put her hand on his chest and shifted closer to him. "But you'd have to build it yourself."

"Ah so it's going to be a dilapidated shack then." He laughed.

"I'll help. What matters is we're away from all of this. Nobody can touch us, and nothing is on fire."

"So, are we retired, or did we win all the battles and secure Stability for everyone forever?" he asked.

"Neither. This is my goddamn daydream." She poked him with one finger playfully. "In this version of the world, there's no such thing as the Harbingers, or the United Entities. No war, no Stability. There's just us, and that's all that matters."

"Sounds nice." He leaned forward then and kissed the top of her head and became momentarily lost in her scent. She'd looked up at him then, and he saw tears in her eyes. "What's wrong?"

As an answer, she'd kissed him, long and hard. He kissed her back and felt what she'd been trying to say. Her kiss had said, "It may not be possible, but that doesn't make me want it any less."

Alone and cold in a room beneath millions of pounds of rock, he opened his eyes to the reality that had been his fate. The penny clutched in his hand was all that remained of Brooke. He looked inside himself, trying to find the hate he'd used to push himself across the desert and into the Hollows. He found only ashes and tears.

~

Turner pushed open the flap of his tent. The sky in the east had turned a pale blue near the horizon. He hadn't been able to sleep, but a few hours of silence had allowed him to calm his mind a little. When he stepped outside, those already out and about in the camp followed him with their eyes. He approached the Nanook and found Kalen already below it with the rest of the crew.

"She's all yours," Turner said. "You know, I think Zimmer would be proud of you."

"He'd be proud of all of us," Kalen said. "I just hope I don't screw it up."

"You'll do fine." Turner felt confident in saying that. Kalen had always been a strong leader, even if only from the sidelines. In truth, Kalen may have been the better pick to lead them all along, but at least he was getting a chance now. "We're counting on you to keep them busy."

"And we're counting on you and your science nerds to pull off a miracle." Kalen laughed, with only a hint of nervous energy. "We've got you covered."

Turner looked over Kalen's shoulder and was surprised to find Payne standing with the rest of the crew. "What can I do for you, Payne?"

"Sir, I'd like permission to resume my post." Payne took a deep breath. "I promise I won't let you down, sir."

"That's up to Kalen. This is his show now," Turner said with a wink. "But I'll put in a good word."

Turner saluted both of them and walked to the truck he'd equipped to move out ahead of the main formation. Plime and Black were already in the backseat, with Vesnina driving. Plime was making final adjustments to the devices they'd put together from radios and other equipment cannibalized from the mechs. If everything worked, they would be able to program Turner and Vesnina's optics to scan for the frequency of the Ston device. If that didn't work, they also had two modified handheld radios that could do it.

Turner got into the passenger seat and flipped a switch on the truck's comms radio. He had tried all night to think of what to say to everyone but hadn't been able to come up with anything. After a deep breath, he held down the button and prepared to speak. He spoke the only words he could think of, "Let's go be heroes."

The roar of the mechs behind him powering up their engines was the only answer he received. It had been enough. The ground trembled with each step as they advanced, and he was amazed, as he always was, by the sheer size of the machines as seen from below. Vesnina drove their truck forward into the trees, racing out ahead of the advancing storm.

CHAPTER 21

Katherine got up early and immediately headed for the mech hangar. When she got there, Jim was welding on the shoulder of an Ursidae class mech they'd brought from Taycher. He climbed down and brought her over to a workstation set up underneath the four legs of the mech.

"Hey, what's going on?" Jim asked. "You look like shit."

He poured some coffee from an insulated container into two paper cups and gave one to her. Katherine hadn't been able to sleep at all the night before, and it evidently showed. He motioned for her to sit down with him in two folding camp chairs.

"I don't know..." She trailed off. "I don't know if he was serious or if this is some sort of test. He can't be serious, right?"

"I'm not sure what you're talking about, Katherine." Jim took a drink from his cup and looked around the garage. No one else had arrived yet, but he stood and turned on one of the large shop fans just in case, before returning to his seat.

"Breaks, the guy in the suit who's always around..." Katherine waited to make sure Jim knew who she was talking about. "He canceled the board meeting, or had someone else cancel it, I guess. And he told me something about that device we brought from Taycher."

"That Ston thing? I've heard some stuff about it. People talk."

"They've got a lab set up around it. They're trying to replicate it to send out to the other Cones," Katherine said.

"Sure, that makes sense. If you could put a big dome over anything you wanted, why wouldn't you want to replicate it?" Jim shook his head, apparently unconcerned with the idea. "That's not exactly news. We know they've got other Cones, or whatever, that could use one of those things."

"One of them is different, though," Katherine said. Her hand began to tremble, and she hated that her emotions were affecting her this much. "If he's telling me the truth, it's being engineered to send a pulse underground. At first, I thought he was just going to use it to collapse the Hollows. He clearly doesn't believe in what Garrin is trying to do."

"You know, that could work." Jim sat back in his chair and took a drink of coffee. "I mean, it's a bit extreme, but it could be worth it in the end to make sure the technology doesn't start popping up everywhere."

"You're not listening," Katherine said, setting her coffee down. "That might be what he's telling other people, but do you know why they're digging that hole outside?"

"The guys call it the Grave of Civilization." Jim laughed nervously. "Nobody really knows what's up with it. A lot of people think it's just to keep everyone busy."

"Breaks is going to use it to shatter the Earth." Katherine looked at Jim, pleading with him to believe her. "He—and whoever else he's got in on this—think that the Harbingers need to take out humanity entirely. Not just the power structures and systems of oppression. I don't know, he could be testing me to see where I stand, but I believe him. He said that variables were coming into alignment or some other unhinged crap."

Jim wore a look of concern and confusion as he tried to process what she was saying. It looked like he'd decided on how to respond when a siren blared in the hangar. A voice called out through the base-wide comms system.

"Enemy forces have been detected. All personnel, report to dispatch locations or to your designated support positions. This is not a drill. Repeat. All personnel, report to your dispatch locations or to your designated support positions."

"We've got to get to the excavation site, Jim," Katherine said. "I think the pieces are coming into alignment."

Jim opened a drawer in his toolbox and pulled out a pistol. He checked to make sure it was loaded and then put it into his holster. "Lead the way."

Mark was working in the hole with the same team he'd been with during his previous shift. He'd woken up sore and tired, but he'd followed Gonzales and worked to break up the ground with the jackhammer yet again. He was halfway through his shift when Henry pushed him with his good arm and signaled to cut power to the hammer. Mark let go of the handle, and the hammer slowed to a stop. Everyone was scrambling to get in line for the elevator when a deep rumble shook the earth. Loose rocks fell from the sides of the shaft and peppered the area.

No one bothered to properly store their equipment. A furious tension had instantly changed the people at the bottom of the hole. Arguments broke out at the elevator as people tried to squeeze inside. Thankfully, an additional hoist descended from above, and the tension eased somewhat. The new platform was little more than a metal plate attached with four cables, but people climbed on board anyway.

"What the hell is going on?" Mark asked.

"I've got no clue, but we just got the order to get back inside immediately," Henry said. "Come on, let's go. We've already missed three lifts."

Together, they queued up and took the next ride up. On the surface, the crowd was haphazardly exiting the building from every door. Just as Mark was about to pass through a large rolling garage door, the crowd parted. A team of people wearing the clean grey coats of the research lab ran into the building hauling something underneath a tarp. Along with them were armed soldiers and the man in the black suit, Breaks. Mark allowed himself to be caught in the commotion of the tidal crowd as it surged back toward the door. He fell back and kept his eye on the research team, managing to linger behind a forklift as the final workers fled the building.

"Hey, Alder!" Henry called out. He hadn't continued to the mountain, then. "We need to get inside before everything goes to shit. What the hell are you still doing in here?"

Mark thought quickly and brushed some dirt from his pants. "I fell down in the crowd when those guys came running in." He jerked a thumb back at Breaks and the others. "What the hell are they doing, anyway?"

"Got no clue." He put his good arm around Mark and started leading him away. "Above my paygrade, boy. Of course, no one gets paid here, so I guess—"

Something shook the building, sending debris raining down from above. Henry dropped and covered his head. He cried out in pain and Mark instinctively bent down to check on him.

"Were you hit?" Mark asked frantically. He managed another look at Breaks and saw him standing among the smoke and chaos, completely still, as he checked something on his clipboard.

"Just my goddamn shoulder. Shouldn't have used it. Help me up," Henry reached out a hand and Mark helped him to his feet.

"Let's get the hell out of here," Henry pushed Mark and he obeyed.

Once they were out of the building, it was clear that the Harbingers were under attack. The crowd had mostly finished its crush to get back into the mountain. Another rumble sounded, and Mark looked up just in time to see camouflaged guns positioned higher up on the mountainside unleash a volley of projectiles. A second later, one of the guns exploded. Its flaming debris rained down on them as they crowded their way into the Hollows.

Alison was at the back of the truck, packing away the last of their supplies, when a sound like thunder came from the direction of the mountain. She looked up just in time to see orange flames rolling into the sky. This was followed by several rockets launched from positions on the mountain. They sailed by overhead, their flames illuminating the area momentarily with unearthly red light. Brilliant bursts of light preceded the deep bellow from their explosions. As the sound faded, a hot wind pushed back through the forest. In the momentary hush, she heard a new sound. Someone very close by was screaming. A child. Eva.

Alison stopped breathing and listened for the sound again, her heart seeming to skip several beats. Just ahead, she saw a truck pull onto the road from behind a stand of trees. Her own truck's engine rumbled to life. Zak had started it, and she wasted no time climbing into the passenger seat.

"That's John!" Alison yelled as she slammed the passenger door. "Drive!"

Zak spun the tires as he pulled onto the dirt road, barreling into the cloud of dust pulled up by the truck ahead of them. As they sped down the narrow road between the trees, another volley of projectiles flew by overhead.

Every time John's truck came into view, it seemed to be at the next bend in the road. Rounds filled the sky above, now passing in both directions. It felt to Alison like being in a small rowboat between two battleships engaged in a broadside exchange.

As they came to a straight stretch of road, Zak managed to close the gap to within just a few car-lengths of John's truck. A bump in the road sent both vehicles momentarily into the air. As the trucks came back down, John must have overcorrected, because his truck flipped violently onto its side in front of them.

"Shit!" Zak yelled as he slammed on the brakes. Their vehicle slid along the loose dirt, narrowly avoiding hitting John's. Alison opened the door before they were completely stopped and jumped out as soon as they were.

"Eva! Eva, are you okay? Eva!" She pushed through her pain and went to the overturned truck.

"Allie!" A small voice came from the cab as an explosion rocked the area.

Several trees along the road behind them had already caught fire, sending thick black smoke through the trees and into the sky. It choked the narrow roadway they were on, making it hard to see. A low continuous rumble told her that the mechs behind them were advancing. Eva screamed again, and Alison tried to look through the windshield. The glass was shattered and opaque. Finding a strength she didn't know was possible, she climbed the truck and pulled the back door open. In the shaft of light that pierced the dark interior of the truck, Eva looked up at her.

"Allie!" Eva yelled, her voice cracking at the edges with fear.

Alison lowered herself into the truck and swept Eva into an embrace. "It's going to be okay. I'm going to get you out of here. You're going to be okay."

Above her, the door to the front seat opened. Eva screamed again, snatching a stuffed whale from the ground and clutching it to her chest. It was Zak. He was silhouetted briefly against the sky before he climbed down to where Alison now saw John was lying motionless. Zak immediately began working on the roof hatch which, in the overturned truck, now opened out to the side. He pulled four release pins, and it fell away to the dirt with a dull metallic thud.

Smoke began to fill the inside of the truck as Alison crawled out with Eva. She ran as best she could back to her truck and opened the driver's door. Eva scrambled across to the passenger's side and looked at Alison in a way she couldn't read at first. Zak was still back at the other truck, having just managed to pull John through the opened roof hatch. Alison climbed into her truck and put her hands on the steering wheel. She felt the low rumble of the engine. The impulse to drive away was strong. The longer they stayed out on the road, the closer the approaching mechs would get.

"John!" Eva cried out. "We can't leave him! Allie, we have to help him!"

"Shit." Alison took her hands off the wheel and stepped back out onto the road.

~

Someone was pulling him from the overturned truck. There was smoke everywhere, and John couldn't see Eva. He wrenched his hands away from the figure above him and pushed at them to leave him where he was.

"No…" John mumbled as he became aware of his surroundings. He forced his voice from a hoarse whisper to his usual commanding tone. "The girl. Get her out."

"We got her, John." Alison said, crouching down near his head. "I've got her."

His vision was still blurred, but he recognized her voice, and relaxed.

"Help me get him up," another voice said. It was familiar too, but his mind couldn't quite place it. "We can't stay here."

Then he was rising, and he found his legs were responsive now. Accepting the help from Alison and the other figure, they made their way back to a second truck in the middle of the road. Relief flooded him as he spied Eva in the front seat. He shook off the help and walked under his own power the rest of the way. His vision was cleared now, he realized, and he looked for the owner of the familiar voice.

"Lockwood?" John asked. "Is that you?"

It was unmistakably the boy, the man, of course. Zak said nothing and opened the back door of the new truck. John could read everything Zak wanted to say in his expression. Fury, disappointment, and pity were all plain to see. All of it was tinged with panic as John remembered the battle brewing all around them. He got into the truck and began to catch his breath.

Alison got into the driver's seat and looked over at Eva beside her. She smiled, and John felt tears coming to his eyes. He'd wondered for so long what the moment would be like, and it was before him now. Alison and Eva were together. Two tattered lives joined once again among the chaos he'd created. Then, just as Alison was about to drive away, something slammed into their truck from behind.

CHAPTER 22

Turner listened through the truck's radio as his team began their assault on the Hollows. Vesnina drove their truck, pushing to get as much speed from it as she could without sending them tumbling into the trees. Volleys of explosive ordinance screamed by overhead in both directions. He felt helpless as Kalen commanded the tiny core of mechs as they provided what amounted to cover fire for his advance.

"Get some heat on the turrets!" Kalen yelled, his voice already fading from the low frequency. "Keep the Harbingers occupied, or they'll never make it."

Turner looked in the side mirror just as one of their lighter mechs, the Icarus, took a direct hit and stumbled forward into the trees. It was lost for a moment beneath the canopy. Then a blinding light signaled a catastrophic failure of its core. Who had been assigned to that unit? He tried to remember, but couldn't find the names.

"I've got new heat signatures out there, everyone." Payne's voice came in over the comms. He sounded calm and sure. "Looks like they've dispatched their own forces. I see at least ten units, but they're all clumped together. There could be more."

"Get some rounds into the trees in front of us," Kalen said over the radio. "I saw this work once."

Turner smiled. They were setting a fire to create a smokescreen. It was smart, he thought, the fires might obscure their small numbers. Kalen had been the right choice for this task. He gave orders in a way that was both emotional and reassuring. He exuded an infectious confidence that sent a chill through Turner. They were going to win or die on this mountain, perhaps both.

The unmistakable and terrifying sound of a jet screamed by overhead, and Turner watched with dismay as it passed in front of him.

"Oh shit," Vesnina said quietly.

Turner felt the hairs on the back of his neck go up as he imagined what that jet might have fired as it passed by overhead. Moments went by and they weren't hit. Then, bizarrely, the jet released a flurry of missiles that lit up the mountainside in a line of fire. A friendly unit? Turner looked to Vesnina for confirmation.

"Anybody call for reinforcements?" Barkley called in over the radio. Turner felt lightheaded. "Hold on just a bit longer, groundhogs. Sorry we're late. I've got some friends of yours behind me."

"Oh, hell yeah!" Turner yelled, relief washing over him. He punched Vesnina in the arm lightly. He reached for his radio and clicked the handset. "Banks, you back there?"

"Get off the comms, cadet." Banks said over the radio. "We have forces gathering up just inside the barrier. Keep on mission and let us get to work."

Turner wanted to scream. Their almost certain deaths had just become a little less certain.

"How the hell did Barkley get through the barrier?" Vesnina asked as she took a sharp curve in the road.

"The cargo lift he's flying can take off vertically so all they'd need to do is get it under the barrier," Turner said. "If a command mech showed up at Taycher after we left, its cargo bay would be big enough. Or maybe they just loaded it on a truck and drove it under."

"This doesn't make any sense," Plime said suddenly. "I'm getting two signals. They have different signatures, though."

"That would make sense if they've managed to replicate the Ston," Black said. "I'm picking them up as well. One signal is steady, likely holding the barrier up, but the other one looks like it's cycling up."

"Why the hell would they be cycling up now?" Plime asked. After a moment of thought, she went pale. "They must have figured it out. They're going to trigger a pulse around the mountain."

"We're going to need two teams." Black said stoically. She immediately began dividing the modified radios and other equipment for disabling the devices between them. "If we can't disable the second device, our forces will be destroyed."

"I'll go with Black and target the one cycling up," Turner said. "Vesnina, you go with Plime and whoever gets—"

"Shit!" Vesnina yelled as a thick cloud of smoke cleared. Suddenly there was another truck in front of them. She jerked the wheel to the side and managed to only hit the truck with the front corner of their vehicle.

"Where the hell did that come from?" Turner yelled. "Is everyone okay?"

He looked over to see Vesnina pulling herself off the steering wheel. A cut near her eye dripped blood down her face, but she was conscious. Turner checked the backseat and saw Plime and Black were okay as well, though their equipment was in disarray. He opened his door and staggered out into the road. The impact had dazed him, but he shouldered his rifle and aimed it at the truck they'd hit. He noticed at once that it was one of their trucks. It had the identifying marks for the vehicles based at Taycher. It was the one that had been stolen, he realized.

"Everyone out!" Turner yelled in his most authoritative voice. He coughed, choked by the increasing smoke, but kept his rifle trained on the new truck. The sound of aircraft passing by overhead added to the already overflowing soundscape. The Harbingers must have released their own jets, because it sounded like a dogfight was going on.

Zak stepped out of the truck in front of Turner. Turner remembered Hartley, her leg gushing blood on the top of a ridge, and almost shot Zak on the spot. He held his fire as another person got out of the vehicle. Sergeant Major John Phillips was standing there in front of him, looking more disheveled than he'd ever been during any of their Live Piloting classes.

"Get everyone out," Turner said. "I don't know why you're here and I honestly don't have time to figure it out. We just need the truck."

The rebel woman they'd briefly held prisoner exited the truck on the driver's side with a child behind her. The woman aimed an ancient-looking pistol at Turner and backed away with the girl slowly. He tightened his grip on his rifle and contemplated taking the rebel woman down. The child looked around the woman then, and the terrified look on her face stopped him. He felt his rage die like a flag in the eye of a storm. The girl squeezed a stuffed whale tightly and looked at him like she was looking at a monster.

"Alison, put down the gun," Zak said. "Turner isn't going to shoot us. Right, Turner?" Zak took a step away from the truck toward Turner with his hands out. "Just let us go. All we're trying to do is get Eva to safety." He gestured behind him at the woman and the child. The woman, Alison, lowered her gun but looked at Turner, defiant.

"You're in the wrong place…" Turner's voice was drowned out by jets passing by low overhead. He lowered his rifle and yelled over the sound. "This is the last place you want to be right now! Get out of here before I change my mind. We're all probably dead, anyway."

A series of explosions rocked the area, causing Eva to scream and cover her ears. Vesnina took this moment to exit the truck. She marched up beside Turner and aimed her pistol at Phillips.

"How long have you been a goddamn traitor?" she asked. "Do you understand what you've done? Do you have *any* idea how much damage you've caused?"

"What the hell are you talking about?" Turner asked. He hadn't figured out if Phillips was a traitor or a captive, but right now, it wasn't important. They just needed to get the truck and keep moving. With two vehicles, they could chase down both Ston devices and disable them.

266

"How the fuck do you think they managed the attack on Taycher?" She kept her weapon on Phillips. "This sack of shit. I found your goddamn manifesto in your room, Phillips."

She shoved her hand into her pocket and pulled out a small red data chip. Turner looked at Phillips and saw him recognize the object she was holding.

"What the hell is she talking about Phillips?" Turner could feel vibrations in the ground now. Mechs were approaching from both directions.

"I thought you died," Phillips said. He was looking at Vesnina with a mix of confusion and apparent relief. "Did you read what's on that chip? All of it?"

She threw the chip at the dirt in front of Phillips. "I read enough." Her finger slid through the trigger guard and she steadied her hand.

"I can't make up for what I've done," Phillips pleaded. "But I need to get this woman and her daughter to safety. Just let them go and you can do whatever you want with me."

"He has no idea." Vesnina barked a manic laugh at the sky. "Always acting like he's this wise mentor, and he's got no fuck-ing idea."

"Turner, we have to go now," Plime called out from the truck. She and Black were still sorting through their gear inside. "The Ston is still heating up, and we don't have much time. They'll be able to level everything around the mountain for miles if we don't get there soon."

"Move, now." Turner tightened his grip on his rifle, but kept it lowered. "We do not have time to argue. There are at least two of these things now."

"Two of what?" Alison asked. "What's going on?"

He turned toward her, and the girl behind her shrieked. Turner let his rifle dangle from its strap and extended a hand in front of him. "Please, just move away. Somewhere up ahead, there is a device powering up that will level anything for miles. Anyone outside the mountain is at risk, unless we can stop it."

A moment of silence passed between the groups. Smoke drifted on the wind, and the sounds of battle came ever closer.

"Take me with you," Phillips said suddenly. "I know these people, and they know me. If you're telling the truth, you'll stand a better chance of getting inside if I'm with you."

"Why the fuck would we trust you?" Vesnina asked. She hadn't lowered her weapon.

"Because I'm tired of being the reason that people die." Phillips looked tired. "Shoot me or let me come with you." He didn't wait for an answer, just picked up the data chip from the dirt and got back into his truck.

Vesnina seemed to be at a loss for words. Her gun was still pointed at where Phillips had been. Slowly she lowered it, looking defeated and angry.

"He's right," Turner said. "We stand a better chance with him."

"Fine, but if he tries to pull anything I'll shoot him." Vesnina gave him a wary look and then went to get into the forward truck.

"I'll go too," Zak said. "You're going to need all the help you can get. Alison, just go. Take Eva and get as far from here as you can. I won't be any help to you from here on, anyway."

"Yes, you will." She was fighting tears. "They'll need me in the other truck. Just let me say goodbye, okay?"

~

Alison turned to Eva and took her small hands in hers. She looked into her child's eyes, a mirror of honey brown. "I'm going to need you to be brave for me again, all right? I want you to go with Zak. He's going to keep you safe now."

"The fuck I am!" Zak sounded frantic. "Alison, you need to take Eva and go. You need to go *now*. We worked this hard to get you here."

"Based on what they're saying, we won't survive if this thing goes off." She said this in a calm, final tone. "They need two people who can get them inside, one for each truck. And besides, Zak, I can't run on this leg. I'd never get her clear."

Alison let the tears run down her face unhindered. Zak looked for a moment like he was going to argue but nodded and stepped back. She hugged Eva, hard, picking her up. She could hear activity behind her as everyone sorted themselves and their equipment into the two vehicles. Alison ignored this as best she could. She was intent on trying to remember every detail about Eva in that moment. The way her hair smelled, like the smoke and pine around them, but with a hint of something sweeter underneath. The faintest scent of a house that would never again need its roof repaired, or its paint touched up. She smelled of a place only they would ever remember. She smelled of home.

"I love you, Mommy," Eva whispered through hiccupped sobs.

269

Alison sank to her knees. A vicious pain shot through her leg, but she pushed it all away. How had Eva known? It didn't matter, she decided. She knew now, and that was enough. She held on tight to Eva and then found the strength to pull back. She took out the pack of crayons she'd taken from the gas station and slipped them into Eva's hand.

"I love you too, Eva." She brushed a stray hair back behind Eva's ear, then held her face in her hands for a moment. "You take these and make something pretty for me, okay? I'll come find you. Be brave. Be strong. Your mommy loves you very much. Please, never forget that."

"No!" Eva cried as Alison stood and walked quickly toward Turner. "Allie! Come back!" Eva tried to run after her, but Zak held her back. A rogue round impacted just a few hundred yards from them in the trees, and the heat was instantaneous. The fight was getting too close. They all needed to start moving. Zak had to get Eva as far from the mountain as he could, and they needed to go stop whatever was about to destroy everything around the mountain.

Alison watched as tears cut rivers in the dust on Eva's face, and then she was moving away, receding into the distance once again.

~

The Hollows were in a complete frenzy as Katherine and Jim tried to work their way toward the north exit. They started seeing people in dirt-stained uniforms, and it was clear the workers from the excavation site had already been called back inside.

As they turned one corner, Katherine was confronted with Garrin striding toward her. He was wearing a mech-piloting suit, pulling six other mech pilots in his wake. She averted her gaze and hoped he wouldn't see her, but was disappointed when he called her name. Katherine waved Jim off with a discreet hand gesture.

"Katherine, where are you going?" Garrin smiled at her in a way that made her sick. "Go get suited up. I want you with me on the Anansi."

"Sure," she said. She tried to dart past him but was stopped suddenly by his huge hand around her upper arm.

"Unless you've got somewhere else you need to be." Garrin turned and nodded at the other pilots, dismissing them to continue on toward the mech garage. When they were gone, Garrin pulled Katherine in close to him. "It'll be just like old times. Let me help you out of that uniform."

Katherine's arm twitched as she tested his grip. He closed his hand more tightly and directed her toward an open supply room. Katherine saw Jim moving in from behind a throng of other people and managed to warn him off again.

"We've got a few minutes before they get the Anansi pulled out of the hangar," Garrin said as he moved her along the corridor. "Let's make the most of what time we've got left."

She allowed herself to be led into the room. Once he had her inside, he gave her a sick smile, like they were getting away with something together. She did what he expected and backed slowly toward the nearly empty shelves at the back of the room. When he turned and closed the door behind them, she drew her pistol and aimed it at him.

"Open the door, motherfucker," Katherine said. "Open the door and go on your merry fucking way or I'll blow your goddamn head off."

Garrin laughed as he turned around. "Oh, sweetie, you're not going to shoot me."

Katherine shot him. He yelled out in pain and grabbed his shoulder, then flailed toward her in a rage. She swept her pistol squarely across his face, redirecting his inertia and sending him sprawling toward a rack of toilet paper and hand towels. His head made a sharp crack as it connected with the shelving, and he fell onto the polished concrete floor. As a pool of blood began to form, she stepped over him and left the room.

Katherine closed the door behind her and found Jim waiting for her, trying to look like he was lost. No one in the hallway seemed to have noticed the gunshot over the clamor of the crowd. She holstered her gun, and they ran toward the north exit door at the end of the hall. Katherine slowed down when they got close, straightened her uniform, and walked the final few yards calmly.

"I'm needed out at the excavation site," she said to the guards.

One of them eyed Katherine and Jim, trying to discern their intentions.

"I'm sorry, but we're stealing off this exit. If we let you out, we won't be able to let you back in."

The other guard stood up straight at their post and said, "We have orders not to let anyone out through these doors."

"Mr. Breaks is expecting me," Katherine said calmly, with only a hint of calculated superiority. "Open the door, soldier."

For a few heart-pounding seconds, she was convinced the guards weren't going to open the door. But the guard she'd addressed first slumped a little and put his key in the wall next to the door. The guard on the other wall did so as well. Once the door came up waist-high, Katherine and Jim ducked underneath it and ran for the fence that surrounded the excavation site.

CHAPTER 23

The truck bounced along an uneven forest road as they followed
the steady signal of one of the Ston devices. John, Plime and
Vesnina had taken the front truck while Turner, Black and Alison had taken the other. Their paths had diverged a while back,
and John's group was around the eastern side of the mountain.
Plime was giving John the most basic rundown of their predica-
ment, occasionally calling out corrections to their heading. All
of this she accomplished while continuing to work with the
equipment. An almost supernatural ability to multitask was on
full display, and John wondered if she could have done the entire
mission herself.

"So, the Ston isn't just a shield, it's a weapon?" John asked
rhetorically. "That would explain why they risked so much to
get it."

"That's basically it, yeah." Plime said as she looked up from
her device. "The one we're after is going to be inside the mountain. I'm done with the modifications to your optics, Vesnina.
If you activate your comms display, you should have a new channel with a simple directional sensor."

Vesnina brought the truck to a stop and waved her hand in
the air in a semicircle. Information was now being displayed

onto her retinas. John watched her as she studied whatever she was seeing, moving her head to get a feel for how the new feature responded to her movements.

"I've got it. It says it should be below the road up ahead." Vesnina looked ahead, where two trucks were parked across the road. She glared at John in the rear-view mirror. "Phillips, we're going to need you to get us inside."

"Let me drive." He opened his door so they could switch seats. "Be ready if things don't go like I hope."

Vesnina got out of the truck and eyed him suspiciously as he got out as well. She drew her pistol but kept it out of sight, her meaning clear. If he tried to warn the guards, she'd shoot him. They got back in the truck, and he drove up to the checkpoint.

There were four guards at the checkpoint, all with rifles drawn. Two of them stepped out into the road, and one of them raised a hand for them to stop. John complied.

"Just hold steady, everyone," he said. "If this goes south, I'll hit the gas." He rolled down his window and put his hands on the steering wheel. Before the guards reached them, he said quietly, "There's a large blast door just beyond this guard station. You see it?"

"I do," Vesnina said. "More guns hanging around there too. It's open, though."

One guard, a thin man who looked no older than a first-year cadet came to John's window. The other began circling around to the back of the truck.

"Are you a traveling man?" the guard at John's window asked. He looked scared.

"Yes, across the River Styx to meet my fate," John said. "I put that bit into the initiation, kid. I'm the Voice of the Fall. Please stop wasting our time. My name is John Phillips, and I have business with Katherine Scholl."

John hated invoking the unofficial title he'd earned. But, if there ever was a time to use it, it was now.

"Sure, but I'm going to need all of you to step out of the vehicle." He looked up nervously as one of the jets flew by, spraying rounds at one of the large artillery guns higher up the mountain. "I don't even know how we'd get you cleared. Things are kind of complicated right now."

"I'm carrying an extremely valuable asset," John said, trying to take advantage of the soldier's nerves. "I've been ordered to get it inside as quickly as possible. Radio Katherine Scholl. Tell her John Phillips is here and get clearance to let me inside. As you just said, we don't exactly have a lot of time."

As if to punctuate his point, a rocket slammed into the mountainside a few hundred yards above them, raining debris in front of the entrance to the mountain.

The man paused, then reached up to his shoulder for his radio. "West gate requesting permission from Katherine Scholl to grant access to John Phillips and valuable asset." While he waited for a response, he asked John for identification.

John retrieved what he had, a military ID from the Academy. This didn't seem to disturb the man. With how many of the Harbingers were defectors from the UE, a lot of people probably came through with military identification.

"Let him through," a gruff voice came through the radio. The soldier stepped away to continue talking to whoever was on the other end. John couldn't hear most of what the guard said, but the kid seemed concerned about protocol and screening. He was contemplating how to ram through the barricade when the guard turned and called out to the others.

"He's clear," the kid called out to the other guards. He waved at John to pull up. "Park in one of the spots up ahead and get inside as quick as you can. I don't know how much longer they'll have this entrance open. It's good to know the Voice of the Fall is here with us, sir."

John gave the kid a dry grin and drove forward. He parked in a dirt lot next to a pair of dirt-encrusted ATVs and examined the entrance into the Hollows.

"Vesnina, I need you to hit me," John said. "Not too hard, but—" John's head rocked back as Vesnina used a closed fist to open a gash in his forehead. "Shit! That should do fine. We just need to look like we're in a hurry. Just carry me inside and we should be okay. No one is going to stop someone dragging an unconscious old man."

"You're a fucking traitor," Vesnina said. "Give me a reason not to shoot you instead. I've seen bodies being carried inside, too. You've gotten me this far and you'll get me in, dead or alive."

"Because I am still useful." John held her gaze as blood began to drip down his face. "I can still do some good with whatever time I've got left."

"You don't get to change sides in the final minutes of the game because you feel bad. There's no coming back from what you've done."

"I know," he said.

"Let's go," Plime said from the backseat. "There are some casualties being brought up now. We can blend in with them."

John stepped out of the truck and allowed Plime and Vesnina to half-carry him toward the entrance. His weight nearly pulled Plime and Vesnina to the ground, but they managed to stay up and keep moving. More people came up from behind them. Two were carrying someone with severe burns to their face, and a few others were hurrying inside under their own power. A familiar sound came then. Like the heartbeat of a giant, it steadily increased until it was a constant, deep hum.

A voice called out from one of the people hurrying inside, "Our command mechs are deploying!" A collective cry of jubilant relief followed them into the darkness as they entered the Hollows.

~

An explosion in the forest brought Zak out of a daze. He was still on the side of the road as smoke and dust swirled around him. He pulled Eva off the road and sat with his back against the massive trunk of a redwood tree, trying to collect his thoughts. He closed his eyes and fought against the growing fog of panic in his mind to ground himself. Both groups were gone, trying to stop the Harbingers from using the Ston device to obliterate the forest and anyone unlucky enough to be in the area. And here was Eva, alive, and now she was his responsibility. He looked at her and saw she was staring at him with those same honey-colored eyes he remembered from the house in the woods. She still had tears streaming down her cheeks, but she looked fierce in the flickering light as trees around him burned.

He had no idea what the radius of the Ston device's destruction was, and they needed to get moving. If turner and the others failed, he had to get Eva as far from the mountain as possible. His easiest route for escape was back down the road they'd been on, but metal titans were approaching from that direction, each one firing at enemy units and guns stationed closer to the mountain. The forest, then, was his only choice, even as fires were quickly spreading through it.

"We need to go," Zak said, and got to his feet.

Eva held her stuffed whale to her chest and looked west, already seeming to know which direction they should go. Zak leaned down and picked her up. She was light, nothing compared to the backpacks and gear they'd had to train with back at the Academy, and he would be able to make good time carrying her through the forest. He set off at a run into the trees. As he leapt over a fallen branch, an explosive round blasted a nearby redwood, erupting in a gulp of fiercely hot fire.

Eva cried out and clung to him tightly. Splintered wood from the exploded tree blew past him, stinging his hands and face. He pressed on. He needed to get clear before the two lines got into close range with each other. This was a dense forest, and traditional open-range tactics wouldn't work here.

Zak felt a tremor in the ground before he saw its source. He stopped in a small clearing, trying to gauge which direction it was coming from, when something landed between two ancient redwoods, sending one crashing to the ground in the center of the clearing. A massive Jotun class mech blotted out the smoke-shrouded sun, casting its massive shadow over them. It was too late. The mechs had made more progress than he'd thought.

Zak stood helpless as a lighter and more agile Aves class mech arrived. It came directly from above, belching smoke from its jump jets, and landed behind them with a tremor. The impact rattled his teeth. They were stuck between these two machines, directly in the line of fire. He didn't even know which side either of these mechs belonged to. Zak had only a moment to decide what to do as the two units sized each other up. He threw himself and Eva behind the fallen redwood tree, just as the Jotun fired a round from its main gun at the Aves. It connected, sending the mech stumbling backward. It was quick to recover, however, and engaged its jets to propel it directly over the tree they were using for cover. The two mechs collided in a thundering cacophony of metal and fire. Zak had only trained for mechanized combat this close a handful of times. It was exactly as he remembered it; like a cage fight while holding pistols.

As the mechs grappled and fired at one another at close range, Zak took the opportunity to run. He managed to get across the clearing the mechs were fighting in and continued into the trees. The trees behind him groaned, and he chanced a look back. The Jotun was stumbling backward toward him, firing wildly into the sky. Massive trees bent under the weight of it as the Aves leapt into the air again. It seemed suspended in the sky above them for a moment, silhouetted by the blood-red sun, before it crashed down onto the Jotun while firing. The ground seemed to lift beneath Zak's feet as momentum carried the two units toward him.

The trees that had been groaning under the increasing pressure finally splintered and shattered at the base. Zak cradled Eva's head and shielded her with his body as the huge trees came down around them. One slammed into the ground next to them, one of its smaller branches pressing down onto his back painfully. Mercifully, it stopped before it crushed them. He managed to scoot Eva out from under him and then got to his feet.

A blast from the Jotun's main gun connected with the Aves, blowing one arm completely off the unit. It spun and then landed on the fallen tree where he'd almost been pinned. The Jotun lifted one massive leg and slammed it down on top of the Aves, causing the mech to stop moving. The Jotun pointed an arm-mounted gun down at it, seeming to dare it to move.

Sunlight sliced through the smoky haze, glinting off the surface of the Jotun, and Zak recognized its features. It was the Cronus, the mech he and his class had put together at the Academy. Visible though a constellation of bullet impacts on the windshield was a face he also recognized. Rebecca Lund had been too focused on her skirmish with the Aves to have noticed Zak and Eva before, but now he saw her head jerk in his direction.

They stared at each other for a long moment: Lund, piloting a huge frame of high-carbon steel, and Zak, standing weakly below with a child cowering beside him. Zak saw rage bloom across Lund's face. It was the same expression she'd worn after he'd shot Hartley in the leg. He picked Eva up and prepared to run at the slightest movement from the Cronus. The moment stretched on as they both contemplated their next move.

The downed Aves mech moved first, evidently having regained power. It tried to claw out from underneath Lund's mech, and Zak turned to run. As he did, he saw Lund move the controls of her mech, lifting the leg of the Cronus again and slamming its full weight down on top of the Aves. A groaning crunch, like the hull of a submarine succumbing to the pressures of the deep sea, indicated a structural failure of the Aves's cockpit.

He turned back to see if Lund was going to come after them. She inclined her head briefly, telling him to run, and looked back at her controls.

Zak managed to shield Eva's ears only a moment before the Cronus's main gun let loose a series of concussive blasts directly into the Aves cockpit. Zak's ears were immediately filled with a high-pitched ringing. He pushed through the branches of the fallen tree to get away from the madness that was closing in all around them.

Turner drove along the road leading around the western face of the mountain base. They were chasing the second signal Black and Plime had isolated. He thought he might have to cut through the trees when a road leading toward the mountain finally appeared in front of them. He took it.

From the backseat, Black said, "This is good." She looked at a display panel that was hooked into one of the composite radio devices. "Our signal is directly ahead, and it's still picking up intensity. The other signal is steady, maintaining the protective barrier over the mountain."

Alison turned to her. "What exactly does 'picking up in intensity' mean? Is that an 'oh, that's interesting' or an 'oh no, we're fucked' sort of thing?"

"I don't know. It's spooled up more than enough energy to let off a massive blast already. If I had to form a hypothesis now, I'd say it looks like it's going for a complete overload of the device." Black said this coldly and didn't look away from her screens. "I can't imagine why they're still going. A pulse this big could be apocalyptic."

Turner's blood ran cold at the last word. In all his meetings with Black, she'd chosen every one of her words very carefully. She'd meant to say that one.

"When you say apocalyptic..." Alison began.

Black waved one hand at her dismissively. "Turner, I'm transferring the update for your optics now. You should be able to access the frequency of the Ston devices as a channel of your communications application." Black continued studying her screen while Turner made a hand gesture in the air to activate his optics.

"You privvies get computers in your brains?" Alison asked. "Sounds awful."

"It's an optical implant." Turner made another gesture to access the new tracking channel. "Displays information on my retinas. Transmits information on encoded channels to keep teams linked in combat scenarios."

The fighting on this side of the mountain was almost nonexistent, so as they approached a guard station, the soldiers stationed there immediately fanned out and aimed their rifles at the truck. They'd been waiting for something to happen.

"Looks like we've got some eager soldiers here," Turner said as he slowed down. "Alison, you're up. I hope you can talk us through this."

"You have to be kidding me." Alison leaned forward in her seat, peering through the dusty windshield. "I think I know one of these guys."

A man broke away from the line and stepped forward with his hand out. Turner brought the car to a stop. The checkpoint was little more than a break in a fence line with small cement building and a truck parked across the road.

"Everyone out of the vehicle and on the ground!" the man yelled.

"Stay in the truck and run through them if you have to," Alison told Turner. She stepped out of the truck. "Hey, Herm. What the fuck are you doing all the way over here? The action is that way!"

"Alison?" His face softened and he lowered his weapon. The soldiers behind him relaxed a bit but kept their aim. "Hey, what the fuck are *you* doing here? A bit late to the party, aren't you? Fuck, you look pretty rough, girl. Really, what are you doing out here?"

"Retrieval and recon assignment." She pointed down at her injured leg. "Went a little sideways, but I made it. I do have to get these guys inside ASAP, though. Command is gonna want to hear what they've got."

"And what do they have?" Herm asked her.

"I could tell you, but then I'd have to kill you. You know the drill, compartmentalization of information."

Turner hoped that would be enough, but wasn't sure. He put his hand on the gear shift and was ready to floor it if he had to.

"Yeah, sure. You'd better get inside before the heat works its way around the mountain." He stepped aside and waved at the others to move as well. "It's good to see you again. I'll radio up to the main gate. Watch out for the big hole on your way over, though."

Alison got back into the truck, and Turner drove forward carefully. He looked at Herm as they passed the soldiers, offering what he hoped was a confident smile. When they drove past the row of soldiers, he let out a breath.

"I can't believe that worked," Alison said. "Herm never was the brightest, but damn."

As they followed the road, Black updated them on numbers Turner didn't understand. It seemed more important for her to vocalize them than for him to understand. She was working something out. Soon, they came up on a large, excavated pit with a broad spiraling dirt ramp that went down to a building.

"Stop," Black said firmly. "It's in there, but according to this, it's deep underground. It's cycling up still, and it's a half mile underground."

Turner stopped the truck and turned around to face Black. She still hadn't looked up from her screen and was muttering something under her breath.

"Black, should I relay this information to Vesnina and the others?" He waited for a response, but she still didn't say anything. "Black, you need to talk to us. This is your show now."

When she looked up from her screen, he saw tears in her eyes. Her normally stoic veneer had cracked. She was somehow both more present and further away than he had ever seen her.

"If it's left unchecked, it will soon exceed the tolerances of the housing, triggering a resonance shell collapse," she said.

"Meaning what?" Alison asked, her voice tense and sharp.

"If my readings are accurate, we're nearing the point of no return. Unless we can stop it very soon, it's all over. Everything. Nothing will survive what happens next. Not just for miles, everything, everywhere." Tears rolled down her face as she seemed to work through some mental and emotional arithmetic. "You have to get me to the device so I can get it cycled down. Tell the others if you can."

Turner nodded and turned back to the wheel. He took the truck down the ramp, headed for the building below.

~

Mark moved through the packed corridors with the other diggers from the excavation site, keenly aware of his surroundings. The Hollows were under attack, and he was on the inside, out of his normal sphere of surveillance. Henry seemed to be the only person with even a cursory interest in his whereabouts. The workers were all heading deeper into the mountain, headed toward where the bulk of the living quarters were. The announcements over the base-wide intercom made mention of what people should be doing if they were going to be involved in the battle. Non-essential personnel weren't mentioned.

"Why don't you come with me to my quarters," Henry said. It wasn't a question. "Procedure for us serfs is to get outta the way. They'll come get us if they need anything."

"We're not supposed to do anything to help?" Mark asked as he fought to stay with Henry in the crowd. "Seems like a lot of manpower to waste."

"Maybe for people like you, but I've spent my whole life moving heavy crap from one place to another. And what they told me to do if this ever happened was to move my heavy ass outta the way." Henry gestured for them to make a turn. The crowd was thinning a little as they got closer to the residential section of the Hollows. If he was going to do something, it would have to be soon.

Mark tried to think through the map he'd been able to create in his mind of the mountain complex. While he had this opportunity, he could finally do something to help the United Entities. A coordinated attack was underway, and he was behind enemy lines. Of all the places he'd seen since he'd been here, there were very few that he had immediate access to with any tactical significance. Classrooms, mess halls, barracks, and a slew of other low-level areas weren't worth his time. The mech garages and research areas were much more secure, but would be infinitely more valuable targets. The garages would be packed with personnel and equipment. Gaining access might be hard, but the damage he could do might be massive. The research lab was more of an unknown, but might be less guarded.

Mark stopped suddenly in the middle of the hallway, causing a moderate traffic jam behind him. People began pushing past him roughly and Henry turned to see what was going on. The crowd spilled around Mark, as they mindlessly made their way forward. Henry called out to Mark, but was having trouble moving back toward him.

Mark could turn and get away now with little effort. Henry wasn't as nimble as Mark was. Offering some parting words might smooth things over greatly though, and so he decided what to say.

"I can't just sit and wait while there's real work to do," Mark called out. "I have to do something."

Henry called after him to wait, but Mark had already turned upstream. He made his way toward the wall where he'd have better luck moving against the traffic. Henry might try to chase after him, but he doubted it. He also might alert someone that a recruit was running around unaccompanied. Or, and Mark thought this was the most likely scenario, Henry might just go to his room and wait like he'd been told. Alerting someone that he'd lost Mark wouldn't look good for him. And Mark suspected that he'd been at least marginally convincing when he'd said he had to do something. It wasn't even technically a lie. Henry might think Mark was off to do some heroic thing for the Harbingers.

Once he was against the wall, Mark was able to move back the way he'd come, only needing to worry about traffic on one side of him. He slipped back to a juncture and turned down it. Mercifully, the crowd was much thinner in this hallway, and he was able to get his bearings. He examined the painted lines on the wall and found a green line easily. Research it was, then. Maybe there was something valuable he could smash in there.

CHAPTER 24

Vesnina and Plime stopped supporting John so he could stand on his own. The chaos inside the Hollows was even more frantic than outside, the confined space serving only to amplify it. They worked their way through the throng, along a white corridor, and further into the mountain. When they came to a junction in the tunnels, Vesnina consulted the readings on her optics and turned left.

As they walked through the complex, it became clear to John that they were hopelessly lost. He assumed that her optics told her which direction the Ston device was, but not how to get there through the labyrinth of corridors. Apart from being lost, they had another problem. As they got deeper, the chaos was subsiding, and he was beginning to feel more exposed. They weren't wearing the right outfits to blend in, and it would only be a matter of time before someone stopped them. He'd been watching the walls as they walked and had noticed a pattern. A few groups of people wearing grey lab coats always seemed to be following the green lines on the walls.

"Green line," John said quietly. "And we need to get out of these UE uniforms."

Vesnina grunted in assent and took the next green line turn. Someone was walking toward them, and Vesnina swore under her breath. "Shit, I know that guy."

John looked up the corridor and recognized the man as one of the cadets Zak had been close with at the Academy. Mark Alder stared at the group for what felt like an age and seemed to be assessing his options. He was wearing the standard uniform of the base, though his was covered in dirt. Apparently making a decision, he smiled and continued walking toward them.

"Follow me," he said in a low voice. "You guys stick out like wolves in a sheep herd." He walked a few doors down the hall and then opened the door to a large room with two rows of industrial washing machines and dryers. Plime was the last one in and closed the door behind them. She leaned against it and continued to work with her radio devices. John, not wanting to be the one to explain the situation, left Vesnina and Alder to talk and busied himself by pulling together uniforms his team could use to blend in.

"What the hell is happening?" Alder asked. "Why are you all here? How did you even get inside?"

"I could ask you the same question." She put her hand on her sidearm. "There's a lot going on, and I don't know whose side you're on."

"You're going to have to trust me," Alder said, his voice taking on an edge. "Based on your uniforms, I can guess you just arrived. With a whole lot of friends, I hope. What's going on, why are we attacking now?"

Vesnina looked at John, seeming to contemplate how to proceed, and then spoke. "There isn't a lot of time, but are no sides anymore. Not right now. We have a much bigger problem."

"What could be that important?" Alder shot a suspicious look at John and Plime.

"I assume you know about the device the Harbingers stole way back at Taycher?" Vesnina asked.

"Sure," Alder said. "Dropped some planes right out of the sky. We assumed it was some fancy tech they stole from the research labs."

"Well, it is. Plime here helped develop it." Vesnina pointed at Plime, who was still busy with her devices, frowning at something on the screen. Vesnina continued. "But we discovered something very important. The device doesn't just protect, it can also be modified to destroy. The way I understand it, it can destroy an entire city if they need it to, probably more. And you know the Harbingers won't hesitate to use it on whatever targets they deem necessary. They're charging one up for a pulse to take out our forces outside right now."

"So, you're all here to take it out. Sure, that makes sense." Alder said. "Let's wreck some expensive shit. How did you even get inside?"

"Plime is with me," Vesnina said. "We came up from Taycher with Turner and the others. I'll let Phillips tell you why he's here." Her tone darkened as she turned to John. He'd been hoping that Vesnina would simply omit his betrayal, but she hadn't.

John stood in the middle of the room with an armload of uniforms, trying to think of how to explain himself. He didn't know what to say. He'd never had to justify his allegiance with the Harbingers to anyone but himself.

"I don't expect you to understand," John began. "But I have been with the Harbingers of the Fall for a long time. From the very beginning." He saw Alder's hand twitch toward a sidearm he didn't have. "I wrote many of the words that formed the basis for how the organization works." John felt tears coming to his eyes. Faced with accepting responsibility for what was happening, what had already happened, he felt powerless and small. "But nothing I wrote could have ever justified the amount of destruction the Ston can cause. That amount of power can't be in anyone's hands. I will do whatever I can to make it right."

"Make it right." Alder looked somehow tired instead of angry. "I've heard that a lot recently. You know, we wouldn't have to keep making things right if they weren't already so goddamn broken."

Suddenly Vesnina held up a hand. She blinked and made a motion in the air, evidently doing something on her internal optics. "Plime, does the term 'shell collapse' mean anything to you? I just got a really degraded message from Turner, and that's what I think it says. The mountain must be interfering with our optics communications."

Plime didn't answer immediately, but looked up a few seconds later, her face pale. "What did you say?" she asked.

"Shell collapse," Vesnina said slowly. "That's all I can get from the message."

"That's why these readings make no sense." Plime gestured to her modified radio and display. "Someone is trying to use the other Ston device to trigger a resonance shell collapse."

"That sounds bad," Alder said, shifting his focus away from John. "Is it as bad as it sounds?"

"It means someone has basically put the second Ston device into a self-destruct sequence," Plime said. She looked up at John and the others. Her chest was heaving, as if she was suppressing an outburst. "They won't be able to get it cycled down now. The device is going to go off half a mile underground. Everything is over. Not just this base. Everything. The forces at work in that device are so powerful that it's going to shatter the Earth's crust like an eggshell." She turned to face the wall and vomited.

"This is your fucking fault!" Alder's voice cracked. He lunged at John, but Vesnina managed to get her arms around him.

"We don't have time for this," Vesnina said, shoving him back violently. "There still has to be something we can do."

"Why would anyone do this?" John asked quietly. Then he remembered his own thoughts. Just a day ago, as he'd been driving on a long desert road, he'd imagined the end of humanity himself. Eva had interrupted that thought process, simply by reminding him of the cost, but not everyone had a reminder like that. If he hadn't been completely divorced from the Harbingers before, he was now. He'd created a monster. "What do we do? How can we stop it?"

Plime was still facing the wall, and for a long moment, she said nothing. Then she whispered something John couldn't hear. She turned around quickly, her eyes wide. "Destructive interference! We've still got the other active Ston somewhere in this mountain. I think I can modify it to cancel out the other signal the moment it triggers. If we can get it cycled up and synchronized, I should be able to mitigate most of the damage. We have to get to the other device now. We have to go."

John felt relief wash over him and dropped the armload of uniforms he'd been holding onto a table. He picked out a set for himself and they donned the dull grey uniforms as quickly as they could. Just as everyone was finishing up, the door flew open. A large man covered in blood stumbled into the room, a gun held out in one unsteady hand.

"So, you thought you'd use that cunt's name to get into my base?" The man pointed his weapon at John and walked further into the room. "Got cold feet when the fight got real, eh, Phillips? Did you even really believe any of the shit you wrote?"

The man had caught them all unprepared. Alder didn't make any sudden moves, as he was still without a weapon. Plime backed against a wall and looked back and forth between John and the intruder. Vesnina had been caught while still getting into the new uniform, and her weapon was still on the bed in front of her.

John was the only one with quick access to his weapon, but it was in its holster. He stood firm in the center of the room. He recognized the man as Garrin Kingston, a career military man who had run in many of the same circles with him. He'd disappeared a few years before, and the rumors held that he'd either been conscripted into a classified UE Intelligence unit or had defected over to the Harbingers of the Fall. Now John knew which of those was true.

The man was already badly injured. Blood was smeared across most of his face, and he was swaying in a way that belied a tentative relationship with consciousness. If John worked the situation well, he could outmaneuver him.

"You have no fucking idea what it took to get all this accomplished!" Garrin yelled. "All you did was write your pretty words in your room at your precious Academy. We did all the hard work out here to make it real. And we're going to see it through. In the end, the only power that will be left is this base and others like it already primed for what comes after the Fall. We will build this world however we see fit. I will build this world how it should have been built to start."

"No, you won't," Vesnina said, straining to keep her voice calm. "If you don't let us go, there isn't going to *be* a world left to build on."

"Listen to her," John said, taking a tentative step forward. He had only just been given this news, but the truth of it burned within him. Nothing could stand in the way of them getting Plime to the other Ston device. "We're here to disarm the Ston devices. One of them is about to rupture very soon, and if we don't stop it, all of this is over. Not just the Harbingers of the Fall, not just the United Entities. All of it. Garrin, you have to believe us."

Garrin had been holding his gun out in front of him while they spoke, and his arm was beginning to waver. "Those are some fancy words that amount to you destroying the most valuable war asset ever created. Your words aren't getting you out of this one, you fuck."

"Maybe not, but they bought me some time." John ducked down while pulling his pistol from its holster and fired two shots quickly without looking down the sights. He fired two more once he'd gotten it level. Garrin pulled the trigger on his own weapon as his blood painted the back wall with a constellation of spatter.

Garrin fell backward, his heavy frame smacking the cold white floor and landing in a heap. John stood motionless for a moment. A surge of adrenaline coursed through him as he waited to see if Garrin would get back up. He didn't. Then, as the adrenaline subsided, John felt a spreading pain in his chest. He sank down to his knees, let go of his gun, and it clattered to the floor.

"Phillips!" Vesnina ran over to him and helped him onto his back. "We could have taken him together."

"No, you have to go." John coughed and tasted blood. "I'd started to feel like there were no right choices left." He looked up at the ceiling, his vision blurring and fading with each ragged beat of his heart. "I've lived too many lives already. Please…" He blinked and made an effort to finish his thought. He looked at Alder, who was standing above him. "Please, tell Zak that I'm sorry. He won't understand why, but tell him for me, okay?"

Alder looked at him with apprehension, then nodded. He picked up the gun John had dropped and left to help Plime. Vesnina stayed by his side, not seeming to know what to do next.

"Take this." John reached into his pocket and pulled out the red data chip with his final essay for the Harbingers on it. Read it all, and maybe you'll understand. Now go."

Vesnina took the chip and he tried to push her away, but her hold persisted. "I forgive you, Phillips. I'm not sure if that means anything to you, but I do." She looked down at him for one long moment, then let him go.

Before he could respond, she was gone from his view. He heard the door open, and then quick footsteps told him they'd left. The room was quiet now. John coughed again and reached back into his coat pocket. He took out the photograph of his family he'd kept with him through everything. He unfolded it and held it close to his eyes as the world around him continued to dim. His wife and daughter smiled back at him from across time, and he ran his thumb along the fold in the image. He realized, for the first time, that the crease hadn't actually separated him from them. It had brought them closer together, each time he'd folded it and tucked it back into his pocket.

As he looked at their faces, he asked himself, for the last time, if they would understand the man that he had become. And, for the first time, John finally felt like the answer was yes. He drew in a final breath, allowing it to fill him completely. When he exhaled, he envisioned his guilt escaping with it. He closed his eyes and the photo fell from his hand into the slowly expanding pool of blood that surrounded him.

CHAPTER 25

Katherine and Jim made it to the perimeter gate of the excavation site. To her relief, it was still open. Across the rim of the pit, she saw a truck turn down the dirt ramp. Shouts came from the large building at the bottom that contained the vertical mineshaft. When the truck didn't stop, gunshots started pouring from open windows in the building. The truck swerved off the ramp, landing hard at the bottom of the pit. As shots peppered the truck, someone inside it returned fire.

"Look, we've got friends," Jim said.

"We have to move while they're distracted," Katherine said. Together, they slid down the steep dirt embankment to the level of the building.

She ran across the open equipment yard, doing her best to stay behind cover. More shouting came from inside the building, and Katherine ducked behind a cluster of barrels as a spray of bullets kicked up dust around her. She looked around and saw Jim peeking out from behind a forklift a little further back. He took two deep breaths, then sprinted out and dove for cover next to her.

"Our friends are moving up toward the building too," Jim said. "Let's lay down a bit of suppressive fire as a show of good faith."

They leaned out and fired off a few rounds toward the open windows. Katherine thought she heard someone yell out after her third shot, but she couldn't be sure. Three people from the truck were on foot now and had advanced to within hand signal range of Katherine and Jim. They found cover behind more construction equipment.

She couldn't recognize any of them through the dust being kicked up by machine gun fire. One person was carrying some sort of radio, and another had a noticeable limp and what looked like an antique gun. The third person, tactically outfitted, and currently firing short bursts from his rifle, seemed to have combat training.

Katherine signaled for the other group to advance on her mark, and they acknowledged. Being shot at by the same people had made them quick allies. Before she could signal, three soldiers burst out of the front doors of the building. They quickly took up position behind a stack of large tires next to the entrance.

"We can't just run in the front door," Jim said. "I'll circle around and draw them off."

Katherine grabbed his arm. "Stay with me, Jim. I don't need you getting yourself killed."

While they were talking, the groups continued to take shots at one another, but no one was breaking from cover. The only weapons Katherine and Jim had were their pistols and very limited ammunition. Katherine worked through the scenario in her mind, trying to find some analogy that would help her solve the puzzle. The best she could come up with was the thought that they were like moths drawn to a blazing bonfire. This was hardly useful, but she pushed forward with the idea. She'd taught soldiers how to think through these situations for years, and it was her turn now. Not moths then, rats facing off against a snake. Jim was right, they needed a distraction. She looked up at Jim to convey this, but found him already looking at her, smiling.

"Do you remember the Anansi stories my mom used to tell me?" Jim asked.

"What the hell are you talking about?" She let go of his arm and looked at him with stern confusion.

"Well, my mother used to tell me stories about how Anansi would deceive people to get the things he wanted." Jim looked down and saw that Katherine had let go of his arm. He winked and stood up. "This one goes like this."

He stood and sprinted from cover, heading around the side of building. Katherine watched in shock as bullets rained down around him. One hit him in the shoulder, sending a spray of blood into the air. He went down behind a stack of coiled metal cabling. More bullets sprayed on Jim's position, but he fired off two more shots toward the building.

Katherine managed to shake off her initial shock and signaled to the other group to advance. As they all moved, she took down a distracted soldier with a well-placed shot to the head, then tucked herself behind a pile of stones. As the other group advanced all the way up to the building, the man with the rifle took down the other two soldiers who'd been defending the door.

Katherine looked frantically back at Jim's position and saw him rise and shoot toward the building again. She hated what he was doing, but made use of the opportunity to dash for the building.

Once she was up close, Katherine recognized two people in the other group. Alison, the courier John had left to go find, was somehow there, struggling to reload an ancient-looking revolver. She was pulling cartridges from a pouch and sliding them into the chambers. On more than one occasion, a cartridge fell to the ground instead and Alison pulled a new one from the pouch. Katherine also knew Black, though only minimally, as the head of the research department back at Taycher. Katherine didn't know the man with the rifle, but he was wearing the uniform of a cadet from the Academy. The name Turner was printed above the right breast pocket.

"What the hell are you doing here?" Turner whispered as he relieved one of the dead soldiers of their weapon. She saw distrust in his eyes, but also a deep sadness. She'd been the highest-ranking officer at the Academy, and his response to seeing her wearing the uniform of the enemy was understandable.

"It's a long story," she said. "Just know that we're on the same side right now. I can promise you that much. I don't have time to explain, but we have to work together. What's inside this building is more important than anything else."

Turner took a deep breath and nodded. "We know."

"So, you're here for the same reason?" Katherine asked, wanting to make sure.

Alison raised her eyebrow. "Big fucking bomb in the ground, yeah?"

Before she could answer, Turner's head twitched and he looked off to the side momentarily, seeming to receive a message on his optics. He whispered something to Black that Katherine didn't hear.

"That could work," Black said. She turned to Katherine with a faint trace of hope in her eyes. "We can stop it. I can stop it. I just need to get down there."

Katherine took a rifle from one of the other bodies and checked the digital display to make sure it still had ammunition. The display flickered at first, but then displayed half capacity. Turner signaled for a breach of the door and counted down from three with his fingers. On zero, he kicked the door open. Katherine moved into the building first, sweeping the area with her weapon. She didn't see anyone. Turner and Alison followed, making sure to keep Black behind them. They found easy cover just inside the door behind a bulldozer with a large rolling toolbox next to it. When they were secure, Katherine joined them and listened for movement.

She was about to suggest they continue to move in when she heard a scuffle. Jim's voice echoed through the huge open room.

"Just do it, Katherine!" he yelled. "Take them out!"

She glanced around their cover and saw a woman forcing Jim onto his knees in the dirt. He clutched his shoulder, which was soaked through with blood. His face was pale but he seemed as alert as Katherine had always known him to be. The woman stood behind Jim, pressing a large knife to his throat. Katherine recognized her. It was Sima, the woman who'd delivered the phrase that had both signaled the end of her authority and

302

allowed them to approach the Hollows. Breaks did have people everywhere, it seemed.

Breaks stepped out from the shadows and stood calmly in his clean black suit beside Sima and Jim. The dust on the floor had dirtied his normally immaculate leather shoes. "I thought we had an understanding, Katherine," he called out. "But I suppose you've reminded me of man's true weakness in our final moments. In a way, I suppose it makes sense. Mankind has been a lot of things during its brief existence, but meek was never one of them. It's already over, though. The device is primed and set. From what I understand, we've got about twenty-two minutes left before it breaches. A resonance shell collapse, they called it."

Katherine tried to formulate a plan that would keep Jim alive, but couldn't find one.

"Katherine, come on out," Breaks said. "I promise we won't shoot you. More to the point, we couldn't, even if we wanted to. The device has crossed a threshold and it's putting off enough interference in here that all our weapons are inoperable. Let's not spend these final moments as enemies. This is what you wanted, isn't it? There is something beautiful about mankind creating the only thing which can truly end their reign."

"We don't have time for this bullshit." Turner raised his rifle, ready to leave cover, and then stopped. "He's telling the truth. This goddamned thing isn't working."

"They've got Jim," was all Katherine could manage to say. She closed her eyes and flew through scenarios, but no new plan came to her. Jim was the one person who'd understood her in a very long time, and she didn't want to lose that.

From beside her, she heard a sharp metallic click. Katherine's eyes flashed open. Alison broke cover and held her ancient revolver out with both hands. The hammer was already pulled back.

"Never aim your gun at anything you don't want to kill," Alison whispered. She steadied her hold, put her finger against the trigger, and sent a bullet flying across the room with a thunderous shot. Breaks' face was frozen in a look of surprise, his right eye now merely an empty socket. A thin river of blood flowed from it, and then he limply collapsed face-first onto the dirt floor.

Sima pulled her knife against Jim's throat and jerked it sideways. He immediately fell to his side, writhing in the dirt. Alison turned her gun on Sima and fired again, hitting her in the chest.

"Let's move!" Turner yelled. "I don't see anyone else, but we can't be sure."

Katherine leapt from behind cover and ran to Jim. She was thankful for Turner's decisive nature as he maintained command of the others. He had them move toward the elevator cage perched at the edge of the wide hole in the earth. As they moved ahead, she reached Jim. She fell to her knees beside him and grasped the sides of his face in her hands.

He looked panicked as he attempted to take deep gurgling breaths. Blood pooled around him from the gash in his throat, but he stopped thrashing and managed to look up at her. She didn't know what to say, and knew that Jim couldn't say anything to her. He reached up and put his hand on her cheek. Tears fell from his eyes as she brought her lips down to meet his. She kissed him lightly.

When she pulled away, his eyes met hers. His breathing slowed, and his hand slid away from her cheek, leaving a smear of blood that immediately began to cool. He took two more short breaths and then lay still. She fought against the urge to collapse into him, to surrender to her grief. Instead, with a trembling hand, she closed his eyes.

"Fall with grace," she whispered.

She stood and left Jim's body. By the time she made it over to the others, Black was already inside the elevator cage with her devices, looking down into the Earth. The hole was dark, an abyss that seemed to have no end. Black was working with the equipment she'd brought, seeming to be rewiring them even as she spoke.

"Are those even going to work?" Alison was asking.

"They're shielded," Black said dismissively "Any instruments we use with the Ston have to be. Now, stop asking questions and start running. As long as Plime makes it to the other Ston in time, we can alleviate the damage. But there are going to be some inevitable variations that will need to resolve themselves."

"Can't you do it remotely?" Katherine asked.

"That isn't possible. I need to be there to monitor any last-minute calibrations. Besides, the amount of energy being built up down there is so high that no one is going to be able to survive being within a hundred yards of it for long. I won't be coming back up."

Turner looked like he wanted to argue, but before he could, Black pulled a lever in the elevator cage, and began to descend. She went back to work with her devices, and they watched in silence as the elevator carried her into the darkness.

Mark led the others as they sprinted through the complex. With everyone else in the facility moving from place to place, they met no resistance as they made turn after turn in the labyrinth of hallways. He knew where the labs were from his tour with Breaks.

"Keep up," he said. "We're not far now."

They made a few more turns and ended up in front of a set of double doors that would open up into the research lab. Mark saw immediately that the guard next to the doors was someone he knew. Gonzales smiled instinctively before noticing his drawn weapon.

"What brings you down here?" she asked cautiously. "Shouldn't you be with your fellow diggers?"

"I was asked to bring these two to the research labs. Finally got my chance to help out." He gestured back at Plime and Vesnina, hoping his rapport with Gonzales might carry him through this interaction. "Garrin sent us."

She seemed to relax at the mention of a well-known figure in the Hollows.

"We've got fifteen minutes," Plime said quietly as she continued to work with her equipment.

"We don't have time for this," Vesnina raised her weapon and pointed it at Gonzales. Mark had only a moment to react and managed to push the barrel of Vesnina's weapon just before she fired. The round impacted the wall behind Gonzales, and she reacted by raising her own weapon instantly.

"Stop!" he yelled and stood between both of them. "Just stop. Gonzales, I need you to trust me. You need to get out of here with everyone you can. Please, just let us pass."

"You know I can't do that, Mark." Gonzales raised her own weapon. "I'm going to need all of you to drop your weapons and lie down on the ground."

"Fourteen minutes," Plime said, her voice trembling nearly as much as her hands. "Please. If you don't let us pass, everything we know is gone. Everyone. The United Entities, the Harbingers of the Fall, anyone you've ever loved or hated. All gone. All we need is for you to step aside."

She was crying hard now, wiping the tears from her eyes as they formed, but unable to keep pace. Gonzales stared at the group for a moment and then lowered her weapon. Plime and Vesnina rushed forward and pushed the doors open, leaving Mark outside with Gonzales.

"Thank you," Mark said. "Now you need to get out of here as fast as you can."

"Tell me, Mark," Gonzales said, disregarding what he'd just said. "You can't tell me why you joined the Harbingers, because you never really joined us, did you?" She didn't wait for confirmation. "Just tell me why you're here, then."

He shrugged, feeling small and young. "My family thought the military would be a good fit for me." It was apparent to him now that Gonzales was more adept at reading people than he knew. She'd probably been more involved in his intake assessment than anyone.

"That's bullshit," she said. "Nobody does what we've had do just because someone told us to."

307

"I wanted to be a part of a team doing something important," he said, trying to find the words. "I found friends, and then all I wanted was to keep them safe. All of this happened, and I lost them all. I wanted to make someone pay for it."

"I think that's only the second true thing you've ever told me." Gonzales said. "The first was when you asked me to trust you just now. Now, I don't know what the hell is going on in that lab, but your techy girl seemed pretty convinced that we're all going to die."

He nodded. "Yeah, like thirteen minutes and this place is going to be very unsafe. Get as many people as far away from here as you can."

She took a deep breath and then set off at a run toward where the bulk of the living quarters were. It would be close, but Mark thought she might have enough time to get herself and some of the others out.

Mark turned and went through the double doors into a large room packed with both ancient and modern computer equipment. No one else was there. The stillness, after so much chaos in the halls, was jarring.

In the center of the room sat an egg-shaped device. Dozens of wires and cables were plugged into it, like a patient hooked up to life support. One of Plime's devices was plugged into the Ston and she was working with it carefully, almost reverently. She worked in a graceful way that spoke of years spent in labs. Vesnina was watching her, seeming unsure of what to do next.

"Hurry and get that thing set up so we can get out of here." Vesnina looked nervously back at the double doors.

"Give us fire, and we will burn things," Plime whispered.

"What?" Mark asked as he walked up to the device.

"You need to go," Plime said as she continued working with the Ston. Sweat was beading up on her skin, but her movements were still fluid and precise. "I can handle it from here."

"Just set it up and let's go," Vesnina insisted.

"I'll need to monitor it until the very end." Plime allowed her tears to flow unhindered as she continued her work. "And the radiation it's going to give off will be lethal. You two should go. Even minor fluctuations at the end will have seismic repercussions. This whole complex isn't safe."

"I can't just leave you here!" Vesnina said.

"Yes, you can." Plime didn't look up from the Ston.

"Come on, Vesnina," Mark said. "Send a message with your optics and warn whoever you can."

Vesnina glared at him but nodded and turned away. She spent a moment sending a wide broadcast message to anyone using United Entities encryption channels to retreat. Mark hoped at least some of the message would make it through to the forces outside. As she did, Mark saw an ancient base-wide communications station near the front of the room. He walked over to it and set John's gun down next to a faded chrome microphone plugged into the system. He picked it up. With his other hand, he pulled the penny necklace from inside his shirt and held it in his palm. In that moment, he wondered what Brooke would have wanted. Part of him believed that she'd want him to leave the Harbingers to be crushed within the Hollows. Another part of him struggled against this assertion.

Then, for a moment, he was with her again. They sat in Rec. Six back at the Academy, playing chess as the sun set beyond the high walls outside. Her smile flashed, and he saw within her eyes a hope for a world without the need for the brutal skills they'd been trained to employ. They'd spoken frequently about living alone in the woods, at peace with their surroundings. Would she want her memory tied to the deaths of the entire population inside the Hollows?

No, he decided. Allowing them to die without a chance for escape would be like using the device himself. He would fight the Harbingers another day. And so, Mark held down the button on the microphone. A sharp squeal of feedback came from the speakers throughout the room, and hopefully the others in the base as well, resolving quickly into a low static hum as he debated his words.

"All stations, abandon duty assignments and postings." He said in a halting voice. Vesnina flashed a look of alarm at him, but then she too seemed to understand. "A seismic event is imminent. Repeat, all stations abandon duty assignments and postings. A seismic event is imminent. Evacuate the Hollows immediately." He put the receiver down and turned to Vesnina.

"We've got a ride out of here." She didn't seem to believe the words herself. "If we can get to the north exit before Plime and Black do their thing, we have a way out of this."

~

Zak broke through the brush at the edge of a tree line and continued up the slope of a grassy hill. His head was spinning, and he'd begun to see stars at the edges of his vision. Reluctantly, he put Eva down and collapsed onto the cool grass. His lungs were in constant, searing pain and he dry heaved as he tried to get enough air. The pain in his legs was excruciating, like being stabbed with a thousand hot needles at once.

A massive smoke plume drifted by overhead like heavy storm clouds. Beside him, Eva picked at the blades of grass and watched the forest burn. Constant gunfire and explosions continued to strobe like lightning from inside the forest. Zak studied Eva's face, marveling at her ability to stay calm in the face of such destruction. It occurred to him then that this was the second time in her short life she'd watched helplessly as her family was ripped away from her. He saw in her a mirror of himself and understood his role more clearly than ever. Eva would not feel like a ghost in her own life, not if he could help her. This responsibility went beyond guilt or forgiveness, and felt more akin to duty. It was something he owed her, something he owed Alison as well. He finally got control of his breathing and laid back.

"Will the trees grow back someday?" Eva asked him quietly.

"Yes, they will," Zak said. "Someday."

Out on the mountain, the flashes from the fighting were coming less frequently. Something had changed in the rhythm of the chaos. He could see mechs moving away from the mountain. His legs were in less agony now. They needed to get moving again. The more distance they could cover, the safer they would be.

~

Mark ran to the doors of the research lab with Vesnina and looked back at Plime. She was still working feverishly with the

Ston, so focused that he doubted she even noticed they were leaving.

"Thank you," Mark said quietly, and shut the doors behind them.

The Hollows had previously been merely frantic, and it was now in a state of frenzied panic. People were running through the halls at breakneck speed for any exit, while others were trying to calm everyone down and keep them at their posts.

Mark found the blue line on the wall that would lead them to the excavation site and sprinted for the exit with Vesnina behind him. They turned a few corners, and then the door was out ahead of them, a bright white square of light in the distance. Other people were with them, pressing in on all sides, as they streamed toward the door. A voice came over the base intercom system.

"Attention all personnel. Disregard evacuation order." The voice stopped for a moment, then came back. "Repeat, disregard evacuation order. Enemy forces are retreating. The danger has passed, and we will be engaging a full lockdown, effective immediately."

Ahead of them, the blast door started to close. Mark poured on more speed, almost losing his balance as they got closer to the door. So many people were still around them trying to get out that by the time they reached the door, it was already below waist level. Vesnina threw herself to the ground, pulling Mark with her. Together, they scrambled underneath the door as it continued to close.

Mark thought he wasn't going to make it, but then a pair of hands grabbed his and pulled him outside. He pushed himself up quickly and looked around for Vesnina. To his relief, she'd made it out as well. A woman was helping her to stand up.

"Thanks," Vesnina said, and then started running. "Let's go!"

The woman turned and looked at Mark. Her eyes widened with fear as she recognized him. Mark knew her, as well. This was the same woman he'd captured in Tonopah. The rebel woman Zak had gone off to play hero with on the day Brooke died. Why was Alison here now?

Turner stepped in front of him, breaking his concentration. "Run, Mark! We need to get back to the excavation site. I'm not sure if we're going to make it."

They started running, pushing up the sloped path toward the excavation site. Alison had trouble keeping up because of an apparent injury. She stumbled on the uneven ground and collapsed. Mark focused on the path ahead. He wasn't about to risk anything for the woman who'd taken Zak from him. Then, a flash of something he'd forgotten, or perhaps something he hadn't wanted to remember, came to him clearly.

As he'd aimed his gun at Alison beneath the crumpled remains of his command mech, he had seen her grief. They'd been the same in that moment, united in the horror of losing everything they loved. He hadn't wanted to see it. Zak had tried to tell him, had pleaded for him to understand, but he hadn't listened.

Mark turned around and ran back to where Alison was struggling to stand. She looked up at him, still terrified of what he might do to her. He leaned down and grabbed her arm, threw it over his shoulder, and began pushing up the hill again. She was trying to help, but he was mostly dragging her as they finally made it to the gate.

A jet screamed by overhead and banked hard, pushing the smoke away from them for a moment. It looped back, then came in for a vertical landing in front of them. A torrent of dust blasted them as they pushed across the final yards. A loading ramp extended from the back of the jet and people began to stream into the cargo hold. Mark watched with relief as Turner and Vesnina made it inside.

He screamed with effort and pushed across the open construction yard. His eyes filled with tears when, suddenly, Alison became lighter. He looked to his left and saw that Katherine Scholl had joined him. Together, all three of them reached the loading ramp and collapsed on the cool steel deck of the cargo bay. Dozens of people were crowded into the modified cargo lift.

"I heard some groundhogs needed a lift," Barkley called from the cockpit. "Hold on. This is gonna be a rough takeoff."

The jet lifted from the ground. Mark looked outside as the cargo ramp began to close, at the imposing mountain that contained the Hollows within it. For a moment, he could smell the forest in the dust that was being pulled up around them. It was sweet, like flowers fresh in spring. It was how Brooke had smelled on the day he'd met her. He felt for the coin necklace dangling in front of his chest and held it close. The jet pulled up sharply, and he felt the maneuver like a weight.

An uncanny stillness replaced this weight as a strange inversion of force passed around them. The jet, and everything around him seemed to hang in the air, suspended for just a moment. The mountain below them sank in, and then erupted, sending a plume of debris hurtling into the sky. A new feeling of intense pressure came from below, and their jet lurched upward, seeming to ride an unseen wave of force. Mark grabbed hold of someone's hand, he didn't know whose, and squeezed tight. They squeezed back, and then the cargo ramp closed, sealing them in darkness as they were borne safely into the sky.

EPILOGUE

My mother always said there are two sides to every story. She'd then go on to say that those two sides are the right one and the wrong one. I've always believed there are as many sides to a story as people in it. She had a lot of stories; they all did. I think that's why our little group made it out to Harbinger Lake every year. On each anniversary of the Battle of the Hollows, we would gather around a roaring fire and tell stories no one else could really understand.

The soft canvas of my tent, set up on the north rim of the lake just outside of Ember Springs, fluttered in the morning breeze. After unzipping my sleeping bag, I stepped out of my tent into the crisp first light of the day. I stretched, letting the sun warm the exposed skin on my arms and face. I wasn't the only one camped along the lakefront. All along the bank, large group campsites and occasional single tents were set up. I preferred the northern rim. It was the least crowded, and I got to watch both the sunrise and sunset.

It was a pilgrimage, and not just for our group. It was a sort of unofficial day of peace; a welcome reprieve from what had become a world of chaos. If anyone else from my group was going to show up, today would be the day. The water was calm, and only small waves lapped at the edges.

Though it was hard to imagine, the lake hadn't always been here. After the Battle of the Hollows, the landscape had been irrevocably changed. I still remembered how it looked before, in the distant way of childhood memories, peppered with facts and details that I was never quite sure were my own. There had been an imposing mountain once, surrounded by redwood trees at the base, and carpeted with deep green pines at the higher altitudes. The mountain had erupted, though, spreading debris for miles. What remained was an almost perfectly circular open caldera that had eventually filled with water to become the highland lake it was now.

The eruption, and accompanying geologic repercussions, had caused volcanic and seismic events around the globe. Tsunamis raged for thousands of miles and pushed further inland than any on record. Geomagnetic fluctuations from the blast had disrupted electronic systems worldwide. The destruction was so profound that most people assumed it had been the entirety of the intended result. Someone had flipped the breaker on society, and we were all left scrambling in the dark. Very few people knew the truth of what almost happened that day, what my mother and the others stopped.

A haze of smoke drifted on the wind, tinged with the scent of cooking food. Hundreds of small fires were cooking breakfast, boiling pots of water for herbal teas sourced from the local plant life, or, if a camp was lucky, making coffee. I still had a few plastic packets of the instant stuff in my pack. I'd been saving it for a special occasion and figured today was as good a reason as any likely to come.

I set about the task of rekindling the previous night's embers. There was no shortage of firewood around the lake. Thousands of felled redwood trees still lay on the ground, fanned out radially from the blast center. Seen from above, it must look like the iris of a massive eye. Some trees had miraculously remained standing. There were quite a few, but the four positioned at roughly the four cardinal directions around the lake tended to be where people congregated.

I was close to one of those miraculous trees. This one had died in the fire caused by the battle. It was a massive black pillar with twisted arms that seemed to reach for the stars at night. Hundreds, perhaps thousands, of words were carved into the charred wood at the base. Names, dates, short messages, and the occasional crude drawing were among the offerings. My contribution on my first visit had been my name: Eva Harrow. I'd put a single hash mark beneath it and then added a new one every year since.

There were fifteen hash marks there now. Perhaps that accounted for the increased turnout for this year's pilgrimage; nice round numbers always seemed to stir additional emotion in people. For me, though, this anniversary was different for another reason. I wasn't sure if I would be spending it alone.

As my kindling began to catch, I added a larger piece of wood. I warmed my hands as the flames curled around it, adding my smoke to the communal haze.

While there weren't official lines or rules here, people tended to stick close to their own kind. To the east, followers of Stability gathered and mourned the loss of the once-great order of the world. On the west side, the Harbingers celebrated their victory in bringing down what they'd seen as the rotting tower of civilization. It was a subdued kind of celebration, though. I'd attended gatherings on both sides of the lake, and the mood was remarkably similar. Humanity had always been more united than they knew. To the north and south were sort of buffer zones. No one asked whose side you were on in those areas, and that was probably the actual reason I preferred the northern rim. I never felt quite at ease with the other groups.

I added my kettle to the fire, settling it in to heat up some water for my coffee. While I waited for it to boil, I went to my bag to get the instant coffee. I pushed aside my childhood toy, a stuffed whale I called Meeple, and saw there were four packets left. I'd begun to wonder again if anyone else was coming when I heard a twig snap behind me. I whirled, scared even on this day of peace of being caught unaware.

"Sorry I'm late," Zak said. "There are a lot of people this year."

He looked older than when I'd first met him, of course, but somehow his aging seemed inexplicably advanced. His once-dark brown hair was already streaked with grey, and his face seemed set into a stoic neutral that felt like a defensive measure.

"Fifteen years," I said. "Big anniversary, I guess." I gestured for him to sit as I continued to tend to the fire.

"Anyone else coming?" He took off his heavy pack and let it fall to the ground with a thud, then took a seat on a fallen log.

"Hell if I know." I shrugged and checked on my kettle. "Doesn't matter."

Truthfully, I did hope at least my mom would show up. Things had ended poorly at the previous year's pilgrimage, and I wanted a chance to try again.

"She'll be here," Zak said, as if he knew what I was thinking. "Alison's never missed an anniversary. Katherine probably won't make it, though. She's on the western rim with the Harbingers. I heard she's not doing so hot. Needs help getting around. Turner is camped right at the base of the eastern tree with the rest of the old UE people this year. Probably regaling them with stories of his heroism and all that."

"Have you talked to Mark?" I asked.

Zak raised an eyebrow. "Have you talked to your mom?"

"Point taken." I took the kettle out of the fire and put it aside, then gathered two cups. "Coffee? I won some of the instant crap in a poker game a few weeks back, if you want some."

He nodded and looked out over the lake, no doubt wondering where Mark might be among the flickering campfires all around the rim. We drank our coffee in silence. After he finished his cup, Zak began setting up his camp. I thought about offering to help, but I knew he enjoyed the process of doing it himself. Instead, I retrieved a pad of paper and a pencil from my bag.

By flipping through the pages, I saw scenes from my travels the previous year. I'd always been interested in art, and I was actually getting pretty good. I spent most of the day sketching the landscape and Zak as he went about setting up his camp or making lunch on the campfire. I'd spent two years with him after the Battle of the Hollows, and his mannerisms were something I had come to rely on. Back in the beginning, we hadn't known who, if anyone, had survived the battle. He'd kept his word to my mom and made sure I was safe.

It was his idea to camp here on the anniversary every year. The first time, we'd been surprised to find a few other like-minded people camped here as well. It hadn't been a lake yet back then, just a big ugly hole in the ground. The second year, even more people showed up, and we asked around for information about my mom and the others. Eventually, we found out that my mom was camping near the south rim and had been looking for us, too. I remember holding my joy inside, pushing it down so hard that I'd cried the entire time we walked. I hadn't wanted to get my hopes up.

She was cleaning dishes in a big bucket of water, too engrossed in the task to hear us as we entered her camp. Her hair was pulled back the way I'd always remembered, and she looked tired. Finally seeing her again unlocked everything I'd been holding in for two years. It had felt like a floodgate opened up inside me.

"Allie!" I said as I ran to her.

She turned, and froze, seemingly unconvinced I was really there. I ran into her, and she swept me into an embrace I never forgot. I cried for what felt like a day.

We were inseparable for years afterward. I traveled with her and learned everything I could about how to survive on my own in the wilderness. She took me to far-off places I had never imagined I would see. I saw the ocean.

I never wanted to leave her side again, until last year's pilgrimage. Almost everyone had been at that one. Things were going as they usually did, and as the fire was starting to die down at the end of a long night. I stood up to say something I had been thinking about for months. I insisted to our group that we had to choose a side. The fighting hadn't stopped with the Battle of the Hollows. If anything, the bloodshed and chaos had only grown worse. I didn't even know which side I wanted us to join up with, I'd just gotten it into my head that we needed to be doing *something*. All that did was ignite a blowout fight among our group. Old allegiances resurfaced in a flash, and everyone eventually went their separate ways amid a sour cloud of resentment. Once everyone else had cleared out of the campsite, my mother had argued with me.

"You can't go get yourself caught up in this damn conflict," she said. "I fought so that you wouldn't have to."

"It's not like this thing is over, Mom," I said. "People are still dying. People are still oppressed. Nothing's fixed!"

"It's not our job to fix it." She sounded tired.

"Someone has to." I grabbed my bag and stood up, unsure of what I was going to do next. "I can't keep following you around while we pretend like the world isn't on fire."

She looked up at me with what I had interpreted as annoyance at the time, but now knew was probably more akin to tolerant amusement. To her, my rebellion must have looked familiar. "And where would you even go?"

"Anywhere but here." I turned and left the camp without another word.

It wasn't the first time I'd stormed off and wandered the woods by myself for a while. I liked to think that it was normal for a mother and daughter to fight occasionally. It was, however, the first time I hadn't come back. I was here now, though, and I hoped the others might take a chance and show up too.

The sun began its final descent behind the far mountains. As Zak cooked dinner over the fire, I started to lose hope that anyone else would show up. But, as a swath of paint-stroke clouds in the west were illuminated with pink light, I heard footsteps. I turned around slowly. Standing at the edge of our camp was Mark, looking unsure of his next move. The firelight, overpowering the fading daylight, played across his face in a way that made his intentions seem ambiguous. He seemed to make a decision and walked confidently into camp, tousling my hair as he walked past me toward Zak.

Zak stood, a pair of metal tongs in one hand, and waited as Mark approached. I started to wonder if I should get up to defend Zak when there was a sudden movement. The two embraced like brothers. In a lot of ways, that's what they were. I smiled, happy that Zak would at least have this day with his friend. No one quite knew what Mark did with the rest of his time. He never offered that information to anyone, and people respected that barrier.

They parted, and Zak waved me over.

"You're looking more grown up every year," Mark said it like something an uncle would say at a family reunion. "What are you, like, fourteen now?"

"Twenty." I punched him lightly on the shoulder.

"Ow, watch it." He wrapped me in a hug and squeezed hard. "Really, though, you look so much like your mom." I saw Zak try to stop Mark from asking, but he was too late. "Is she here yet?"

"Not yet," was all I could manage. I turned away to hide my tears and walked a few steps from the fire into the dark. I could hear Zak chastising Mark, and that made me smile a little. I wiped at my tears and looked up into the sky. The clouds were holding onto the last color of the sunset, mostly grey with faded highlights of pink and red. Trees that had begun to grow back after the battle were silhouetted against the sky. I made a mental note of the arrangement so that I could recreate it in my sketchbook later.

"Did you seriously think I wasn't coming?" I heard her voice first, then her approaching steps. Allie was there, she must have walked up while I was admiring the scenery. I recognized her movements more than any physical features in the low light. Her careful, intentional gait seemed to unconsciously avoid the twigs and other forest detritus that would betray her movements. And then she was there in front of me with that same battered old backpack she refused to replace slung on one shoulder. "You're going to have to tell me what was so interesting it kept you away for a whole year."

"Allie," I managed to say, my voice rising sharply at the end. "Mom?"

"Yes, honey." She smiled and held out her arms.

I slid into them like I was a child again and curled into her embrace. I'd been so worried that the last thing we would ever share was an argument. Now that she was there, I had things to tell her. I'd spent the last year on an adventure that even she and the others might be impressed by.

As I pulled back from her, she reached out and wiped away my tears. "Hey, it's okay, honey. I love you. A little argument is never going to change that."

I nodded, feeling small and young again but slowly regaining my composure.

"Oh, I brought you something." She swung her bag around and unzipped one of the smaller pouches. She pulled out a pack of crayons and handed them to me, a tradition she'd kept up since I was old enough to remember. "I'd ask you to make something pretty for me with these." She wiped away another of my tears. "But you already have."

ACKNOWLEDGEMENTS

I always wait until the very end to write this part. And, other than writing the paragraph that goes on the back of the book, it might be the hardest part. It's hard because there are so many people I want to include. These books have felt like an entirely personal project at times. Looking back though, I can see that's not even remotely true. Throughout the journey I've had hundreds of conversations about From Rust with people. If you are one of those people, I want you to know that your contributions are not forgotten.

I'd like to thank Deanna specifically. Writing can be a weird journey. Even though I'm ostensibly the one guiding the process, it can often take on a life of its own. It will sometimes tug me deep into the night, or leave me alone for days, or keep me in a fog of ideas that can cloud my ability to function normally. You endure these things and allow me the space to explore. You're also there to bring me in from the wilds when I get too lost. I don't know how exactly you manage to do that, but you do a magnificent job. Thank you.

To everyone at Vulpine, thank you for taking a chance on my story. I'd only published one short story before you decided to take on my three books. You've allowed me the creative freedom to take these stories and make them real.

Editors make the word soup make sense. I've had many eyes on this series. My mom, my brother, Kaleigh, Lisa, Grigory. Each of you has provided everything from overall critiques to line edits. Without your guidance, these things would be a mess.

Finally, I want to thank everyone who has trusted me to tell them a story. There are millions of stories to choose from, and that you've chosen mine is no small thing. Thank you. I humbly invite you to stay close, though. There are a lot more tales rattling around in this world factory of a head.

Daniel James Clark was born on a U.S. Navy base in Naples, Italy, and after a number of brief stops across the world early in life, settled in Henderson, Nevada, a suburb of Las Vegas. He began writing early but didn't begin seeking publication until 2019. His first short story, *A Sky Made Black*, was published in the Bell Press anthology *Futures* in November of 2021 and received a nomination for a Pushcart Prize. His first major publication is the *From Rust* trilogy of military science fiction mech novels from Vulpine Press. When not writing, he divides his time between professional photojournalism, nonprofit website management and design, and homemaking for his wife and two children.

Find him on Twitter @DClarkWords